HEROES IN THE CROSSFIRE

FOUR ROMANTIC SUSPENSE NOVELLAS

LYNN H. BLACKBURN   LYNETTE EASON

ELIZABETH GODDARD   LISA HARRIS

INDEPENDENTLY PUBLISHED

OUT OF TIME

DEFEND AND PROTECT, 2.75

LYNN H. BLACKBURN

1

"I need your help. *Please.*" The thready voice hitched for a moment. Then, "Call me back."

As an attorney, Hope Malone was used to hearing those words, but rarely did they hold such desperation. No. It was more than that. The woman who'd left this message was terrified.

Hope paused the message. She'd been in a hearing all day, and she wanted nothing more than to go home, take a hot shower, and go to bed, because that was the wild and crazy life she lived. In bed by 8:00 p.m. on a Friday night.

She checked the time stamp. 4:42 p.m. She backed the message up and played it again from the beginning. "Hope. It-It's Gloria. It's time and I need your help. Please. Call me back. I'll . . . I'll be waiting. I'll have my phone on me at all times." Gloria left a number and the call ended.

Gloria . . .

Not a particularly common name. But it was familiar. How did she know a Gloria? She hit Play again, trying not to let the fear permeating each word distract her from the voi—

Gloria! She grabbed her phone and returned the call.

No answer.

She called again.

Nada.

She called once more, and this time she left a message. "Glory. It's Hope. Got your message. Here's my cell. Call me whenever." She left the number and disconnected. No one hearing that message would know who she was or why she was calling. She couldn't imagine what Gloria had gotten mixed up in, but if it was bad, there was nothing in the message that should put her in any danger.

Gloria had said she'd have the phone on her at all times, so she must have given Hope a mobile number. Maybe she was in a situation where she couldn't answer, or had the phone on silent. Hope sent the same message in a text.

Come on, Glory. Respond.

But no little dots appeared on her phone screen. Hope turned to her computer. Ten minutes later she had an address. Gloria lived in Raleigh. She double-checked the address. North Hills. Okay, so Gloria lived in a swanky part of Raleigh. If Gloria could afford a house like the ones common to that area, she probably knew lots of attorneys.

Why would she call? Why now? And what did that mean about "it's time"? Time for what?

Gloria and Hope had met on their first day of law school. Hope had moved into her apartment two weeks earlier, driving to the campus every day so she could learn how to get to each of her classes and important locations on campus. The more modern buildings were easy enough, but maneuvering her wheelchair through some of the older buildings required a plan—one she mapped out well before the halls were filled with students.

Gloria was staring at a map of the campus and walked right into Hope, tripped over the wheelchair, and landed in a mass of books and the remains of Hope's coffee.

She scrambled to her feet, eyes wide in a mixture of humiliation and horror, and grabbed Hope's shoulders. "Are you all right? Did I hurt you? Did I break your chair? Are you all right?"

Hope had tried not to laugh. But Gloria was covered in coffee, her books were everywhere, they were holding up traffic in the halls, and somehow the combination struck her as hilarious.

Once she started, she couldn't stop. And then Gloria joined in. After a few more minutes of chaos, Hope convinced Gloria that the only thing that had suffered any damage was the coffee. They walked to class together, and when Hope settled on the front row in the only space available for her chair, Gloria sat beside her. When class ended, they exchanged numbers and promises to "bump into each other" soon.

Hope was fresh off a painful breakup and perfectly content to study in the library. Gloria was in the first throes of a heady romance, but her new man traveled a lot. When he was out of town, she didn't want to be at home alone, so she joined Hope, and their friendship blossomed as they studied Civil Procedure, Contracts, and Torts.

Gloria didn't return for their second year. She was pregnant and engaged to the father of the baby, and when she called to share her news, she didn't sound all that broken up over putting her dreams of becoming a lawyer on hold.

They met for lunch a few months after Hope graduated. Gloria was eight months pregnant with baby number two. Despite promising to meet again after the baby was born, they'd lost touch. Nothing more than an occasional Christmas card in the years since.

And now this? It didn't make sense.

She mulled over the situation as she shut down her computer, packed her bag, and exited the building. She wrapped a scarf around her neck but didn't bother to put on the heavy jacket she'd worn today. She had an office on the ground floor now and covered access to her parking spot. By the time she was in the car, she'd made up her mind.

She punched the address into her navigation app and followed the directions through the evening Raleigh traffic. Twenty minutes later, she eased to a stop in front of an imposing home. The blinds were open, and the light pouring through them created patches of glowing grass that formed a kaleidoscope in the yard.

She tried Gloria's number again. No answer.

The driveway was steep and led up to where the house perched at the top of the cul-de-sac. She could manage the driveway in her chair, but there was no graceful way for her to make it to the top of the stairs that flanked the double front door.

The truth was, most homes weren't designed for wheelchairs. Her sister Faith and Luke, her sister's fiancé, had spent one of their first weekends together as a couple adding a ramp to Luke's home. The gesture had cemented the bond she'd already formed with the man she now claimed as her brother, even though the wedding was still several weeks away.

It would be reckless to attempt to get any closer to the house than she already was. But . . .

Her phone rang. She didn't recognize the number, but under the circumstances there was no way she was letting it go to voice mail. She accepted the call.

"Hello."

"Ms. Malone?" The male voice was deep and held a stern edge that had her straightening in her seat. She had no idea who this was, but if he wasn't the headmaster of a snooty all-boys prep school, he'd missed his calling.

"Speaking."

"Ms. Malone, it has come to our attention—"

"I'm sorry, but with whom am I speaking?"

"Ms. Malone—"

"We've established that I'm Ms. Malone. What remains to be determined is who *you* are."

"Yes, ma'am. My apologies. This is Special Agent Richard Smith."

Richard Smith? Like that was a real name. This should be interesting. "And which agency do you work for, Special Agent Smith?"

"I'm with the FBI, Ms. Malone, and we would greatly appreciate it if you would move your car."

2

FBI Special Agent Charles Romero listened in as Hope talked to Smith.

"Am I impeding an investigation, Special Agent Smith?"

"In a manner of speaking, ma'am."

"I'm a law-abiding citizen here to visit an old friend. You're going to need to give me a little bit more to go on than that."

This could go on forever. "Hope. It's Charles."

There was no response. But from the camera they had on the Kepler home, he watched as Hope pulled away from the curb and drove several houses down before putting the car back in park.

"Hope, we were wanting you to leave the area."

"I'd like to speak to you on a private line." Her voice was frigid in a way he'd never heard before.

"Done." From his position in the surveillance vehicle, he hit the button to disconnect the call. Then he pulled his phone from his back pocket and called Hope. "Hi."

"Are we on speaker."

"No." The *of course not* went unsaid.

"Gloria called me at 4:42 p.m. this afternoon. She asked me to return her call. She sounded terrified and said she would keep her phone on her at all times. I didn't get the message until 5:15. I tried to call her several times. She never picked up. I drove over here, and as you can apparently see for yourself, the lights are on, but if someone is at home, they aren't responding. I called her again from here. Nothing."

Charles wasn't expecting this. He grabbed a pen and notepad and scribbled down the salient points. "Was she at home when she called?"

"I have no idea."

"You can't go in that house, Hope."

"Can't?"

Hope did not appreciate being told what she could or could not do. He knew that. He loved that about her. But it was clear Smith had set her off, and she was in no mood to be forgiving. Still, he tried. "It has nothing to do with your chair. We have the home under surveillance. That's really all I can say at the moment. But going inside would not be good—for you or our investigation." He forced himself to continue. "And the house is as far from wheelchair accessible as it can be. There are stairs at every door."

Not something he'd noticed before Hope Malone came into his life and rearranged everything inside him. But he noticed now.

"Then you need to go inside. Check to see if Gloria is okay."

"Hope—"

"Snarls." Hope had given him that nickname last spring when he was assigned to protect her for a few days. She hadn't used it in a while, and he wasn't sure if her using it now was a good sign or a harbinger of doom. "She was afraid, and she called me for help. I cannot rest until I hear from her or know that she's okay. Can't you have someone knock on the door? Peek in the windows? Something?"

"We're in the middle of an investigation."

"And going to the door would mess that up? Come on. Use your imagination. You can send someone to the door without giving yourself away."

"I'll make sure we check the house. But I would really appreciate it if you would leave the area."

"No problem. I'll grab dinner."

Great. "Let me guess. You'll be dining nearby."

"There are so many delicious places in North Hills."

"Tell me where you're going. I'll join you."

"You—"

He tossed out a few names over her continued spluttering. Hope was rarely rattled, and he loved that he could throw her off her game. Of course, when she regrouped, she would hit him with everything she had, but for now—

"Fine. I'll see you in ten minutes." He would have to jog four blocks to his car, but it would be worth it.

"Fine."

He watched as she drove away. "Smith. Send someone in."

"But—"

"I don't care how you do it. Gas company. Door-to-door salesman. Get Stevenson—he looks like he's twelve—have him take an order form for cookies. We have reason to believe Gloria Kepler is in trouble. She isn't answering her phone. And we've been watching the place long enough that it's making me twitchy. There's usually more activity at this time of night. The daughters have soccer practice. But no one is coming in or out."

"What are you going to do?"

"I'm going to have dinner with a lovely lady."

"Same one who's been blowing you off the past month?"

There was no denying it. She'd said no every time he'd asked her out. And it hadn't been for the past month. It had been for the past seven weeks. "Same."

"Man, sometimes you gotta learn to let go."

Charles grabbed his jacket. "And sometimes you have to fight for the right to hang on."

HOPE WAS BREATHING hard by the time she settled in at the table she'd told the hostess she preferred. A table large enough for Charles, all 6′ 6″ of him, to stretch his legs. How on earth had this happened?

She tried to force her heart rate to settle, but it was a futile exercise. It wasn't that getting into the restaurant was difficult. She could maneuver through far more crowded spaces without expending any extra energy.

It was Charles. She'd successfully avoided seeing him for weeks. Not because she didn't want to see him. Because she wanted to see him too much.

"Esperanza." Charles addressed her as he often did, with the Spanish version of her name, and sat beside her. Not across from her the way normal people did. Nope. Not Charles. Beside her. As if he were still her bodyguard and she was still in danger from the homicidal maniac who'd threatened her sister in the dead of night.

She pointed to the chair across from her. "Unless you've invited someone else to join us, that seat is available."

"I prefer this one. Better sight lines."

"You are so full of it."

He turned in his chair so he was facing her, his right arm propped on the table, his left hand gripping the back of his own chair. Two months ago, that hand would have been on her chair. It was a subtle distinction, but he was telling her that he didn't believe he had permission to come into her personal space—not now.

"I am not full of it. I'm in the middle of an investigation. One you have managed to insert yourself in. As much as I enjoy playing bodyguard with you, I'd much prefer to be with you when I can lavish all my attention on you, in the way you deserve."

Okay, so maybe he'd gotten the message, but he hadn't bought into her plan just yet.

"Charl—"

"You and I are long overdue for a chat, but it will have to wait."

The server appeared, bringing chips, two bowls of salsa, and a sweet tea that she set down in front of Charles. A sweet tea that Charles hadn't ordered, but which he thanked her for with an onerous level of familiarity.

Their conversation, entirely in Spanish, made it clear that Charles was a regular, and that as far as the server was concerned, Hope might as well not even exist.

You brought this on yourself.

Charles wanted to date her with an eye toward forever. He made no secret of it. She was the problem. So she had no right to the jealousy clawing through her chest.

But that didn't mean she wasn't considering the removal of the server's hand from Charles's shoulder—with a machete.

She took a sip of her water and practiced the "nothing fazes me" face she'd perfected in law school.

After three full minutes—not that she was counting, but who could help seeing that ginormous clock on the wall?—the server condescended to take her order.

Hope ordered her tacos and a tamarind *agua fresca* in perfect Spanish. *That's right,* chica, *I understood every word you said.* The server scuttled away, and Charles had the decency to wait until she was out of hearing before his grin turned into a guffaw.

"That wasn't very nice, *querida*."

What could she say? "I didn't like her touching you" seemed

a bit presumptuous under the circumstances. Better to keep them on task. "Are you having someone check Gloria's house?"

"I am."

Relief flooded through every pore. "Thank you."

"You're welcome." He took a chip and dunked it in the salsa. "How do you know her?"

"We were in law school together. Just the first year. But we're not in constant contact. I didn't even realize she was in Raleigh. I guess my Christmas cards have been going to someone who tossed them in the trash."

"Maybe. But they haven't been in the area long."

"And you know this because?"

"I'm not at liberty to say."

She didn't roll her eyes. She didn't snort. She took a chip from the basket, stared straight into his eyes and said, "Then why are you here?"

3

The server, who Charles couldn't help but note was making as little eye contact as possible, delivered Hope's *agua fresca* to the table, along with a fresh basket of chips. "Your food will be right out."

Charles waited until Hope brought her drink to her lips to say, "I miss you."

Hope choked.

He wouldn't apologize for not playing nice. Hope had him so tied up in knots he could barely breathe, barely sleep, and the only thing that had kept him from coming apart had been that he'd been neck deep in the Lucius Kepler case for weeks.

He handed her a napkin and gave her his most charming smile. "You okay?"

"Fine." She gasped and coughed again. "Perfectly fine."

"As I was saying," he paused as she took another drink, "I miss you. I wanted to see you. You were in the area. This seemed ideal."

"Charles—"

"We're not doing this here."

"Doing what?"

"Whatever it is you have in your head."

"That makes no sense."

"I'm not an idiot."

She threw her hands out in frustration. "I never said you were."

"You like me." When she made no response, he chuckled. "No snappy comeback?"

"Charles—"

"See, when you say my name like that, I get the feeling you're going to say something we'll both regret. Maybe you could table that, just for tonight."

"Communication is a key component of any relationship."

"I'm delighted to hear you acknowledge that we have a relationship."

"That wasn't what I meant!"

Charles took another chip. "Another key component of a relationship is choosing the timing of your battles. When we have time to discuss whatever it is that has you running away from me, we will do that. I can't wait to hear what sort of arguments you've come up with."

Hope didn't speak, but he had well and truly broken through her normally calm exterior. Her mouth was even hanging open, and her eyes—mercy. She had the most amazing eyes. Brown with flecks of gold. Although if she could shoot lasers from her eyes, she would be slicing him into ribbons at the moment.

"But we don't have time for that," he said. "I have to get back to work. You have to get back to not hanging out in front of Gloria Kepler's house, and we both need to eat before we do that."

The server, bless her for her timing, appeared with their food. When they were alone again, Hope picked up her silverware and unwound it from the napkin. "You—"

"Let's pray, shall we?"

She narrowed her eyes at him but conceded with a quick nod. He resisted the urge to reach for her hand and hold it while he blessed the food. As soon as he said "amen," he took a huge bite of his taco. Hope took a bite that wouldn't have filled the belly of a baby bird.

"Why are you watching Gloria's house?"

He chewed longer than was necessary, swallowed, took a sip of his drink, cleared his throat, and tried not to laugh at the annoyance written all over Hope's beautiful face. "The better question is why is Gloria Kepler reaching out to you? And why now?" Hope's mouth tightened. Her throat flushed scarlet, and the color crept upward to her cheeks. "You're not usually so easy to rile."

Hope set her fork on her plate, straightened her shoulders, and leaned toward him. The effect was surprisingly threatening from someone so small. "Special Agent Romero, if you wish to question me, please feel free to contact my legal counsel. Otherwise—"

"Hope—"

"You may address me as Ms. Malone."

"You're really angry, aren't you?"

Her eyebrows nearly hit her hairline. "Astute deduction, Special Agent Romero."

"Then I apologize, Ms. Malone." He watched her, waiting for any sign of a thaw, but her features remained glacial. "Hope, come on. What's the deal? This isn't us."

He held her gaze and refused to break the eye contact. She didn't look away. On a scale of 1–10, her anger had dropped from a 10 to a 9.5. Maybe.

His phone buzzed. He ignored it.

It continued to buzz. Her lips twitched. "Are you going to answer that?"

"Are you going to tell me what's going on?"

"Snarls, answer the phone."

The tightness in his chest that he hadn't realized was there released at her use of the nickname. If she was calling him Snarls, she couldn't be too mad. He'd missed the call, but it rang again as he pulled the phone from his pocket. "Romero."

"Gloria Kepler is dead."

ALL THOUGHTS of standing her ground, maintaining her independence, and making Charles understand that their relationship was not going to work fled at the words she heard through the phone. *Glory? Dead?*

She sat in silence as Charles spoke. "Yeah. I'll be there in a few minutes."

He slid the phone into his pocket.

"She called me. This afternoon."

"Yes."

"She was alive."

"Yes."

"How did this happen?"

"I don't know."

"I should have called the police. Called Faith. Called—"

Charles stretched his hand across the table and covered hers. "I know you gave me the short version of what happened today. How about you give me the long version? Start at the beginning."

So she did. She explained how they met, how they lost touch, and the phone call that led her to the cul-de-sac where he'd found her tonight.

He listened without interrupting, his thumb brushing over her hand in slow, comforting sweeps. When she was done, he laced his fingers through hers. "Will you come to the office with me?"

"Yes."

"Do you want to finish your food?"

"No."

He looked around the room until he caught the eye of their server. When she approached the table, he was all business as he asked for the check and to-go cups. The poor server backed away from the table and all but jogged to the kitchen.

Despite the seriousness of the situation, Hope couldn't stop the smile tugging on her lips.

"What?" Charles asked.

"You scared her."

"I just asked for the check."

"Yeah, but it was in your FBI agent voice."

He frowned. "I don't have a—"

"Oh yes you do."

The server appeared with the check. "The drinks are coming."

Charles handed her his credit card. "Thank you. I really appreciate it."

"Sure."

Charles watched the server leave, and then turned wide eyes to Hope. "I didn't mean to."

"I know." It was her turn to pat his hand. "You can't help it."

"What is that supposed to mean?"

"It isn't a criticism. It's just you. You're huge. Your voice is deep. And when you're in a serious mood, you don't get loud, but your voice gets even deeper and there's this sense that you are not a man to be messed with."

Charles, bless his heart, looked horrified. "I don't want to scare people. Well, not accidentally."

"It's okay." She was still patting his hand.

He flipped his hand over and once again laced his fingers through hers. "Do I scare you?"

There was no doubting the sincerity of his question, and she couldn't bring herself to tell him anything but the absolute truth, even though she knew it would make things so much harder later. "No. You make me feel safe."

His face lost all worry, his expression filled with a tenderness that she knew he rarely directed at anyone but her. "I will always protect you. Body and soul."

He meant every word, and that was part of the problem. But now wasn't the time to get into it. "I know."

The server returned with their drinks and Charles's credit card, then hurried away. He took the pen to sign the receipt and mumbled, "I'll leave her a good tip."

The man was a two-hundred-fifty-pound muscle-bound marshmallow.

He stood, their drinks in his hands, and she backed away from the table. They didn't speak as they made their way through the restaurant. He held doors for her and walked beside her to her car, and then waited as she transferred into the car and heaved her chair into the seat.

When she was settled, she closed the door, cranked the engine, and rolled down her window.

Charles handed the to-go cup to her, settled both hands on the top of her car, and bent down so his face was level with hers. "I'm going straight to the office."

"I'll be right behind you."

"Hope?"

"Yes?"

Before she realized what was coming, he reached in and wrapped his hand around her neck, pulling her toward him until his lips pressed against hers.

She forgot all the reasons she'd had for staying away from him and melted into the kiss. His lips were soft, the kiss gentle, his touch on her neck a feather-light caress. He had always been this way with her. A decadent mixture of intensity and tenderness that made her feel cherished. It was addicting.

A horn beeped and a shrill "Whoop! Yeah man!" shattered the moment.

Charles moved both hands to the door. "Drive carefully, *querida*."

She managed a whispered "You too."

He winked as he turned away.

She was in so much trouble.

4

Charles waited in the parking lot of the FBI office as Hope transferred from her car to the wheelchair—a maneuver she made look easy thanks to years of practice. It was difficult to stand still and not step in to help, but she didn't want his help. Not with this.

It had been an intense forty-eight hours with her that had taught him an important lesson regarding chivalry and manners. When he'd complained at Hope's unwillingness to let him help, she'd adopted what he now referred to as her "closing argument face" and proceeded to demolish his entire understanding of what it meant to be a gentleman.

"Why it is important to you that you help me with the wheelchair? I've already told you I can manage it."

He knew she was leading him somewhere, and he wasn't going to enjoy the trip, but he answered her truthfully. "I was raised to be a gentleman, Hope. I'm a big guy. I'm strong, and I can be intimidating. My mother made sure that I knew that it was important for me treat everyone with respect. My father enforced polite behavior in all scenarios. I've spent my entire life standing on the bus, giving up my seat in a crowd, holding doors, and generally trying to assist wherever I can."

Hope's smile was gentle, which confused him to no end. "Your parents sound like wonderful people."

"They are."

"And I'm not saying they were wrong. About any of it. But ultimately, why do we believe those things to be the hallmark of good manners?"

"I'm not following you."

"Why does it matter if you give up your seat to an elderly woman, or hold the door for a mother with three kids?"

"Because it's rude not to."

"Why is it rude?"

He found her delightfully infuriating, although at the moment she was leaning heavily in the infuriating direction. "Why don't you tell me, since you clearly know the answer."

She settled herself in her chair. "I apologize. I'm being a jerk."

"Not a jerk." He'd known her all of four hours, and he already knew that no one would describe Hope Malone as a jerk.

"Fine. A brat then."

He laughed as he settled into the overstuffed chair beside her. "Spit it out, Counselor. Explain your theory of chivalry to me. Please."

She laughed with him, and then proceeded to do just that. "Most of the time when we show good manners it's because we decide to forgo our own comfort to ease the path of someone else. And while there are many reasons for choosing to do that, ultimately, it's about respect. It isn't about one person being stronger or weaker."

"Okay, then how is it disrespectful for me to help you with your chair?"

"Because I don't want you to."

He threw up his hands. "I don't get it."

Hope held up a finger. "Okay, let me ask you this. If you were sitting in a crowd of strangers, and you tried to offer your seat to a pregnant woman who was standing along the wall, and she declined your offer, would you pick her up and put her in the chair?"

"Of course not!"

"Would you think less of her for refusing to take your seat?"

"No."

"Why not?"

"Because it's her choice. I've offered her the seat. Maybe she finds it uncomfortable to sit. Maybe she's been sitting all day. It's none of my business. I made the offer in good faith. She declined. Done."

"I agree. And it's the same for me. I know you're willing to help. I appreciate the willingness. I really do. But it's actually harder for me transfer into a car, or out of a car, when someone helps, than it is when I do it myself. So if the goal is to show me respect, then it's actually more chivalrous for you to trust me to know whether I need help or not."

"I can see where you're going with this."

"There are a lot of people who see my chair and immediately make assumptions. Most of which are wrong. I will admit that early on, when every day, every hour, sometimes every minute was a fight to find my independence, I was more sensitive, and I would turn down offers of help that I genuinely needed. But I've grown and matured. If we run into a situation I can't manage, I will allow you to help in whatever way necessary."

That was a relief.

"What you're going to have to come to terms with is when I insist on doing something on my own, and other people are watching, why does it bother you? Because if the goal, truly, is to respect me and my wishes, then it shouldn't matter."

"What you're saying is that some people are chivalrous not so much because they genuinely respect the other person, but because others will assume they are a jerk if they don't help."

Hope shrugged. "That's not the entire motivation, but it's part of it. You wouldn't believe the people, men and women, I've had to argue with who got downright aggressive in their desire to help me. As if I don't know what I need or want. It's dehumanizing."

They talked the rest of the afternoon, and she told him about the events that led to her injury. The early years of life in a wheelchair. College. Law school. What she found most frustrating about her life. How much she adored her sister, who happened to be his coworker Faith Malone, and how much she hoped Faith would get her act together and snag Secret Service Special Agent Luke Powell so Hope could have the brother she'd always wanted.

Charles was putty in her hands by the time the danger had passed and he returned her to her home in Raleigh. He was thrilled when Hope said yes when he asked her out. She was busy with a case that was going to court and had very real reservations about dating anyone, but especially an FBI agent.

They'd taken things slowly. But she took his calls, responded to his texts, and met him for lunch or dinner. They went to the movies twice, to a concert, and cooked in each other's homes. Until seven weeks ago, things were going great.

They went to dinner, went back to her place, watched a movie, and spent several delightful minutes kissing before he went home. But when he called her the next day, her tone was less than welcoming. Two days later, when he called again, she told him it was best if they didn't see each other again.

He'd accepted her decision even though he knew it was a mistake. He prayed for wisdom, prayed for patience, and prayed that somehow, if it was God's will, she would come back into his life.

He was thrilled with this opportunity to find out what went wrong and fix it. But he never imagined it would happen because of a murder.

HOPE WAS ABOUT to close the car door when she saw her *agua fresca* sitting in the cup holder. She couldn't reach it from her current location, and she didn't want to climb back in the car to retrieve it.

But it was delicious, and she hated to leave it behind.

Charles leaned against the door. "Do you need anything out of the car before we go in?"

"Would you grab my drink?"

"Of course." Charles ducked into the car and handed her the to-go cup. He closed her door and then walked beside her as she maneuvered up the ramp to the door. He stayed by her side as they wound their way to his cubicle.

"Let me grab a few files and my computer, and we'll go to the conference room."

"This is fine." Hope looked around his work area. "I can squeeze in here while you sit at your desk."

His eyebrows rose. "Are you sure?"

It would be a tight fit, but it made no sense to go to the conference room. "I'm sure."

He sat at his desk, and she positioned herself behind him. He turned to face her and their knees touched. It wasn't an unpleasant experience, being this close to him.

He leaned toward her. "I'm sorry about your friend."

"Thank you. I am, too." Should she have tried harder to stay in touch? Maybe. They'd been close for a time, but it was Gloria who'd put the distance between them. "I wish I knew more about her life now. I assume that if you're watching her home, either she or someone in her household was up to no good. But it's hard for me to believe it was her. People change, but the Gloria I knew would never willingly be involved in anything criminal."

"I wish I could answer that question fully. I can tell you that there are criminal activities that warranted our surveillance of the home. We don't know how much she knew or how involved she was. Our primary interest is in her husband."

"I was afraid you were going to say that."

"Why? Do you know something about him?"

"Not really. I was very rarely around him, even when she and I were close. But from what she said and some of the things he did, I never imagined that he was the marrying type. Then she got pregnant, and everything changed. She told me he proposed almost as soon as she told him about the baby."

"Was he trying to do the honorable thing?" The way Charles asked the question, she knew he was playing devil's advocate.

"I remember at the time thinking the whole "I got her pregnant so now we're getting married" approach seemed a bit old-fashioned. The last time I saw her, she was pregnant again and made a few comments that gave me the sense that her husband was very possessive and protective."

"Shouldn't a husband be protective of his family? A man wanting his pregnant wife to stay safe doesn't seem like a bad idea."

"True. I've been racking my brain to remember our conversation. I recall feeling that the protectiveness might have a rational basis, but that the possessiveness was a bit much."

Charles did not seem surprised by her observation. "I would agree with that assessment. He isn't the type of man to share. And he's not the type to let go of anything he believes is his."

"Including Gloria?"

Charles inclined his head. "I have reason to believe that he was unfaithful to her, but he wouldn't have accepted any infidelity on her part."

Hope had a sinking sensation in her bones. "Do you think he killed her?"

"Way too soon to call. But the officers who found her said that your name and number were written on a notebook on her desk. There's a good chance that whoever killed her knows she called you."

This was why he'd wanted her to come back to your office. It made sense now. "You have got to be kidding me."

"What?"

"Are you going to try to take me into protective custody again?"

Before Charles could answer, a far-too-familiar voice responded. "No." Faith, Hope's sister, came around the corner. "But *I* am."

This was what she got for encouraging her baby sister when she wanted to pursue a career in the FBI. "I do *not* need protective custody. It's a name and number. And we were friends years ago, but we've had no contact beyond a few Christmas cards in the last five years."

"True. But . . ." Faith trailed off and widened her eyes at Charles.

"I know that look, Faith Malone. What aren't you telling me?"

Charles tapped Hope's knee and she turned her attention to him. "Lucius Kepler is not someone who presumes innocence. If he suspects you know something that he doesn't want you to know, he won't hesitate to kill you."

"Seems like someone that trigger happy would have a hard time holding on to whatever power base he has." Hope was impressed that her voice was steady and didn't hint at the terror slithering along her nerve endings.

Charles snorted. "You aren't wrong, but I doubt he cares."

Hope ran her hands through her hair. "How do I wind up in these situations? I don't know another person—not one!—who has ever been put into protective custody because some nutcase wanted to kill them for no reason. And I'm going on round two."

"Oh come on." Faith's exasperation was evident in her tone. "You know plenty of people who've been in protective custody."

"Sure. But for a reason. Because they were whistleblowers, witnesses of crimes. Not because they just happened to know good people who knew bad people."

Faith reached around her from the back and leaned over to rest her head on Hope's shoulder. "It's not full-blown protective custody. But I don't want you to go home tonight. Come home with me. Or go to Charles's house. But don't go to your home. Not until we have time to check it out in daylight. Make sure it's safe. Please?"

Hope looked at Charles, and he did a horrible job of fighting a smile. "I told you. Didn't I."

His smile broke free. "You did."

Faith released her. "What did you tell him? Was it about me?"

"Oh yeah. It was about how my big, bad FBI-agent sister has a wheedling, manipulative side and I'm the only one who ever gets to see it."

Faith let out an affronted gasp. "I'm not wheedling or manipulative."

"Not usually. Just when you want me to do something I don't want to do. And you know what makes it so awful? I'm not the type to fall for manipulation. Usually." The truth of the matter was more complicated. Faith wasn't manipulating her. She knew it. Faith knew it. And she suspected Charles knew it.

Faith was giving her a way out. A way to go home with someone who was armed and dangerous, someone who could protect her. But this way she could say she did it to keep Faith from worrying, rather than having to admit that she was scared and didn't want to go home alone.

"Fine." Hope twisted as much as she could and looked at Faith. "I'll come to your house. For tonight. But tomorrow—"

"Tomorrow we get you safe in your own home."

She turned back to Charles. "Does that work for you?"

Relief shimmered from him in waves. But before he could respond, the phone on his desk rang.

"Romero."

As he listened, Charles went rigid in his seat for a full ten seconds, then he reached for a pen. Whatever he was writing, he was doing it with firm, short strokes. He didn't contribute to the conversation with anything more than a few grunts and one, "Yeah. I'm on it."

When he hung up the phone he turned around and reached for Hope's hands. "Gloria's daughters are missing."

5

Charles had no doubt that Hope would hold it together, but that didn't mean his news wasn't going to hit her hard. She made no move to pull her hands away as she processed what he'd said. "What else do you know?"

It was a smart question from a woman who understood how law enforcement worked. "We don't have enough manpower to keep the entire family under surveillance. We're watching the house and Kepler. We've been able to confirm that the girls didn't attend their practices this afternoon. We know they didn't return home. Raleigh investigators are obtaining security footage from the schools and making phone calls to try to determine where they went when they left the school."

"Is it possible they're at a friend's house?"

"Yes."

"But what is your gut telling you?"

"My gut has no clue. I don't know where they are. They didn't come home. They aren't currently with their father."

"How do you know?"

Charles considered how best to answer her question. Hope was an attorney. This was an active investigation, and she was now a part of it, for better or worse. But Hope wouldn't do anything to jeopardize the case. "We had a local sheriff's officer give the news to Kepler. He was still at work. The officer treated him the same way we would treat any spouse of a murder victim."

Hope quirked an eyebrow. "So, guilty until proven innocent?"

"Hey, it's not our fault that it's almost always the spouse."

"Right."

"Anyway, the officer explained that they'd received an anonymous phone call that there'd been a murder in the house. The officer who responded to the call saw something suspicious from the back kitchen window, investigated, and found Kepler's wife. According to the officer, Kepler's first question was, "What about my daughters?""

Faith squeezed Hope's shoulder. "How old are the girls?"

"Seven and five." Charles focused on Hope. "We've had eyes on their home for weeks. The girls were not in the house."

"If you've had eyes on the house, how did someone kill Gloria?"

"There's always a possibility that someone snuck in. They could have been helped by Kepler, or by the household staff. We haven't ruled out that possibility, but we do know who entered the home today. Besides Gloria, there were three people who came and went. All of whom had reason to be in the home, all of whom have been in and out of the home since we began surveillance, and none of whom were suspected of being anything other than what they claimed to be. There was no reason to suspect them of foul play when they left the house this afternoon."

"Were they household staff?"

"One, the chef, was in the home daily. The others were the

technician from the pool company and an interior designer Gloria was working with to redesign their theater room."

Hope rubbed a thumb across his hand, her brow furrowed. "None of those people sound dangerous."

"I agree. The chef is known to us. We'll watch her, but it's unlikely she's responsible. The pool company sends different people out, so he could be an imposter. The designer is also a possibility. She has well-known clientele in the Raleigh area, but we didn't vet her. We weren't trying to protect Kepler or the family, so the people in and out of the house were persons of interest, but only in the sense that they could be facilitating his crimes. Clearly, at least one of those people isn't who they seemed."

"Do you suspect they might have been working together?"

"Anything is possible at this point." He laced their fingers together. "But for tonight, there's nothing you can do."

"I—"

"Hope, *querida*, we'll find the girls. There's been no ransom request and no demands. Kepler is not a good man. He has enemies. The kind of enemies who wouldn't hesitate to use the girls as leverage. But while there are always exceptions, the criminal element we believe he's involved in has a family side that cannot be disputed. The wives and children are off-limits. Always."

"Honor among thieves? There's no such thing."

"I agree, but as hard as it is to believe, it is possible for a person to be a horrible individual and a loving parent at the same time. Of the three men we suspect Kepler to be in competition with, all of them are doting fathers and in two cases, grandfathers. These men wouldn't hesitate to destroy Kepler's business, but they wouldn't go after his kids."

"I agree with Charles," Faith said.

Hope turned toward Faith. "That doesn't mean the girls aren't in danger. They could be afraid. Or hurt."

"Or they could be hanging out with friends, still blissfully unaware of what happened to their mother." Faith reached out and gave Hope's hair a gentle tug. "If they're together, they'll figure it out."

Hope released one of Charles's hands and reached for Faith's. "I hope you're right."

"I'm always right." Faith flashed a smile that was full of teeth and absent of humor. "Charles is usually right as well. For tonight, the best way you can help is to get some sleep so you can be at your best tomorrow. Come on. Let's get home before Luke starts blowing up my phone."

Hope threw up both hands in defeat. "Fine. Are you going to tell Luke what's going on?"

"Are you kidding? He'd cut me off from Cherry Coke for a week if I didn't."

"If you tell him, he'll come over and pace around the house all night."

Faith winked. "All the more reason for him to know."

Hope turned back to Charles. "You'll call me, no matter what time of day or night, when you know more." It was not a question.

"I will. And you'll call me when you get to Faith's house. And in the morning. And if I call, you'll answer."

Hope dropped her head, and Faith found a reason to be elsewhere and disappeared. "Hope?"

"I . . . I shouldn't have ghosted you." He'd never expected her to admit that. "It was . . . I was . . ." She swallowed and looked at him. "I'm sorry."

"Apology accepted." He meant it. "But we still need to talk about why."

"You deserve more, Charles."

"I deserve the best." He placed a finger under her chin and lifted it until her eyes met his. "Which is why I want you."

"CHARLES—"

He traced her jaw with a finger and leaned toward her to place a soft kiss on her forehead. "I want you to go with Faith. And when you get settled, I want you to think about how much you dislike it when people disregard your wishes. When they assume they know what you need better than you do."

Hope's heart threatened to self-destruct as he turned her own words back on her. Was that what she'd done?

Charles continued to speak in that soft way he had, a way she suspected very few people knew he was capable of. But the softness didn't minimize the sharp edge of his next words. "And then I want you to consider the possibility that I might know my own heart and mind better than you do."

He held her gaze, and there was no anger, no hostility, no drama. Nothing but a deep hurt that he made no effort to hide from her. She had no idea what he saw when he looked at her. But whatever it was, it generated a flicker of a sad smile before he dropped his head and pressed his forehead to hers. "I want you to give us a chance."

He was waiting on her to speak. She knew it. And she had so many things she wanted to say. To explain how confusing this was to her. How much she cared for him and how afraid she was of hurting him. How she'd convinced herself that he was too much of a gentleman to hurt her, so she'd decided to take care of it for both of them.

How she now saw that she'd done to him the very thing she hated when it was done to her.

But the words refused to leave her mouth.

He shifted his position so he could whisper in her ear. "Why are you running away from me?"

She swallowed, and in the quiet intimacy he'd created as his body hovered over hers, it sounded like some sort of gurgling sea monster preparing to wrap its tentacles around a ship and drag it to the deep. Charles pulled back enough to look at her. His entire face grew solemn as he traced her lips with his finger. "Are you so afraid that you can't speak, *querida*?"

Her skin heated. She was ruining everything. "No," she gasped out. "Yes." Oh, as if that was better. She shook her head in defeat. "Maybe?"

He flinched at her words, which finally loosened her tongue.

"No. I'm not. I mean. I am." She groaned. "Why can't I talk to you about this?"

"I don't know, but please keep trying."

Something about the pleading in his voice broke her, and before she could stop herself, it all flooded out. "I don't want you to resent me someday."

Charles pulled back like she'd slapped him.

"I know you see me, as a person, not as a person in a wheelchair. And it isn't anything you've ever done or not done that makes me think this way. But I know how difficult it can be to accommodate me. And how will you feel when I can't go hiking with you, or camping with you, or join you on a leisurely stroll on the beach holding hands?"

Charles's mouth had literally fallen open, his shock evident.

She should have stopped then, but did she? No. "You're extraordinary. You're smart, strong, funny, gentle, loving, charismatic, charming, and seriously good-looking. You could have anyone. And you deserve someone who can take care of you. Love does that. Love takes care of others, and I can't be the one who is always taking and never giving. That's not fair to you. I need to find someone that the scales can stay balanced with. I'll always be out of balance with you."

Charles had gone so still that Hope began to wonder if he really had gone into shock. All she could do was stare at him.

Had she really said all of that? She'd never articulated some of that before, not even to herself.

Charles sat all the way back in his seat. Face drawn, eyes hooded. Every few seconds his head would shake a tiny bit, and she knew without him speaking that his mind was frantically processing what she'd said, and the implications of her fears.

When he spoke, it was nothing she was prepared for. "I'm not sure what I thought was going on," he said, "but it wasn't this." He cleared his throat. "Did you hear anything I said before? You nodded in all the right places, but I'm wondering if you were just pacifying me. Because I just told you, not five minutes ago, that it's not nice for you to make decisions for me. And listening to you right now, I'm wondering if we've been in the same relationship this whole time. Because if you knew me at all, you would never even consider the possibility that I would resent you."

That sounded ominous, but she couldn't blame him. And if he decided she was way too messed up for him to bother with her, well, he would be right. But Charles wasn't done. Not even close.

"Do you really believe we would always be unbalanced? That I would resent you because I have to do more housework, or put the glasses on the top shelf all the time? Or because you'll never be able to mow the grass or paint a room and I'll have to do it all?"

He pointed to his chest. "If you don't think I'm capable of figuring out that you love me with something other than acts of service, then I'm not sure where any of this is going. I believed I knew you and you knew me. Not completely, but well enough to assume that this kind of junk would never come up. But if this is what you anticipate life would be like with me, then what reason do we have to pursue a relationship so doomed to failure from the start?"

He closed his mouth, clearly fighting the desire to say more.

He stared at her for a long moment before he pushed himself back toward his desk and spoke through gritted teeth. "Obviously, I'm going to need some time to process this."

She squeezed her hands on the wheels of her chair and backed out of his cubicle. "That's fine. Of course. I'll find Faith."

He gave her the briefest nod and turned his back to her.

Her last glimpse was of him leaning forward, his elbows on his desk, his head in his hands.

6

Hope didn't have a clear memory of getting out of the FBI office. Or of the drive to Faith's house. Or of what she said to Luke when he stepped out of Faith's home and gave her a side hug, telling her not to worry, that he'd keep her and Faith safe.

She must have washed her face and changed into pajamas, because she was in bed now, holding her phone, finger hovering over the text she'd typed.

> I doubt you want me to call now. But I'm keeping my promise to update you. I'm at Faith's. Luke is here. Faith said there was no sign of anyone following us. Luke's planning to sleep on the couch. The alarm is set, and I have a weapon within reach. She hit Send.

The message showed that it had been read immediately. But there were no blinking dots to indicate that Charles had any plans to send her a reply.

Fair enough.

She set the phone on the bed beside her and settled herself under the sheets. Sleep refused to come, and she lay there, numb, staring at the ceiling-fan blade's shadow visible because of the dim night-light glowing against the far wall.

It felt like hours, but according to her phone it had only been fifteen minutes when a light rap on the door was followed by Faith peeking into the room.

"Are you asleep?"

"No. Is everything okay?"

"Out here? Yes." Faith walked into the room and pushed the door almost closed behind her before joining Hope on the bed. She stretched out beside her on top of the covers and closed her hand around Hope's. "Want to talk about it?"

"No."

"Okay."

Faith made no move to leave. She simply lay next to Hope. Hope fought to hang on to the numbness that had kept her from splintering, but it refused to linger. And when it was gone, the reality of what she'd done, of what Charles had said, of how much she'd messed everything up, of the bleakness of a future without the only man who had ever touched her heart—all of it slammed through her.

The pain fractured the walls she'd erected to protect herself. Her eyes overflowed, and sobs tore through her chest. Faith rolled to her, wrapped her in her arms, and held her close until her body stopped shuddering.

Faith whispered into the silence, "What can I do?"

"Nothing."

"I could shoot him. Luke would help me hide the body."

Hope couldn't bring herself to smile. "Ha."

"See, you think I'm joking, but I'm not. He hurt you. He dies."

Hope had hit the sister jackpot the day Faith was born. Her

loyalty ran deep, and no matter what Hope told her, Faith would always take her side. But she couldn't have Faith or Luke reacting negatively toward Charles. He'd done nothing wrong.

"It was me. Not him."

Faith brushed a hair from Hope's forehead. "You didn't cry the day they told you you'd never walk again. You didn't cry the day Dad moved out. But you're in here sobbing."

Hope heard what Faith hadn't said. Life hadn't always been kind, but Hope had always leaned into the truth of her name. While Faith had once floundered in her faith, Hope had never been without hope. She was a "find the silver lining, there's always a purpose, God has a plan" kind of girl.

"It was my fault. Don't blame him. Don't be unkind to him. Not on my account. He's never been anything but wonderful." Hope's voice broke on the last word, but she held on to her composure until Faith relented with a kiss on her cheek.

"I love you, big sister. And I don't care what you did. I'll always love you. I'll take you at your word and call off the hit on Charles, but I do need to say one thing." Faith squeezed her hand tight. "Don't fall into the trap of assuming all men are like Dad. You were young, traumatized, and processing a life without the use of your legs. He was a selfish jerk who didn't know how to cope when life threw him a curve ball, and instead of being the father you needed, he left." Faith paused to take a breath. "I don't think Charles is capable of anything close to Dad's level of self-absorption."

Hope turned her head toward Faith. "I honestly didn't think about that."

"Not consciously, maybe. But the emotional wounds are there, Hope. And when Charles got close, you ran scared. I'm not a psychologist, but this seems like an easy diagnosis. Your father left you because you were too much trouble, so now you wonder if any man will ever love you the way you deserved to be loved."

Hope wanted to refute Faith's assertions, but . . . "You could be right, but it doesn't matter now."

Faith squeezed her close. "I'll hold on to hope for you until you can hope for yourself again."

Hope lay still as Faith crawled from the bed and slipped out of the room. When the door snicked closed, she picked up her phone. The text remained unanswered.

She closed her eyes and fresh tears slid down her cheeks. The ceiling fan bore silent witness to her pain.

HOPE WOKE the next morning with a raging headache, burning eyes, and a sense of impending doom. She did the bare minimum of her normal morning routine, but then took time to press a cool washcloth to her swollen eyes. After five minutes, when she still looked like she'd gone three rounds in the ring with a heavyweight boxer, she gave up trying to make herself look any better.

Faith wouldn't be surprised by her bloodshot eyes. And Luke would know what Faith knew, so there was no point in trying to cover it up.

She made her way down the hall and into the kitchen. Faith was nowhere to be seen, but Luke was seated at the counter, cup of coffee in hand.

He stood when he saw her. "Coffee?"

"Yes. Please." She sounded like she had a three-pack-a-day habit.

He set his own cup on the breakfast table, and she stopped in the spot that was missing a chair. Luke didn't speak as he prepared her coffee. He set the coffee, fixed just the way she liked it, in front of her, then pulled out a chair and sat beside her. "Need a hug?"

Luke was the brother she'd never had. Oh, her dad had

remarried, and he and his new wife—who happened to be the same age as Hope—had two boys. But the relationship was strained, and Hope had spent little time around the two boys.

They were biologically her brothers, but Luke was the brother of her heart. The one who teased her, who joined her in ganging up on Faith, who had immediately built a ramp onto his house when he and Faith started dating because "you shouldn't have to ever work to get inside," and most importantly, who loved Faith as she was.

Her eyes filled. What was with the tears? Where did they keep coming from? Shouldn't she be completely dry by now? She kept her gaze on her coffee and blinked back the moisture. "A hug would be great." That didn't sound desperate. Not at all.

Luke's arm came around her from the side and he pressed his head to hers. "I'm relieved to know that Faith and I won't need to commit a felony to avenge you." Luke had a deep voice, and the low murmur vibrated through her skull as he spoke. "And I know you don't want to talk to me about this, so you don't have to reply. Just listen for a minute. Okay?"

She nodded and he released her. He took a sip of coffee and stared at the wall across from them. "I gathered from Faith that you believe you've messed up your relationship with Charles, and that it's beyond repair."

"Pretty much."

"If you're right, Hope, then he doesn't deserve you."

She almost dropped her mug. "What?"

"Everyone makes mistakes. Love doesn't ignore them, but love forgives. Love endures. Love never forgets that finding the perfect person for you doesn't actually make that person perfect. Love chooses to see the best in someone, and it makes that choice every single day. If he loves you, he'll listen. He'll give you a chance to explain. Or to make amends."

"That sounds great." Hope took a sip of her coffee. "But we

aren't married. We aren't in a covenant relationship that demands that we try. We were dating. I behaved badly. Then I made it worse."

Luke, bless him, didn't comment.

"There's no rule that says you have to stay with someone who hurt you. He's not doing anything wrong if he chooses to protect himself from me."

Luke cut his eyes at her then, an incisive look that had her wondering what he'd heard in her words that she hadn't meant to share. "I don't disagree with you. What I said was that if he isn't willing to try again, try for more, try for a new start, then he doesn't deserve you and you're better off knowing that now."

"Bu—"

"Faith told me that you two were all kinds of sweet before she left you alone. In the space of five minutes, you went from being on the path to happily ever after to a tumble into the pit of despair."

"That's true."

"I can't believe you did anything that quickly that would justify him refusing to forgive you. Unless you've been carrying on with another man all this time?" His look was sly, his eyes wide.

"Of course not."

"Then he should give you a chance." Luke reached over and squeezed her hand. "In books and movies, love is easy and sweet. In real life, love is hard work. We're sinners who choose to love other sinners. And we're going to mess up. If he's only looking for someone who will be easy to love, he will be eternally disappointed."

"Are you saying I'm difficult?"

Luke laughed, low and rumbly. "Here's what I know about the Malone women. They are fierce." He grinned at her scowl. "They are also fun." He lifted their hands and pressed a kiss to hers before looking her straight in the eyes with unflinching focus. "But if a man can't handle the fierce, he doesn't deserve the fun."

7

C harles tossed yesterday's clothes into his bag, pulled a clean shirt off the hanger, and slid it on. It was warm on skin chilled from the frigid shower he'd subjected himself to. Not because their locker room didn't have hot water, but because he fully expected to fall asleep standing up if he let himself relax.

He'd managed to get three hours of shut-eye with his head on his desk. Now everything hurt. His head, his neck, his back.

His heart.

He'd replayed his conversation with Hope over and over again. Instead of hurting less, it hurt worse. Every time. Until now he was just a raw mass of ache. After everything they'd been through, and everything they'd been to each other, how could she think that of him? That he would resent her? That he didn't have the decency to end a relationship if it was going to be too much work?

Turn it off, Romero. He didn't have time for this. Not that he ever had. Romance worked for others. Not for him. No. Today, he had one job. Support the mission to find the Kepler girls. After that he would worry about who killed their mother. And he would pray their father wasn't responsible, because those kids did not need that.

He was slipping on clean socks when his phone rang. He fought the disappointment that the caller ID didn't read "Esperanza," and answered. "Romero."

"I hear you're looking for a couple of kids." The voice was one he recognized, and he dropped his head to the locker room door. "Sabrina, do I even want to know how you know this?"

She didn't laugh. Sabrina had a sense of humor, but it was . . . quirky. As was the lady herself. "I have my sources. Although in this case it's nothing particularly nefarious."

"That's a relief."

"Faith called."

"Ah." That made sense. Or it did if you could keep up with the connections in central North Carolina. Charles had once asked if someone could give him a chart that listed how everyone knew everyone else.

A chart had been provided. It had not helped.

Charles had met Sabrina the good old-fashioned way—through their work together on a human trafficking task force. As a professor of cybersecurity and computer forensics at UNC Carrington, Dr. Sabrina Fleming-Campbell was a highly sought-after expert who spent her free time analyzing photographic evidence and running facial recognition software—most of which was her own modified and highly accurate creation—to hunt down traffickers.

She was married to Adam Campbell, a white-collar crimes investigator in nearby Carrington County. Adam was also a member of the Carrington Sheriff's Office dive team, and he and his dive team friends were close to the Secret Service agents here in Raleigh. He assumed that connection explained how Sabrina had become friends first with Faith, and then with Hope. He knew that Faith and Hope had joined the dive team and Secret Service agents when they'd all gone to the Outer

Banks in September to celebrate a friend getting out of rehab, and also because it gave them an excuse to go diving.

Normally, Charles wasn't a big fan of using his friends. But when it came to finding missing kids, no one was better than Sabrina, and he had no problem with Faith taking advantage of their relationship to bring her on board.

"What did Faith tell you?"

"The bare bones. But I'm already on it. I have photos of the girls, and I'm checking traffic cams in the area. I've also started running them from the airports and ports and train stations. Neither of the girls has a legal passport, but that doesn't mean they don't have illegal documentation."

"True." Charles did not bother asking Sabrina how she was doing any of this.

"I wanted you to know that I'm on this. It's Saturday and I don't have anything planned that can't be shifted to another time. If this bleeds into tomorrow, my original plans were to go to church and then a family lunch. This type of work is the only thing that would get me out of either."

She cleared her throat. "To be clear, I would miss church, but I don't mind missing the family dinner. Adam's grandmother has decided she likes me, but now she wants to know when we'll be providing an heir. I responded in ways which were honest but may have been bordering on inappropriately rude. Adam finds it hilarious to see me going toe-to-toe with his grandmother and refuses to bail me out. I would not be sorry to avoid that particular familial minefield."

Charles bit hard on the inside of his jaw to keep from laughing. "Thank you, Sabrina. You're a treasure."

"I'm glad you think so. Because before I let you go, I'm going to skip subtle and go straight to blunt."

Charles braced for whatever was coming. With Sabrina, there was no telling.

"Faith told me that Hope cried herself to sleep last night."

That was not what he was expecting.

"Speaking as someone who once tried to shove away the best thing that ever happened to me, if you let her go, you're an idiot. She's got a nice, tough exterior. But that doesn't mean she isn't fragile. At least when it comes to you. So treat her like the delicate masterpiece she is."

Before Charles could formulate a response, Sabrina switched gears. "I'll let you know as soon as I learn anything."

The phone went dead.

Charles stared at it. Had that just happened? If anyone but Sabrina hung up on him like that, he'd be offended. Coming from Sabrina, it was more of a compliment. She didn't bother with the niceties when she trusted you.

He tried to keep his mind on the case as he finished getting dressed and returned to his desk. But the image of Hope crying herself to sleep continued to bloom in his mind on an endless loop.

What was he supposed to do? She'd all but accused him of being so superficial a human being that he wouldn't be able to deal with a future that included a wife in a wheelchair. As if he cared about that. He was in love with her. The person. The lawyer. The sister. The friend.

The woman who made him laugh, who made him think, who challenged him on every level to be a better man. The woman who was *it* for him.

But they couldn't have a life together if she believed the whole time that he was depressed about the need to plan vacations around wheelchair accessibility.

He didn't care. But if walking hand in hand on the beach was so important to her, then he was strong enough to carry her *and* her chair to the dadgum beach.

He paused as a deep knowing settled through his entire being.

He loved her.

He wasn't sure when it happened, but there was no denying it. Not that he wasn't still furious with her and her ridiculous theories.

But when he told her he needed time to process, to consider where things stood between them, that's exactly what he meant. He'd never dreamed she would cry over him.

Maybe he was a jerk of the highest order, but in a very deep place he was glad he could have that effect on her. He never wanted to make her cry. Never again. But she cared enough that the prospect of hurting him, of losing him, had upset her that much? Women didn't cry themselves to sleep over men they didn't care about.

He ran his hands through his short hair. The timing of all of this was horrific. He wanted to find Hope and kiss some sense into her. But he was taking over the surveillance on Kepler in an hour.

If he wanted to have any chance of staying focused, he needed to take care of a few things now.

First, a text.

> Esperanza, it is a mystery to me how such an intelligent woman could have developed such whacked-out ideas about me. When this is over, you and I are going to have a very long talk in order to resolve this. In the meantime, please stay safe and do what Faith tells you to do. I intend to be arguing with you for the next several decades and if you get hurt that will seriously mess with my plans.

He looked over it. It wasn't too mushy. It didn't hint that he knew she was upset. But it was an olive branch of sorts.

He hit Send before he could overthink it.

Then he dialed Faith.

"Charles." Her tone was cool, but not unkind or angry.

"Thanks for calling Sabrina."

"No problem." Faith's voice hardened. "My gut says those girls are okay. But we can't risk it. I wanted the best involved. And we're good enough friends for me to call and ask for a favor."

"I certainly feel better knowing Sabrina's looking at all the footage. If there's anything to find, she'll find it."

"Agreed."

The silence grew as uncomfortable as that time he was on a stakeout with a fellow agent and said, "Hey, isn't that your girl-friend?" right before the girlfriend planted a very unsisterly kiss on the face of the "brother" she had said she was going to meet for dinner.

Actually, this was worse. Because this time he couldn't keep his mouth shut. "Are you planning to bring Hope here this morning?"

"I was."

"I have the surveillance shift until three."

"Okay."

"Faith, please don't let her leave until I get back."

"Charles, she's her own person."

"Yes, but if she wasn't your sister, we would have put her in protective custody last night. She's getting special treatment because of her relationship with you. If I believe she's in danger, I won't hesitate to pull rank as team leader in this situation and lock her down until we can ensure her safety. It will make her angry. She might refuse to speak to me, but she would be safe. I can fix angry. I can't fix dead."

8

Hope stared at her phone and re-read the text from Charles for the tenth time.

He was mad, but not forever mad?

Faith walked into the kitchen, poured herself a glass of Cherry Coke, then took the seat beside Luke. She took a sip, set her glass on the table, and turned to Hope. "I have no idea what happened between you and Charles last night. I do know that he's in a very bossy mood this morning, but I'm not getting the sense that he believes all is lost."

Luke held out his hands, his expression smug. "I told you."

"What did you tell her?" Faith snuggled into Luke's arms, and he tapped her on the nose.

"None of your business. That's between me and Hope. Or is it Hope and I? No. Hope and me?"

"You're trying to distract me." Faith grumbled but didn't seem to mind that Luke continued to distract her, this time with his lips on hers.

Hope ignored them. She loved them. Didn't mean she wanted to see them in a lip-lock before breakfast. Or ever, really. She kept her head down until Luke squeezed her shoulder.

"I'm headed to work. If you need me, call." He pressed a kiss to the top of her head. "Actually, you should just plan to update me every thirty minutes."

Hope rolled her eyes. "Protective much?"

Faith smirked. "What was your first clue?"

She and Faith had breakfast and finished getting ready for the day. Before they left the house, Faith wrapped her arms around Hope's neck from behind and squeezed. "I love you, sis."

"Love you, too."

"If you don't keep yourself safe today, I'll lose my mind."

"I'll do whatever you want me to do."

"Promise?"

"Promise."

Hope drove her car, because it was significantly easier for her to manage in her own vehicle. Faith had insisted that they keep the phone line open between them so they could stay in constant communication on the commute to the FBI office. There was almost no traffic on a Saturday morning, and Faith used the space on the highway to alternate between driving in front of her and behind her.

"Just out of curiosity," Hope asked as Faith again switched her position, this time to beside her, "what do you propose to do if someone comes after me?"

"This isn't funny."

"I wasn't trying to be funny."

"I don't know, okay?" Faith's voice broke. "I just want to make you the least available target I can make you until I get you to the office and in a building filled with armed men and women."

Hope didn't hesitate to apologize. "I'm sorry, Faith. This seems to be my weekend to say stupid things to the people I love most in the world. I appreciate everything you're doing, even if I do think it's unnecessary."

Faith didn't respond immediately. But then the unmistakable sound of laughter floated through the speakers.

"Are you . . . laughing at me?"

"Did you hear what you just said?" Faith's laughter held a hefty helping of gloating.

"What did I say?"

"You said you love Charles!"

"I said no such thing."

"You might as well have."

Hope replayed her words. "You know what I mean."

"Why yes, yes I believe *I* do."

"You're reading way too much into this."

"Methinks the lady doth protest too much."

Hope groaned. "Look, I apologized. Don't make me grovel."

"I won't. But I bet Charles will." Faith sounded far too happy about that prospect.

"No. He won't." She hadn't been sure until she said the words aloud. But she knew he would accept her apology *sans* groveling.

"I hate to be the bratty little sister, but you weren't so confident last night." There was nothing but concern in Faith's voice. "Hope, I've never seen you like that."

"Yeah. Yesterday wasn't one of my better days. I messed up a lot of stuff. But there's a good chance I can fix it. Most of it, anyway." She couldn't fix Gloria being dead. But she could fix the relationships with the people who she did life with. She could hang on, rather than allowing any of them to disappear from her life the way she'd let Gloria go.

When Faith didn't respond, Hope glanced around. Faith was behind her, and slowing. "Faith? Are you okay?"

"Hmm? Yeah . . ."

"Sis, that's hardly a confidence-inspiring remark." Hope continued to drive and kept an eye on her rearview mirror.

"I have to take this call. Hang on."

Before Hope could respond, she had nothing but dead air. The call was still connected, but on hold, as Faith spoke to someone. Hope could see her mouth moving in the reflection.

After a long minute of silence, Faith's voice came through the speakers. "Hope?"

"Yes?"

"When we get to the office, I need you to park, but not get out of the car."

"Do I want to ask why?"

"No, but I'll tell you as soon as we get there."

Hope had promised to do whatever Faith said, and in this case Faith had more information and more skill, so Hope did as requested. Faith parked beside her and hopped into the passenger seat.

"What's going on?"

"Do you remember Detective Morris?"

"Sure. He's the reason Gil and Ivy have to name their first-born son Daniel."

"That's him. He called me."

"And?"

Faith took a deep breath. "Someone broke into your house last night."

Hope shook her head. "He must be mistaken. The security system didn't alert me to anything."

"I said the same." She held out her phone. "He sent me photos."

Hope stared at her home. In the photo it was clear that at least two windows had been broken. She swiped the screen and the next photo was of her kitchen. Every single thing that had ever been in a drawer or a cabinet was in the floor. The next photo was of her bedroom.

The drawers were empty. Mattress slit. Hope couldn't force her mind to process the total destruction of her room. Did that mean she was going into shock? Or was her mind protecting her from the pain that was surely coming?

She handed the phone to Faith. "I don't understand."

Faith squeezed her hand. "The trash guys called it in. Drove by and went to get your trash can, and saw the windows on the back of the house. Freaked out. Called the police."

Hope's eyes filled with tears. "I have the best trash guys. Are they okay?" Her trash and recycling company treated her like a princess. They had told her in no uncertain terms that she was never to pull her trash can to the curb. That they would get it. And twice a year, brand-new cans appeared. When she questioned it, they told her they didn't want her to try to clean them. So they just took her dirty ones and replaced them.

"I told Morris to be sure to tell them that you were alive and well. And then I called Luke. He's already headed to your house. He has Gil. Zane, Tessa, and Jacob are headed to your office. They're going to confirm everything is okay there, then they'll meet Luke and Gil at your house."

"It's Saturday! Did Luke drag everyone from their beds?"

"No. They were in the office this morning. Some kind of training they were going to do and then go to lunch. Apparently, Marty was there, and she's ticked because Jacob told her someone had to stay in the office to answer the phones if needed. According to Luke, she's promised you a chocolate cake."

Hope didn't have the mental or emotional energy to deal with this outpouring of love from everyone from her trash guys to her sister's fiancé's coworkers, who had become her friends over the past few months. If she said anything about them, she would start crying, so she tried to keep her focus on the present. "So are we headed to my house?"

Faith's eyes widened. "Absolutely not. We're going inside.

Right now. The only reason I wanted to tell you out here is because I didn't want to ambush you with this in front of a bunch of strangers."

"Thank you, but—"

"No buts. I'm not saying we won't wind up over there later. But not right now. Let's get inside and we'll figure out our next steps. Okay?"

Hope must have looked calm enough because Faith scrambled out of the car. But as Hope transferred to her wheelchair, her mind was stuck on the image of her bedroom. Someone had violated her privacy, her home, the space she'd made her own.

Whatever was going on, there was no longer any way for her to pretend that it wasn't personal.

Painfully personal.

FAITH'S PHONE call informing him of the destruction in Hope's home had left Charles in a jam. It had taken thirteen minutes to find someone to take his place on the surveillance of Lucius Kepler. Twenty-three agonizing minutes for them to arrive. Seven minutes to bring them up to speed and confirm that everything was covered before he left. Another sixteen minutes to make what should have been a twenty-five-minute drive across town, and three minutes to park and run inside.

In the sixty-two minutes since Faith's original phone call, he'd received two more crucial pieces of information. The first was that Kepler was threatening death and dismemberment to anyone who knew anything about his daughters' whereabouts and didn't share it with him.

The second was that Hope's office, and only Hope's office, had been methodically searched. He had not gotten the whole story on why she was in Hope's office to begin with, but Special Agent Tessa Reed of the Secret Service was the one who noticed that two photographs on Hope's desk had been switched from the last time she'd been there. She'd Facetimed Hope, who had been able to confirm that the photos had not been that way when she left the day before. Further inspection revealed that several files were out of place, and that the contents of at least two drawers had been pilfered.

Someone was after something Hope was supposed to have.

But according to Faith, Hope had no idea what it was.

Charles wanted to find Hope the moment he walked into the office, but his plans were thwarted by the presence of his boss, Supervisory Senior Resident Agent Dale Jefferson. "My office. Now."

Charles took a seat beside Faith at the round table in Dale's office. He managed a quick, "She okay?" to which Faith gave him a brief nod, before Dale settled into a chair across from them. "Talk to me."

Faith didn't hesitate. "It's too soon for forensics to give us anything conclusive—if there's anything to find. But under the circumstances, all signs pointed to Kepler. Hope's security systems weren't defense level, but they weren't cheap out-of-the-box jobs either. Whoever disabled them did so with a certain level of finesse. They were pros."

"I don't disagree with your assessment." Dale tapped his pen in a staccato on the edge of the table. "But I want us to be careful not to make assumptions. It's too much of a coincidence for me to believe that someone would decide to come after Hope the very night Gloria Kepler contacts her, then is killed, and her children go missing. But the reality is, we have no proof."

"Agreed."

Charles leaned forward in his chair. "And there's one more thing. We're bringing the combined might of the FBI, the

Secret Service, and the Raleigh police force, not to mention Sabrina Fleming-Campbell's skills, to the table."

Dale waved his hand in a "keep going" motion.

"Kepler is a criminal. That doesn't make him stupid. It seems strange that he would go after her this way. If he had any clue how deeply Hope is woven into the law enforcement community in Raleigh, it should have generated a different response. Not rush jobs. Nothing so obvious."

Charles turned to Faith. "Although now that I think about it, Kepler wouldn't have had any reason to believe she knows everyone with a badge. It's not like she's a prosecuting attorney."

"True." Faith turned back to Dale. "Hope is a tiger in the courtroom. Absolutely terrifying. But it's rare for her to take a case to court unless it's some of her pro bono work. Hope's specialty is business law. They tend to settle their disputes in arbitration. She isn't in and out of the police station or the courthouse on a regular basis."

Dale nodded. "But Kepler isn't known for being sloppy." He pointed at Faith. "You've been in the news enough in the past year that a cursory search would have connected her to you and should have been enough to give him pause."

"Unless he was in too much of a hurry." Charles spoke as he considered the possibilities. "Let's say Kepler was behind Gloria's murder. He realizes his girls are missing. He gets word that this attorney named Hope Malone was one of the last people Gloria talked to. For all we know, the man had his own phones tapped so he could keep an eye on his wife." Crazier things had happened. "He takes out Gloria, hides his girls so they are safe while he plays the freaked-out parent and grieving spouse, and in the meantime, he has to find out what Hope knows. He might think Gloria had given her more information than she did. Or that Gloria had been making plans to leave him."

"I could definitely see that happening," Faith said. "I never knew Gloria, but I can imagine how a mother who felt trapped might behave. She couldn't leave the girls with their father, but in order to successfully take them, she would have to be prepared."

"Unless," Charles did not like where his mind was going at the moment, "she was just in the beginning stages of her plan, but for some reason felt compelled to rush it and got caught. Something that was big enough to make her risk everything, and that when he discovered it, made him willing to eliminate her from the equation."

Dale stood. "As much as I enjoy hearing all of this, let's try to stick to the facts. And use those facts to figure out what on earth is going on. I should probably pull you both off this case, but that wouldn't be fair to you, Charles. And ultimately it wouldn't serve the case. You know it better than anyone else. Just make sure you are transparent in all your dealings. We don't need anything to blow back on us."

"Yes, sir."

Dale turned to Faith. "You are not officially doing anything on this, and I want to keep it that way. I know you'll work unofficially on it regardless of what I tell you."

Faith dropped her eyes to the floor but didn't protest Dale's assumptions.

"I won't make you sneak around, but don't make me regret it. Is that clear?"

Faith nodded.

"Fine. Get out of here. Keep me in the loop. If you need resources, let me know. You'll get them."

"Thank you, sir," Charles and Faith said in unison.

They took two steps down the hall before Charles turned to Faith. "Where is she?"

Faith cut her eyes in his direction but didn't answer.

"Faith?"

"I'm not sure you deserve that information."

"Regardless of whether I deserve it or not, I can't fix anything if I don't talk to her."

Faith had mastered a look that said, "Fine, but if you mess this up, I'll kill you," without needing to speak a word. That was the look she fixed on him before saying, "She's at my desk."

"Is she alone?"

"No."

"Any chance I can get her alone?"

"That's up to her."

9

W hen Charles approached Faith's desk, he found it surrounded by Secret Service agents. Hope was in their midst somewhere, but he couldn't see her.

He could hear her though.

"You are not going to tell me what I can or cannot do, Luke Powell. And that goes the same for the rest of you. I respect your opinions, but there may be lives at stake."

"Or," Charles recognized the voice of Secret Service Special Agent Zane Thacker, "this is a clever ploy to flush you out."

Charles was large enough to shove his way into their circle, but he was smart enough to ask for entry rather than using brute force. Sizing them up, he determined his best chance of getting through was to approach Gil or Luke. Not because they were easy targets, but because they were both in love with women who had been in the crosshairs of dangerous individuals. They would understand his need to get to Hope.

"Excuse me." He tapped Luke on the shoulder. "May I?"

Luke's expression could have created a glacier out of a tropical island. He stepped six inches to his left, leaving a gap that wasn't big enough for Charles to squeeze his arm through. But Gil Dixon, another Secret Service agent, stepped further to the side. Charles checked Gil's expression. It might have been pity that prompted Gil to give him room. It might also have been an ingenious strategy designed to ambush him.

Regardless, he had his body halfway into the huddle, and he wasn't leaving without Hope. Her eyes landed on him. She swung a hand in the direction of her friends and self-appointed protectors. "Tell them I have to go."

"I would do anything for you, *querida*, but I'm not sure I have enough information to make that call."

She bristled but didn't speak.

"From what I overheard, I'm not sure you have enough information either," he added. "What brought on this sudden desire to throw yourself to the wolves?" Hope may have believed him to be speaking metaphorically, but Kepler had two "pet" wolves. The concept was disturbing on too many levels to get into.

"I got this." She extended her phone toward him, and the circle shifted so he could step all the way through.

"What is it?"

"A map."

"Okay."

"A treasure map," Luke chimed in.

"Not helping, Luke." Hope glared at him.

"It literally has an *X* on it. What else would you call it?"

"I would call it a map. With no guarantee of treasure."

Charles held out his hands between the two of them. "You two are like siblings."

"We *are* siblings," Luke fired back. "And my *sister* seems to think it's reasonable to go to a park where we have no way to control the environment, numerous lines of sight, and more exit routes than we could ever hope to monitor, just because she 'really needs to.'"

"And this sudden need," Gil chimed in, "is something that she has refused to explain to the rest of the class."

"Esperanza," Charles dropped his voice low. "They're making a lot of sense."

"But—" Her eyes filled with a deep pain that Charles would have given anything to remove.

"Guys," he nodded toward Tessa, "and lady, could I ask you to indulge me a moment. Hope and I need to talk."

When no one moved, he added, "Privately."

Tessa gave a delicate snort. "We'll find out eventually."

"Probably. But that doesn't mean we need to hash things out with an audience. Five minutes."

"Come on." Gil slapped Zane on the back and turned to walk to the conference room. "Give them a few minutes. They can't get into too much trouble."

Charles squatted down so he could be on eye level with Hope but didn't speak.

Faith grabbed her iPad charger from her desk and said, "I'll just find somewhere else to be for a little while."

When they were finally alone, or as alone as they could be in a sea of cubicles, Charles returned Hope's phone. "Will you tell me what's going on?"

She didn't answer the way he'd expected her to respond. "Do you think they know I'm here? In the FBI office?"

"It wouldn't be that hard to figure it out. Your car is in the parking lot, you still have your phone, and we aren't trying to hide it."

"That's what I thought, too." Her face was a study in concentration, and Charles waited for her to continue. When she made eye contact, her expression was wary. "Gloria's husband wants to talk to me."

"What?"

"I know." Her shoulders came almost to her ears, eyes wide, the picture of confusion and worry. "It's crazy. But he says he can prove that he hasn't taken the girls. That he knows Gloria called me and he just wants to find his girls."

"And you believe him?"

Hope frowned. "I'm not sure."

"Hope, he is not a good man."

"Yes, but as you said, that doesn't mean he doesn't love his girls. Unlike the Raleigh PD and the FBI, he doesn't have to search legally. He's their father and has a host of criminal contacts he can utilize. Can you blame him for trying to find them using any means necessary?"

"As an FBI agent, yes. As a man, no. But as your"—he caught himself before he said *boyfriend*—"designated protector for the duration, I cannot approve of you putting yourself anywhere in his vicinity."

"My designated protector?"

It was dumb, but he'd said it. He had to follow through. "Yes."

Hope tapped her lip with her index finger as if pondering the mysteries of the universe. "Who designated you?"

"I did." He deliberately put his hands on the arms of her wheelchair and leaned toward her. "You are not going to get yourself killed before I have a chance to love you for a minimum of sixty years. If you want to be a bit reckless in your nineties, fine. Until then—"

Hope grabbed his shirt and pulled him toward her. He almost lost his balance but caught himself in time to fully appreciate the sensation of Hope Malone's lips on his. When she pulled back, she whispered against his lips, "You and I are going to need to discuss your conflict management skills. You keep throwing away your biggest bargaining chip."

"Our future isn't a bargaining chip, Esperanza."

"See what I mean?" She sounded exasperated, but she kissed him again. This time, he was the one who broke the kiss, only to move his lips to her ear.

"You're one to talk." He kissed a line across her cheek, to her nose, and across to her other ear.

"What do you mean?" Her eyes were closed, her faced tilted toward him, and she made no move to escape his lips as they retraced their path.

"If you keep kissing me, I'm not going to be motivated to change my tactics. From where I'm standing, they're working great."

A highly amused, distinctly feminine voice came from behind him. "Should we come back later?"

HOPE NEEDED AIR. She needed a fan. She needed new deodorant. What she did not need was her little sister catching her making out with her—what had he called himself? Designated protector?

Charles held her gaze and brushed her nose with his. "If you could give us another five—"

"Charles!"

He winked at Hope as Faith shoved herself past him and into Hope's line of sight. "Luke is losing his mind about a treasure map."

Before either of them could answer, Faith turned on Hope. "You are not getting anywhere near Kepler. I don't care how public the park is." She turned back to Charles. "You aren't seriously considering allowing this, are you?"

"Faith, Hope is her own person."

Charles's deep voice held a hint of amusement that Hope couldn't figure out until Faith glared at him and said, "Do not use my own words against me."

Hope pointed a finger at Faith and Charles in turn. "Have you two been talking about me?"

"Please." Faith grabbed Hope's finger and squeezed it. "As if you and Luke don't talk about me."

Luke came around the corner on that pronouncement and slid around Charles. "Honey," Luke said with patronizing sweetness, "Hope and I only talk about you when it's for your own good."

"Really." Faith was not amused. Luke reached a hand toward her and brushed his thumb across her cheek. "Hope. Charles. Explain this madness."

Hope held out her phone. "This message came through twenty minutes ago. The sender claims to be Gloria's husband. He wants to meet. The map is of the park with an *X* on the spot where he wants to meet. He claims he has proof that he didn't take the girls. Says he would never harm them."

"Why does he want to give you this information and not us?" Faith asked.

"Oh, I don't know." Hope didn't try to hide her sarcasm. "If I had to guess I'd say it has something to do with the fact that he's under FBI surveillance, and he expects you to arrest him on sight."

"We have nothing to arrest him for . . . yet." Faith's tone held all the annoyance of the frustrated agent she was.

"He may not know that. And I'm harmless. I have no authority to do anything but talk to him. Even if he knows how much of a connection I have to the FBI, even if he knows I'm sitting in this office right now, I'm not a threat."

"No." Charles laced his fingers through hers. "You aren't a threat. But you are far too vulnerable to be anywhere near Kepler."

Hope had to make him understand. "But if he knows something—"

"If he knew something, he would follow up on it, *querida*."

"But, the girls—"

"Every legal means, and like you said, probably all kinds of illegal ones, are being used to locate those girls. You speaking to him in person changes nothing. He can email you. He can call you. He can Facetime you if he wants to see your face when he speaks to you. This," he tapped her phone, "is him playing off your compassion to try to get you into his sphere. He suspects you know something, and if he was responsible for Gloria's death, there's no way to know how far he's willing to go to prevent you from sharing. You cannot give him the opportunity to take you."

Charles took a deep breath, and Hope wrapped her hand around his neck, her thumb brushing his jaw. "Okay."

"Thank you." He held her gaze, and his relief was palpable.

Faith's scoffing snort destroyed their moment. "That's it? Four Secret Service agents tell you this is a bad idea. *I* tell you this is a bad idea. You don't care. Charles tells you it's a bad idea, and you say 'okay' and make goo-goo eyes at him?"

Hope turned her "goo-goo" eyes to Faith. "Maybe if the rest of you had paused long enough for us to have a conversation, it would have gone the same way. But we'll never know. Charles at least had the decency to find out what was going on, get my opinion, and state his own, and we've come to an agreement."

Faith wasn't buying it. "Right."

Luke gave Charles a fist bump. "Glad to have you on board, Romero."

"Glad to be on board." Charles's grin was smug and satisfied.

How had this happened? She broke up with him. She refused to allow this relationship to continue. They had a huge fight. And now he was her designated protector/boyfriend and Luke was welcoming him to the family? Her head might spin off at any moment. She couldn't process all the emotions. Not right now. "Can we get back to the matter at hand? We have a dead woman. Missing girls. A criminal husband/father who might be behind all of it or none of it. And he wants to talk to me."

That shut everyone up.

Until Tessa poked her head around the cubicle wall. "Sorry to eavesdrop. Or not sorry. Either way, why don't you tell him you'll meet him at your office during regular business hours? It's a perfectly reasonable request for you to make, to see him in your territory. You could tell him he can make an appointment with your secretary. It shows that you're willing to talk to him, but on your terms. If he really wants to chat, he'll show. If not, it avoids the messiness of you categorically refusing to meet him." Her lips twitched. "Even if he did send you a treasure map."

Hope groaned. "It's not a treasure map."

"I like it." Faith looked to Charles. "You?"

"Yeah. Hopefully this will be wrapped up before Monday, but if not, we can make sure there's plenty of security. And she can make it clear that there's no client-attorney privilege and the meeting will be recorded."

Hope texted her reply to Kepler and slipped her phone into a pocket on her chair. "I like the 'he never shows up because everything is resolved' plan the best."

10

A s Hope pocketed her cell, Charles's phone rang.
He took one look at the screen and answered the
call. "Romero."

"I need to talk to you." Sabrina sounded . . . rattled. Sabrina
was never rattled. "In person."

"Okay." He wasn't going to argue with her. "Where? When?"

"Can you meet me at the soda shop in Pittsboro? In an
hour?"

Charles glanced at his watch. "Sure. But I'm bringing
Hope."

"Perfect."

The call disconnected.

He put his phone in his pocket and turned to Hope. "How
do you feel about a milkshake?"

"Now?"

"That was Sabrina. She has something she wants to share in
person rather than over the phone. But she obviously doesn't
want us to go all the way to Carrington, and she doesn't want to
come all the way here, because she wants to meet at the soda
shop in Pittsboro."

"Or she wants a milkshake." Hope reached for her purse. "Let's go. I'm driving."

"Not this time." Charles grabbed his own keys. "I have federal plates on my car. And if we need to get back here in a hurry, I actually have the horsepower to do it. I'm not sure your car goes over seventy."

Hope's look was pure affront. "Don't bash my car."

"I can only be in your car for a few minutes before my legs start cramping. I'm driving. Do you want to hear firsthand what Sabrina has or not?"

Hope lifted her chin. "Fine."

It took them ten minutes to get Hope transferred to his car and her wheelchair stowed in the back. Once on the road, Charles reached for her hand. The sensation of her fingers pressed into his settled something in him that he'd never realized was out of sync until he met her.

"This trip is giving me a flashback to the day we met." He gave her hand a gentle squeeze. "We'd been driving for two hours, and you told me in no uncertain terms that if I wanted to keep you happy, I would provide you with a milkshake. Pronto."

Hope dropped her head back on the head rest and chuckled. "I was hungry. And scared."

That was news. "You didn't seem scared."

"I was terrified." The words were a low whisper. "And you were so big and serious. All business. Three guns that I could see—"

"Wait. You were terrified of me?"

Her head whipped around, and her grip tightened. "No. Not of you. Never of you. You promised me you would protect me. I believed you."

"Then what—"

"I was terrified that you'd have to do it. You'd only met me a few hours earlier, but I knew if it came down to it, you would die to save me. I didn't want that to happen. I kept thinking that you probably had a girlfriend who was going to be ticked off when she found out you'd run out of town with a woman you were literally going to have to carry around."

"And I was afraid you were going to figure out that I didn't mind carrying you around." He winked at her. "Still don't mind. Never will."

In his peripheral vision, he saw her take a deep breath. Her shoulders lifted high, then lowered. "I don't deserve you."

He had no idea what to say to that. He didn't consider himself to be a great catch. She was the prize to be won. The woman he would pinch himself for eternity if he got to make his own. That she saw things differently boggled his mind. "You chose those words on purpose, didn't you?"

"Why whatever do you mean?" she asked with put-upon shock. She even fluttered her hand across her chest.

"Because I can't argue with you. If I say you do deserve me, you can choose to take that as me saying that you're a horrible person and deserve to be stuck with a scumbag like me."

"That's not what I meant."

"Or," he continued as if she hadn't spoken, "I can say you do deserve me, and you can take it that I think very highly of you, but also very highly of myself. Either way, I can't win."

"Now who's choosing their words carefully. You know what I meant. You're a good man, Charles. The best. I'll never believe that I deserve you."

"Hope—"

"But I'm not sure I'll be able to get rid of you, either. You're clearly delusional and will need constant supervision to be sure you don't allow yourself to be taken in by other whack jobs who would prey on your gentle nature." She blew out a breath. "Face it. You need me to protect you."

He nodded in mock solemnity. "I do need protection."

"It's big of you to admit it. I'm proud of you."

He wanted to haul her into his lap and kiss the sass right

out of her. She had so much of it, it would take him a very long time. But he was up for the challenge.

They didn't talk much for the rest of the drive, but the silence held nothing ominous. Just a low-grade buzz of anticipation for what Sabrina had to tell them.

They arrived at the soda shop in Pittsboro and found Sabrina and her husband, Adam Campbell, sitting at a table just inside the door. One of the chairs was pulled away, and Hope was able to settle in without difficulty. Sabrina waited for Charles to sit before she said, "I know where they are."

"What?" Hope leaned toward her. "Where?"

Sabrina dropped her head and whispered, "I won't tell you."

HOPE STARED at the top of Sabrina's head for a second. Had she heard that right? She leaned back in her chair and met Charles's gaze. His face was a mask of professional detachment. Then she looked at Adam. He rubbed small circles on Sabrina's back and stage whispered, "Bri, baby, you're freaking them out. You need to explain."

Yeah. She did. Hope cleared her throat. "I want to be sure we're on the same page. You know where the girls are, but you won't share that information. Is that accurate?"

Sabrina nodded, but continued to stare at her hands, head bowed.

Hope knew Sabrina. Considered her a friend. This was not normal behavior. Sabrina was a take-charge, "here are the facts, this is what you should do, thank you I'm done here" kind of person. She was not hesitant. She did not show a lot of emotion.

But she was now.

Hope made a decision. She reached across the table and grabbed Sabrina's hand. At her touch, Sabrina lifted her head and made eye contact. "You're one of the most intelligent women I know. You're also one of the most passionate people I've ever encountered when it comes to children in danger. I trust you to want the best for these girls. If you won't tell us where they are, what can you tell us?"

Beside her, Charles stretched his long arms across the table and placed his hand over Hope's where it held Sabrina's. "I trust you to have your reasons, Sabrina. I'm not interested in doing anything that would bring harm to the girls. If you need me to step outside so you can talk to Hope alone for a few minutes, I can do that."

Sabrina's eyes shimmered, but she didn't cry. "I could be wrong."

Charles scoffed. "When's the last time you were wrong?"

Sabrina didn't smile. "Adam would tell you it was this morning."

"Adam doesn't count." Charles removed his hand and settled his arm around Hope's back. "Talk to us, Sabrina. You've never given us any reason to do anything but trust you."

"I don't want to ask you to do something that could cause you trouble professionally."

"I will always seek to uphold the law. But my first and highest priority is to do what's right. Protecting those girls is what's right."

Sabrina studied Charles, and whatever she saw gave her what she needed to relax. "I found them. They are far from here. And I doubt their father can find them. Especially not while he's being tracked by the FBI."

"Can you tell us if they are still in the US?" Charles asked.

"Yes. My facial recognition software captured them in a small airport. My best guess is that they were flown from Raleigh on a private plane utilizing private airfields. Eventually they landed at a regional airport. The plane was a luxury private jet, and the flight plan and manifest did not indicate there were two children on board. But two children definitely walked off that plane. The software only caught one of the girls, but once I had that, I was able to find both of them. They are together. They do not appear to be in any danger."

"Do you know who has them?" Hope asked.

"I am confident they are with people who care about them."

Sabrina hadn't answered directly, but her answer spoke volumes. Sabrina had to know who the girls were with, and the nature of their relationship, to be so sure.

"I'm out on a limb, as far as I've ever been." Sabrina grimaced. "I want facts. Certainty. Answers. And in this case, if I'm wrong, I could be sentencing those girls to a lifetime of misery."

"But you don't think you're wrong." Hope knew Sabrina well enough to know that.

"No. I won't pretend to know what led to this, but it's difficult for me to believe that it's a coincidence the girls disappeared on the same day their mother was killed. This took careful planning, most likely by their mother. It's possible she forfeited her own life for them. Knew she might be killed but gave them time to get away. I won't cheapen her sacrifice by handing those girls back to their father."

Hope couldn't argue with Sabrina's logic. Or her decision. "Now that you've located them, can you keep track of them?"

Sabrina's eyes lit with the thrill of the hunt. "I won't abandon them. They've lost too much in the past twenty-four hours. So even though they may not need it, I'll continue the watch until there is no hint of concern."

Hope turned to Charles. "Can you live with this?"

"Temporarily." He looked at Adam. "If he goes to trial, we'll need to be able to talk to the girls, to the people who have the girls hidden. They may have key information that we need to put him away."

"I understand. And if we get to that point, we can discuss it again. For now, Sabrina has my full support. No matter what it costs us, we aren't giving those girls up until we know they will be safe."

"Agreed."

There wasn't much more to say. They ordered their milkshakes to go. Hugs were exchanged all around along with promises to keep each other in the loop.

Hope watched Sabrina and Adam walk down the street to their car. "It takes courage to say no to your friends."

"Yes."

"She's one of the bravest people I know."

"I suspect she would consider that to be a high compliment coming from you."

"I'm not brave."

"Sure you are."

Charles helped her transfer into his car. "Not all heroes wear badges and carry guns. Some work quietly to make the world a better place. You do that all the time with your pro bono work. And you were so worried about Gloria that you drove to her home on a Friday night. Your phone call alerted us to her murder. Kepler could have hidden it, disposed of her body, who knows what he would have done? We're where we are now because you chose to follow your gut, follow your conscience, follow your heart, and check on a woman you hadn't spoken to in five years. And right now, you're more worried about those girls than about your own safety and well-being."

He closed her door and jogged to the driver's side. He squeezed her shoulder before he backed out of their parking space. "Gloria knew she could count on you. She must have known that reaching out to you would put you in danger. But she knew you wouldn't have it any other way."

11

Hope considered his words as they returned to Raleigh. She tried to picture herself in Gloria's situation. Imagined what would have led to Gloria's phone call. But nothing made sense.

"I am relieved beyond belief," Hope said when they were halfway home and her milkshake was gone. "But also more confused than ever."

"How so?" Charles took a sip of his milkshake and set it back in the cupholder.

"If she planned all that, why call me? What did she hope to accomplish? She sounded so afraid. That's why I went to the house. There was no way I could leave her hanging all weekend." Hope picked up Charles's milkshake and took a sip.

He cut his eyes at her before returning them to the road. "You owe me a date for every sip you steal."

"Is it stealing though?"

"Well, I certainly don't want it back . . ."

She took another sip before returning the cup to the cupholder. "What's the plan now?"

"We get back to Raleigh. You go back to Faith's for the

evening. I go back to trying to pin something on Kepler. We do all of that without worrying about the girls, which is huge."

She stared out the window. "Would you consider taking me to my office first?"

"Your office?"

"Yes. Someone pilfered my office last night. If I could go through my things, I might be able to figure out what they were looking for. It's hard to do that from photographs."

"I don't like it."

"I have to go back to work eventually. And if you came with me, I'd be safe."

Charles didn't speak for a few minutes. He took a sip of his milkshake and handed it to her.

Subtle he was not. But she took a sip anyway.

"Let me make a few phone calls."

By the time they reached Raleigh, Charles had confirmed that Hope's office was clear, that they could safely enter, and that there would be several agents nearby should anyone try to pull something while they were there.

"Thank you," she said as they entered the building. "I know it's a long shot, but it's all I can do."

"I'm not opposed to long shots," Charles said as they went down the hall. "Those are the most exciting ways to win a game."

Hope stopped at the doorway to her office. Charles didn't say anything. He didn't rush her to go inside. He did slide one hand under her hair, his fingers gentle at her neck. She'd never imagined that someone as physically imposing as Charles would have the capacity for the kind of tenderness he possessed.

While his solid presence at her back held a hint of protectiveness, the overall sensation emanating from him was one of togetherness. He wouldn't take over. He wouldn't interfere. But he also wouldn't let her go it alone. If at any time he sensed that she was faltering, he'd share his strength with her, but he had every confidence that she could handle whatever was coming.

Hope moved into the office, but took the time to scan the walls, floor, and surface of her desk before she settled behind it. "Except for the photographs being out of place, there's nothing that jumps out at me as being disturbed."

Charles leaned against the wall to her left. "They were careful."

"But what were they looking for?" Hope studied her desk. The photo of her and Faith at Faith's college graduation. A more recent photo from a few months earlier of the whole gang in a boat off the Outer Banks. The photo was filled with diving gear, wet suits, and her own joy of having completed her first ocean dive. She pointed to the photo. "This photo—could any of them be in danger?"

Charles studied it. "I doubt it. Kepler would already know the Secret Service agents. Men like him make it a point to know the federal agents in their town so they can avoid them whenever necessary. The Carrington investigators wouldn't be on his radar, but they also pose no threat to him. The only person who might be of interest to him would be Sabrina, and she's already involved."

"True."

She shook her head. "The last time I was in here, Gloria was still alive. I listened to her message. Tried to call her. Left a voice mail. Closed everything down for the night and drove to her house. How is it possible that it's only been twenty-four hours since then?"

Charles shrugged. "I don't know. Twenty-four hours ago, you weren't answering my phone calls. Now? I'm guaranteed at least three dates."

"Will you be serious?" She tried to keep from smiling. Failed.

His answering smile was unrepentant. "I'm trying to distract you on purpose. You're thinking too hard. There may be nothing to see. Turn on your computer. Make sure your systems are working. Go through your drawers. Look through your files. When you're done, we'll go."

Charles took a seat on the sofa at the opposite end of the room and pulled out his phone. If he was restless to return to his office, she didn't see it.

An hour later, she conceded defeat. "There's nothing here."

Charles stood and walked to her desk. "You had to look. Now we know, and we take this off the table."

He was right. She knew it. But she'd wanted it to end. Tonight. She didn't like the sense that someone could come after her at her office. Her coworkers could be in danger. And she wasn't safe in her home either. She didn't even want to think about the amount of work waiting for her there. She needed a new bed. New furniture. New clothes.

She shifted in her chair. "This is why I do business law. It can be cutthroat, but not usually in the literal sense."

Charles came behind her, put his hands on her shoulders, and dug into a tight spot with his thumb. "You carry all your stress here."

"Yeah."

His hand slid down and hit another spot six inches lower. "And here."

"Mmm."

His other hand slid to the left. "And here."

"I get a massage every week. From a trained physical therapist who has magic hands. I wouldn't be able to move at all otherwise."

"This physical therapist a woman?" Unhidden jealousy in his voice.

"Yes."

"Good." He continued to work. "What you need is a live-in masseuse."

She allowed him to push her head to the left, exposing the line of her neck. "Know anyone who might be up for that position?"

His lips brushed her neck. "Maybe."

Her phone rang. His phone rang. Her office phone rang. And from outside, the roar of an engine was the only warning they had before chunks of the wall of her office flew toward them and a Hummer barreled into the hole.

CHARLES HAD no idea what was happening, but he had one goal —keep Hope alive. He reached under her arms and dragged her from her wheelchair. Cradling her body, he jumped away from the vehicle that rested where her desk used to be. The desk was now a mangled mass, her chair somewhere in the wreckage. Dust and debris filled the air, and the vehicle was hissing. Steam billowed from the hood and filled the room around them quickly enough that it prevented Charles from getting a visual on the driver.

"I just wanted to talk." The voice of Lucius Kepler came from the direction of the car. "I heard the phone call and I know you know what she planned. I need my girls. You're going to tell me where they are, or I'll kill you."

"If you kill me, you'll never find them." Hope's voice was strong. Not even a hint of fear. Brilliant woman. Playing for time.

Charles still had no clear visual, but a sound that could have been Kepler trying to free himself from his seatbelt gave him a general direction to point his weapon. He set Hope on the floor in the corner and stood in front of her.

"I need to know they're safe," Kepler shouted. "They are mine. My girls. No one else's. My responsibility. No one gets to raise them except me. Do you hear me?"

"What about Gloria? She was their mother." Apparently, Hope was incapable of keeping her curiosity at bay, regardless of the circumstances.

"She was mine. She could only ever be mine."

"She married you. She was yours."

"She wasn't mine. Not anymore. She betrayed me. Betrayed our family." A loud creak as the door to the Hummer opened. "If you tell me where she hid them, I'll leave you alone."

Yeah, right.

"I don't know where they are. What makes you believe Gloria hid them?"

"Don't lie to me!" The rage in Kepler's voice was tinged with desperation. Not a good combination.

Time to put a stop to this. "Kepler. This is Special Agent Charles Romero. You're under arrest."

"For what?"

"It's a long list." Hope actually managed to say those words without a hint of sarcasm. "Why did you kill Gloria?"

"I didn't kill my wife." Kepler growled. "I would never do that."

"No. You wouldn't. But that doesn't mean you wouldn't have someone else do it."

Charles wanted to turn to Hope and beg her to stop talking. But he didn't dare take his eyes off the spot he expected Kepler to appear.

"Why?" Hope pressed.

"She was mine. The girls were mine. No one else's." Kepler's non-answer was an answer. "I would never let anything happen to them. But she was going to leave me. Take my girls. Take what was mine."

"She called me yesterday." Hope's voice broke. "She was afraid. But you weren't home. So who killed her? Was it the pool boy?"

Kepler scoffed. "Gloria would never have let that punk kid get within ten feet of her. Not that he didn't try."

The "punk kid" was an undercover FBI agent—his cover so well-established that Charles hadn't told anyone, not even Hope, that he was not their target. It had to be the chef or the interior decorator.

"Gloria was too trusting. She let people get close to her when she shouldn't. Now, enough talking. Tell me where my girls are."

"Kepler. Stand down. It's over. You're going to jail. You have no leverage here. No hope of getting out of here a free man." Charles adjusted the angle of his body but made sure he kept Hope completely behind him.

"I need my girls."

"Why would I know where they are?"

Kepler scrambled around the opposite side of the Hummer and stalked toward them. "You were in on it from the beginning. You tell me where my girls are. Or I'll order my men to take care of the people you care about. Starting with this one." He pointed a trembling hand at Charles.

Charles didn't want to shoot him. They needed him alive. But he would not let him get one step closer to Hope. "Stay there, Kepler. Put your weapon down."

As if they'd been waiting for a signal, agents emerged from everywhere. Two agents came from behind the Hummer, one squirmed through the hole in the wall, and three more came from the still intact door to Hope's office.

Two were FBI. The other four were Secret Service.

Charles took advantage of the commotion and charged. He took two strides and tackled Kepler. Charles slammed him to the ground, one knee buried in his gut. The weapon slid from Kepler's hand in Hope's direction. Charles heard her scooting toward it. Then her calm voice. "I have his weapon, and for the record, that move definitely earned you another date."

THREE WEEKS LATER

W hen Charles told her to plan to be gone all day, Hope hadn't a clue what he was up to. Now, she stared in amazement as Charles gently deposited her onto a huge blanket he'd spread out on the sand. He returned a few moments later with her chair.

"Do you want to be in the chair or on the blanket?"

"The blanket's fine for now. Thank you."

The day was cool, but not cold. The breeze coming off the ocean whipped her hair in a million directions, and she pulled it into a messy bun and secured it with a hair band she kept in a pocket of her chair.

"Be right back." Charles pressed a kiss to the top of her head and jogged back toward the car. When he returned a few minutes later, he had a cooler and a sweater. He dropped the sweater beside her. "In case you get cold later."

If she got cold later, she had a much better method for getting warm than putting on that sweater. But she kept those ideas to herself.

Charles opened the cooler and handed her a bottle of

water. Grabbed one for himself and settled in beside her. "Cheers." He tapped her water bottle with his.

"Cheers." She watched the waves crash to shore for a few minutes before lying all the way down and closing her eyes. "I can't believe you brought me to the beach."

"You said you loved the beach." He leaned over her, his big body blocking the sun enough for her to look into his eyes. "And I love you." He pressed a kiss to her lips, her eyes, her nose, then back to her lips. It was several minutes later before he settled in beside her. "I didn't grow up going to the beach the way some people do. We didn't have the money for vacations, and we lived too far away to make it an easy trip. When I moved to Raleigh, I would drive to the coast every time I had a day off. I'd bring a blanket and some food, and I'd park myself out here all afternoon. By the time I made it back to my car, whatever had been stressing me out had faded. Like the waves had taken it out to sea and left me with nothing but peace."

Hope pressed her cheek to his shoulder. "After everything that's happened, I'd say we deserve some peace."

He grunted his assent.

Today was the first time they'd had a chance to spend more than a few hours together since Gloria's death.

Hope was living with Faith, and working from her kitchen, while her home and office were being repaired. The thugs Kepler sent to search her house had been a rough crew who didn't care how much of a mess they left. The people he sent to her office had been professionals who wanted to leave no trace of their presence, but their efforts wound up being pointless after Kepler's visit.

The Monday after Kepler used his Hummer to enter her office, a package was delivered. The postmark was Alaska. The contents held enough evidence to put Kepler away for life. Gloria had been gathering information on her husband for years. She couldn't testify against him, but she'd hoped to have enough dirt on him to keep the girls and herself safe.

The affidavit located in the package indicated that he'd never physically harmed her or the girls. In fact, he'd been a good husband and, in Gloria's own words, an excellent if somewhat aggressively possessive father. Gloria claimed she hadn't known of his criminal activities until the girls were in preschool. By then, she couldn't get out. She was watched too closely. As were the girls. She wasn't happy but was willing to remain . . . until an associate of her husband's showed up late one night. Her oldest daughter overheard the conversation—one that included references to a murder—and came to her mother the next day, terrified. At that point, Gloria began building her own case against her husband, as well as setting up a way for the girls to escape should it ever be necessary. She knew she might not survive but wanted to be sure there was enough evidence to prevent Kepler or any members of his family from ever gaining custody of the girls. She shared her suspicions about the interior designer being in her husband's pocket but had no concrete evidence.

Kepler suspected that she was up to something, and she knew she was being followed and monitored. But when he began ranting about the FBI's investigation into his dealings, she was hopeful that he would be taken out of the picture and she wouldn't be forced to take any of the steps she'd prepared. But then he became so erratic that she feared for her life and the girls.

She'd been right to be afraid. And she'd been right about the interior designer, who it turned out had not only killed Gloria but also the mistress of a client in another county.

The girls were safely in Alaska with a cousin Gloria had grown up with and who was like a sister to her. That cousin had mailed the package to Hope, at Gloria's request.

"Do you think Gloria knew he'd planned for her murder

that day? And that's why she called with that weird message about it being time? Because she knew he was monitoring her phone calls?"

"It's possible." Charles laced his fingers with her. "She knew the paperwork was coming. Knew you would have everything soon. Knew the girls were leaving. If she couldn't join them as she planned, maybe she hoped it would throw Kepler off the scent long enough to let the girls make it to Alaska safely."

"It worked."

"Yeah. But it nearly got you killed."

"I think Gloria knew I would risk coming under Kepler's scrutiny if that's what it took to save her girls."

"Yeah." Charles didn't sound too happy about that. But it was true.

They listened to the waves for a while, both lost in their own thoughts. It wasn't long before a soft snore reached Hope's ears.

Good. He needed the rest. Kepler had gone to jail as soon as the emergency room staff determined that he'd suffered nothing worse than a few bruises from Charles's tackle.

But rather than calming things down, his arrest sent the case into overdrive. Charles worked eighteen-hour days for the next two weeks on paperwork, warrants, more paperwork, and arrests. Which led to more paperwork.

Given the amount of work he'd been doing on the Kepler case before Gloria's death, today was Charles's first real day off in months. And rather than sleeping in and taking her on a normal date—dinner and a movie, no muss, no fuss—he'd packed a picnic, scouted out the most handicapped-accessible beach in North Carolina, and brought her here.

He deserved a nap on the beach. Where the waves would hopefully take away his worries and leave him with peace.

And Hope.

And love.

More from Lynn:

https://www.lynnhblackburn.com/

DEAR READER

Dear Reader,

I hope you enjoyed this glimpse into the life of one of my favorite secondary characters, Hope Malone, and her FBI agent "designated protector" Charles Romero. When I finished writing *Unknown Threat*, Book 1 in the Defend and Protect series, I received numerous messages asking me for Hope's story. And I was all too willing to comply!

The idea for *Out of Time* came from a deleted scene in *Unknown Threat*. I had originally written a fun bit of dialogue between Hope and Faith, and then between Hope and Charles, when Hope was taken into protective custody. I knew the time Hope and Charles spent together would be the beginning of something beautiful, and I'm thrilled to have the opportunity to bring it to the page.

Hope has lived up to her name, her hope and faith remaining strong despite numerous difficulties and challenges in her young life. But in *Out of Time*, we see that even those with a deep and abiding faith can stumble when forced to confront old hurts and face deep fears. I'm so thankful that God is gracious to us when we falter, and that He draws us back to Him with his everlasting love.

Out of Time is just a small slice of the Defend and Protect story world. If you'd like to read more, please visit LynnHBlackburn.com for a list of all the books in the series.

Grace and peace,

Lynn

LYNN H. BLACKBURN BIO

Lynn H. Blackburn loves writing romantic suspense because her childhood fantasy was to become a spy, but her grown-up reality is that she's a huge chicken and would have been caught on her first mission. She prefers to live vicariously through her characters and loves putting them into all kinds of terrifying situations while she's sitting at home safe and sound in her pajamas!

Unknown Threat, the first book in her Defend and Protect series, was a 2021 Christy Award finalist and her previous titles have won the Carol Award, the Selah Award, and the Faith, Hope, and Love Reader's Choice Award. *Malicious Intent*, the second book in the series, released March 2022.

She is a frequent conference speaker and has taught writers all over the country. Lynn lives in South Carolina with her true love and their three children. You can follow her real life happily ever after by signing up for her newsletter at Lynn-HBlackburn.com and @LynnHBlackburn on Bookbub, Facebook, Twitter, Pinterest, and Instagram.

ACKNOWLEDGMENTS

A huge thank you to:

The experts who wish to remain anonymous but who provide critical insight and direction.

My family—Brian, Emma, James, and Drew—for hanging in there with me, again, during deadline drama!

Lynette, Beth, and Lisa – for including me in this project! It's been a thrill to work with you!

Julie Davis – for your editing prowess!

Andi Bradsher – for sharing your insight into managing life in a wheelchair.

The Light Brigade – for your prayer and support.

Debb & Deborah – for virtual Gibbs' slap and hugs and for making the distance over oceans and continents seem not so very far after all.

Most of all, to my Savior, the Ultimate Storyteller – for allowing me to write stories for you.

CODE TRAUMA

EXTREME MEASURES, 1.5

LYNETTE EASON

1

Nurse Practitioner Holly Cooper shut the door of her Honda CRV and clicked the remote to lock the car. She let her gaze roam the hospital parking lot while she turned her collar up against the biting wind.

Was he watching? She walked toward the entrance of the hospital, unable to stop herself from tossing another glance behind her. She'd been doing that a lot over the past two weeks.

Ever since the threats had started.

Notes on her windshield at work, her mailbox at home.

Even a note *in* her locker at work.

Leave and don't come back.

You're not wanted here.

Go away.

She shuddered and hunched her shoulders against another strong gust and the shiver that danced up her spine. She despised the fear that consumed her but couldn't seem to do anything to stop it.

She'd reported the incidents to the sheriff, who was looking into them, but he'd come up empty so far. The same with hospital security.

Holly had closed all her social media accounts and tried to make sure she took precautions when it came to walking to her car before and after a shift.

But she was still scared.

You could call Andy, a little voice whispered.

No. She couldn't. She shut off that line of thought and breathed a relieved sigh when she stepped safely through the automatic doors and into the hospital lobby.

Why would someone threaten her? Who had she angered?

The only person she could think of was Garrett Mann, the doctor who'd repeatedly asked her out and whom she'd consistently turned down. He was flirty and cute, true, but she'd seen the fallout of his relationships and wasn't interested in being his next conquest. But more than that, while her current relationship was in a state of . . . what? Limbo? Uncertainty?

Whatever the word, it didn't change the fact she was in love with someone else. She'd told Garrett that, of course, but it didn't seem to make a difference to him.

"Come on, Holly," he'd cajoled just yesterday, "all this playing hard to get is just wasting time that could be better spent having fun. You know you want to go out with me."

She'd rolled her eyes and walked on while she considered filing a harassment suit against him. Then again, if she went out with him once, he'd probably lose interest. Or she could encourage him to a DEFCON 1 level of annoyance.

Since that held absolutely no appeal, all she could do was pray that if she ignored him long enough, he'd leave her alone. If not, she'd talk to her boss and HR.

She reached the base locker room and pushed inside. Her locker was on the last row, and she scanned the room, noting part of the night shift crew, Carrie and Pam, getting ready to leave. Their presence helped calm her nerves. Slightly.

"Holly?"

She jumped and spun, her heart racing. Okay, maybe she

needed more calming. She placed a hand over her thudding chest and shook her head at the woman who'd stepped up behind her. "Penny. You scared me."

"No kidding. Are you all right?" The redheaded, gray-eyed, Penny Satterfield had been a close friend from the moment Holly had met her. Funny and smart, she had an openness about her that invited friendships and fun. And her skill as a medical helicopter pilot was legendary throughout the business.

"Yes." Holly hesitated then sighed. "Actually, no."

"What's wrong?"

With a glance at the other ladies, she whispered, "Someone's threatening me."

Penny gaped then. "What do you mean? Threatening you how? Since when?"

"Shh!" Holly motioned to the far corner of the locker room. "Come back here. I've got about ten minutes before I need to clock in."

Penny followed her, but it was busy right at shift change. "Hey, Holly, Penny. Good morning." The greeting came from Sylvia Blackmon, one of the flight nurses who often picked up other shifts in the ER when she wasn't working on the chopper.

"Morning, Sylvia," Holly said while Penny waved.

Once the woman had slipped out of the room, Holly opened her locker and Penny leaned against the one next to it.

"Who's threatening you?" her friend whispered.

"I don't know. If I knew that, I wouldn't be so stinkin' jumpy."

"Tell me more."

Holly glanced around. No one was paying them any attention. "It started a couple of weeks ago. Someone on my social media page sent me a private message telling me to leave town or else. I didn't recognize the name, and when I clicked on the profile the person had no friends or even a picture. I think it was a bogus account set up to specifically target me. The sheriff thinks so, too. He tried to track it, but the IP address ended up being from a local coffee shop that tons of people use every day, so there was no way to trace it."

"You've been to the sheriff. That's good, because all of that is so weird. And scary."

"Tell me about it." Holly quickly locked up her personal items and headed to the computer so she could clock in.

"I wondered why you hadn't posted anything lately," Penny said, following her. "What are you going to do?"

"I mean, what can I do?" Holly shrugged. "The sheriff knows." She paused. "Then again, I'm not so sure how hard he's working on it. He's retiring in a couple of months, and right now, there's no one stepping up to take his place."

"Have you called Andy?"

Andy. Holly could no more stop the skip of her heart any more than she could will it to stop beating. She and Detective Andy McKittrick had reconnected from their elementary school days and had been seeing one another on the weekends. She thought he might have been close to asking her to marry him, but then two months ago, his partner had been killed in a nightclub shooting.

Their romance had come to a screeching halt, and no matter what she did, she couldn't seem to reach that place inside him where he'd gone to deal with the trauma. "No. I can't call him right now."

"What? He's practically your fiancé. I can't believe you haven't told him about this."

Holly groaned. "It's complicated." She hadn't told anyone Andy had basically ghosted her. When the subject came up or when someone asked where he was, Holly just said they were taking some time to make sure their relationship was what they both wanted.

"Complicated or not, he'll want to know—and being a police detective, he'll know what to do, too."

"I can't."

"Why not?"

"He's asked me for space, Penny. I promised to give it to him."

Penny's eyes went wide. "Wait a minute. He asked you for space?"

"Yes."

"Oh."

"Right." Holly swallowed the sudden tightness in her throat. How she missed him.

"I still think you should tell him."

"No. I want to, but no. He's dealing with the death of his partner, and I don't want to . . . infringe on that."

But Penny was shaking her head. "I think you're making a mistake."

"Sometimes I think I am, too, but for now, I'm going to honor his request."

Her friend frowned. "Just how much space does he need? Is there more to this than just him trying to work through the death of his partner?"

"Yes," she said, working to keep the tears at bay, "there's more."

"And you didn't think that was important enough to share?"

"I didn't want to talk about it, to be honest, so I've just kind of avoided the topic, but things are up in the air at the moment with Andy and me, and I'm not sure when—or even if—we will work things out."

Penny's eyes were wide. "Wow, I'm so sorry. I had no idea. I'm a lousy friend that I didn't see this."

Holly smiled. "You're not a lousy friend. I'm the lousy friend for not telling you." The smile faded and she drew in a deep breath. "But, now you know. And it is what it is for now."

"I could always ask Holt to look into it."

"Penny, this is not a case for the FBI." And while Penny's husband, FBI Special Agent Holton Satterfield, would come to her aid if asked, Holly just couldn't bring herself to believe she needed that much help.

"Is he at least getting therapy?" Penny's question jolted her out of her thoughts.

"Yes." At least he was. She wasn't sure if he was still going. She glanced at the time. "I'll be over to base shortly. I promised I'd stop by the ER and check on a friend."

"Who?"

"An older gentleman I go to church with." She glanced at her watch. "I've got to go. See you for lunch if you're around?"

"Sure."

Holly hugged her well-meaning friend and hurried off to clock in. She said a silent prayer for the man she loved and asked for wisdom.

And protection. For both of them.

> You're an idiot. We all love you and think you're an amazing man, but you're definitely an idiot.

ANDY PUSHED his half-eaten biscuit away from him and frowned when he read the text from Penny, one of Holly's best friends. He'd thought she was his friend, too. But if it came down to a choice between him and Holly, Holly would win every time. Not that Penny should be made to choose.

> Why is that?

> You're going to lose her. If someone doesn't kill her first.

He sat up on the sofa.

> What are you talking about?!

> Someone's threatening Holly so you'd better do something. Fast.

The breath left his lungs. He rose to pace the length of the kitchen before making his way into the den, where he dropped to the sofa to stare at the screen as though the words might change into something else.

They didn't.

"What's going on?" His brother, Jacob, walked into the den to frown at him.

"Something about someone threatening Holly."

"What?"

"I'm not sure."

"Oh, right, because you refuse to talk to her or let her be with you at the worst time of your life like the woman you plan to marry should be."

Andy scowled. "Shut up."

Jacob planted his hands on his hips and shook his head. "Whatever, man."

Andy ignored him. Like most younger brothers, Jacob could be annoying—even if his intentions were good. Andy dialed Penny's number and grimaced when it went to voice mail.

He tried Holly's. Also voice mail. They'd both be working and probably had their phones on Do Not Disturb. Or they were just ignoring him.

"No answer?" Jacob asked.

"No." He shook his head. "Holly's being threatened, and she didn't reach out."

Jacob huffed. "Why would she? You basically told her to stay out of your life. I'm sure she took that to mean you were staying out of hers, too."

Andy winced. He loved her, and he'd pushed her away. But he'd pushed her away *because* . . . because he was a coward. He'd *pushed* her away before she could *walk* away. His therapist had nailed it when he'd stated that fact three sessions ago. Andy had been wrestling with it since then, trying to find the courage to face Holly and beg her forgiveness. "Jacob, I just . . ."

"What? You think because what's-her-face walked out on you because you showed emotion in front of her that Holly's going to do the same thing?"

Andy froze. Stared at Jacob and swallowed. Even his brother had figured that out? "No. Of course not," he lied.

Jacob raised a brow, obviously seeing right through him.

Andy groaned.

"You need to go to her," Jacob said. "Or you're for real going to lose her. If you haven't already."

He let that sink in. Someone had threatened Holly. As a detective, he'd seen all kinds of things he wished he could wipe from his mind, the latest being the death of his partner. He rolled to his feet and paced to the window to look out. He wasn't able to help his partner as the man lay dying on the asphalt outside the nightclub. What if he lost Holly, too?

He'd asked Holly for space, and she was giving it to him—and he was almost mad that she hadn't stormed his apartment and demanded he let her be with him.

Add *immature brat* to idiot and coward. But, she needed him. Maybe. Regardless, it was time to stop thinking about himself and focus on Holly. If she'd even let him at this point.

"I'm going to her."

"Good. I'll help you pack."

"I got it." He packed an overnight bag and headed for his truck.

"You want me to come?" Jacob called from the doorway.

"No. You have a shift tonight. I'll figure out what's going on and text you." Jacob worked for the local fire department.

"You better." His brother stepped back and shut the door.

Once in the driver's seat, Andy tried calling Holly again.

Still nothing. He backed out of his driveway, his adrenaline pumping.

He'd known Holly since fifth grade—and had vowed to himself that he was going to marry her the day he'd saved her from the playground bully. And then, just a few short weeks later, he and Jacob had been shipped to another foster home.

But he'd never forgotten Holly.

Reconnecting with her a year ago via social media had been an amazing thing, and he only wished he'd done it sooner. They'd dated and made the distance between them a minor inconvenience.

And then his partner, Chris, had died. Killed by a drunk with a gun. They'd responded to the scene of a bar fight because they'd been one street over. When they'd arrived, Chris had rushed through the door and taken a bullet to the head.

Stupid, stupid, stupid. Why hadn't he waited?

But he hadn't. His partner of six years had led the way into the building with Andy pulling up the rear.

Now, Andy sped down the highway toward Asheville, located about an hour away from his home in Spruce Pine. He was thankful for the flashing light on his dash, which made it possible for him to cross the Asheville city limit in just under forty-five minutes.

Now to find Holly.

2

——————

Holly found the emergency department short-staffed, so no one minded that she wanted to care for her friend.

In room six, she checked the IV bag hanging on the pole. "Almost empty, Mr. Carson," she told the man in the bed. "I'll have to get another one." That normally wasn't part of her job, but she didn't mind. The walk would allow her a few moments to think about the threats she'd received and what else she needed to do about them.

He nodded. "It's really good of you to come see me. I know you're busy."

"Aw, what kind of friend would I be if I didn't check in on my favorite drummer?"

He chuckled, but it was a weak sound. She squeezed his hand. "Get some rest. We need to get you well and back up on the stage at church."

"Indeed we do. Thank you, my dear."

"Of course."

He closed his eyes, and she said a heartfelt prayer for God to touch him and heal him.

"Holly, I didn't realize you'd be down here today."

Holly whirled to see the doctor she always did her best to avoid. Garrett Mann. Unfortunately, avoiding people in the emergency room was basically impossible, and he'd caught up with her. "Yep. The place is super short-staffed, and I told Nick I didn't mind helping out." Nick, the head doctor of the ER.

"Well, it's good to see you." He winked at her like they shared a secret. They didn't. "How's your patient?" he asked. "I think I've treated him before. Seizures, right?"

"Right. He's doing fine right now. He was a bit dehydrated in addition to the laceration on his forehead. We're waiting on a room to open up to monitor him for any more seizures. If that'll be all, Dr. Mann, I've got to head to base." She patted Mr. Carson's hand and turned to make her escape.

Garrett stepped in front of her, blocking her way. "It's Garrett, not Dr. Mann. It's good of you to help out. Things can get a little overwhelming. The extra pair of hands is always welcome."

"Not a problem."

She started to head to the next room, but he stopped her once more with a hand on her arm. "What's the rush?"

Holly shot him a tight smile and shrugged him off. "He's not the only patient, *Doctor*. I need to replace this IV bag then head to base." The base for the medical flight team was located in one of the wings of the hospital.

"That's what nurses are for."

She barely refrained from rolling her eyes. "I *am* a nurse, remember? Anyway, I'm here to help, so that's what I plan to do."

"What about lunch later?"

"I already have lunch plans." At least it was true.

"Why doesn't that surprise me?"

The tone in his voice sent shivers up her spine. Was he the one who'd sent the threatening notes telling her she needed to leave? But why pursue her if he wanted her gone? Or did he think she'd come running to him for help?

Ha. Not likely.

She stepped past him, and this time he didn't stop her.

Once out of the room, she let out the breath she'd been holding and aimed herself toward the supply closet.

Another nurse greeted her with a smile. "Hi, Holly, no emergency flights today?"

"Hi Rachel." Rachel Vickers, a respiratory therapist who was often in the ER. She didn't seem to have a problem with Dr. Mann's attentions—even went out of her way to flirt with the man. Rumor had it that they'd dated for a while. So why didn't he leave Holly alone and focus on someone who'd welcome his advances? She realized that Rachel was staring at her, waiting for a response. "Oh, sorry. I'm a little scattered today, but no flights yet. Headed to base shortly." Holly shook off the creepy sensation the doctor always left her with and smiled at the pretty woman.

Rachel frowned. "Tough patient?"

"Tough doctor," Holly muttered.

"Sorry?"

Holly forced a smile. "Nothing. You look like you've been running. Are you okay?"

"Just late and trying to catch up."

"Are you here to work with Mr. Lyles?"

"I am."

"He was sleeping when I checked in on him earlier, so poke gently."

Rachel laughed. "He can resemble a bear, can't he?" Mr. Lyles was a "frequent flyer." He had chronic asthma and didn't always take his meds like he was supposed to. He also didn't like breathing treatments. Rachel nodded to the room. "Is that Dr. Mann?"

"Yes, it sure is."

"Oh good, I have a question for him." Rachel stepped around her. "See you later, Holly. Hello, Dr. Mann . . ." Rachel's voice faded as the door shut behind her.

Holly sighed and headed for the supply room, only to be stopped by Raina Price, the paramedic who was often on the chopper with her and Penny. "Raina, what's up?"

"I was looking for you."

"Well, you found me. I'm headed to get an IV bag. Walk with me?"

"Sure." She started down the hall once more. Raina fell into step beside her. "Isn't that something nurses do?"

Holly cut her friend a sideways glance, and Raina grinned at her. "Sorry, I heard some of the exchange between you and Dr. Mann."

"He's a piece of work."

"I avoid him."

"You're not the only one. And besides, I *am* a nurse."

Raina stuck her hands in her jacket pockets. "Penny said something was going on with you. You okay?"

"I'm fine." And she was fine with Penny sharing with Raina. They were closer than sisters. When one hurt or was in trouble, the others came to the rescue. Or at least tried to. "Just some weird notes. Threatening notes, actually."

"What do they say?"

"Stuff like I don't belong here and if I know what's good for me, I'll leave. Nothing like someone wants to kill me, but someone definitely doesn't want me around."

"When did all that start?"

"A couple of weeks ago."

"But you've been here for ages. Why start wanting you to leave now?"

"Who knows? I've reported it to the sheriff and hospital security, so I'm not sure what else I can do."

"Tell Holt? Andy?"

"Like I told Penny. Not yet."

They arrived at the supply closet door, and Raina checked her watch. "I've got to go clock in. Are you going to be all right?"

"I'll be fine."

"Okay, I'll see you when you come down to base."

"I'm just helping Mr. Carson. I'll be there as soon as I hang his bag and turn him over to Dr. Mann." He might not be her favorite person, but even she'd admit—grudgingly—he was a good doctor and always gave his patients excellent care.

"Okay."

Raina gave her a quick hug. "See you later."

Her friend darted down the hallway toward Life Flight's base. The medical flight team was close, and she loved them like family.

Sometimes more. And her family was amazing. With a mother and father still together and a younger sister in her last year of law school, Holly was blessed, and she knew it.

She held her badge over the security pad and waited for the green indicator to flash, then opened the door. The light came on at her entrance, and in the laptop to her right, she logged in and tapped the appropriate key sequence to indicate what she would be removing from the room.

The IV equipment was in the back, so she followed the shelving unit to the area and grabbed one of the plastic bags.

And the lights went out.

Holly stood still. "Hello? Hey, there's someone in here. Can you turn the light back on?"

But the light shouldn't have gone off. It was motion activated. If it went off, someone had turned it off.

Silence thickened the darkness.

Nothing.

Just the sound of her heart beating in her ears.

And the footsteps walking toward her.

Holly's breath caught.

She backed up, trying to stay as quiet as possible. In her mind, she pictured the layout of the supply room. Sharps to her right. IV bags behind her. Bandages and tape to her left.

Why would someone *turn off* the light to enter the room?

The threats jumped to the forefront of her mind. *God, help me, please.*

She pulled her phone from her pocket and hesitated, her thumb hovering above the home button. Did she want to take a chance on making the light come on? But she couldn't just stand there.

A noise sounded behind her. She spun, listening. Holly heard the person breathing, and a cold chill shivered up her spine. Who was doing this to her?

She moved away from the breathing but was confused. Which way was the door?

She shoved a fist against her mouth to keep from crying out.

She had to get out, get away.

Holly pressed her thumb against the home button. Her screen lit up and provided an eerie glow in the dark room. She swiped a finger across the bottom and saw the missed calls and texts from Andy.

Guided by the light of her phone, Holly moved toward the door.

The hard crash against the back of her head sent her to her knees. She cried out. Her phone tumbled from her hand and her ears rang from the pain. Nausea swirled through her, and she eased backward until her shoulders rested against a supply cabinet.

"Stay out of this hospital," the voice whispered. "Or die. This is your last warning."

ANDY STEPPED inside the hospital and made his way to the base where Holly usually was. When he found it empty, he hurried to Dr. Fitzgerald's office, only find the man out. His administrative assistant directed him to the ER. With each step, the knot in his gut grew. Ever since his partner's death, he'd developed a distinct distaste for stepping foot inside any medical facility. But for Holly, he'd do it. He closed his mind to the memories and focused on finding Holly. He made his way through the triage area by flashing his badge, turned a corner, and found several people clogging the hallway.

"Make way, coming through." A nurse shoved past him. "Here Holly, put this on your head."

"Holly?" Andy pushed his way to the center to find Holly on a gurney with a hand to her head. He stopped beside her. "What happened?"

Her eyes widened when she saw him. "Andy? What are you doing here?"

"We can talk about that later. Now, what happened?"

"Someone attacked me," she said. Tears formed in her eyes and coated her lashes.

He reached for her and pulled her into his arms. "I'm here now." He looked up at the others. "You all can go back to work. I'll take it from here."

"'Bout time you showed up," Penny hissed at him.

"Penny?" Holly frowned at her friend. "How did you . . . ?"

"Know to come out here? I didn't. I was coming to find you because you weren't answering your texts."

"Oh."

Andy took a look at the back of her head. "The skin isn't broken."

"I know, thanks."

"Well, where's a doctor? Someone needs to examine that."

"Take a deep breath and relax," she said, her eyes dark with pain and something else, but he wasn't exactly sure what.

"Someone went to get a doctor. I'm just going to wait here and try not to throw up, okay?"

Andy took the deep breath she suggested.

"Holly, are you all right?"

He turned at the question. Rachel, a nurse he'd met several times during his visits to see Holly, walked up and placed a hand on Holly's shoulder.

"Yes. I'm fine." She started to touch the back of her head, but stopped short, dropped her hand, and grimaced. "Or I will be."

"We're getting her examined by a doctor, and then I'm taking her home." Andy looked at Rachel. "And if a doctor doesn't show up soon, I'm going looking for one."

Rachel raised a brow. "If she said someone is on the way, then someone is on the way."

"I need to make a report and get my stuff," Holly said. "And let my boss know what's happened. Has anyone talked to Dr. Kirkpatrick?"

"I covered that," Penny said. "He said he would find someone to cover your shift for as long as you needed."

"He's a good boss," she whispered.

Rachel shifted. "I can help get your stuff if you want."

"Thank you, but I'll get it."

"Okay, well, if I can do anything, let me know."

Andy stayed at her side while one of the doctors checked her out. "No concussion, and the person didn't break the skin so no stitches. You'll be fine, but you're probably going to have a nice headache."

"I don't know that I'd call the headache *nice*," Holly said, "but I agree that I'll be fine."

"Take it easy for a couple days, and call if you have any nausea or vomiting or changes in your vision. You know the routine."

"Right. Thanks."

After the security officer took her report, Andy said, "I'd like to see the footage leading into that supply closet. It's only accessible to someone with a badge. Let's see who swiped a badge right after Holly."

The officer nodded and walked to the nursing station. With a few taps on the keyboard, he logged into the software and soon had the footage playing. "There's Holly," he said. "And there. The person caught the door just before it closed."

Andy sighed. "No badge necessary. Thanks."

"Yep."

Andy looked up to meet her gaze. "You ready?"

She nodded. Then winced. "Remind me not to do that."

He led her out of the hospital and to his truck. "Let me drive you home. We'll get your car later."

She hesitated, then shrugged. "Sure."

"Who would do this to you, Holly?"

"I don't know. At least, I'm not sure."

"Penny told me about the threats. I'm going to call the sheriff and find out all I can, and we'll get to the bottom of this."

"I've already reported it to Sheriff Lewis as well as Dr. Kirkpatrick, but you're welcome to talk to him."

Andy shot her a look as he climbed into the driver's seat. There was something in her tone that held a chill. A distance. He swallowed. Not that he blamed her. They rode in silence for the next ten minutes until he pulled into the parking space in front of her home. She lived in a three-bedroom townhome not too far from the hospital.

Andy slid out of the truck and walked around to the passenger side. After he helped her from the vehicle, Holly pulled her keys from her pocket. "Let's get you settled," he said, "then I'll call the sheriff. In the meantime, I'm going to stay with you. You shouldn't be alone."

"Andy . . ."

He started to open the door, and she placed a hand on his. "Stop."

"Stop what?"

"Pretending nothing is wrong. We've barely said two words to each other for two months, and now you want to come riding to the rescue? Why are you here?"

3

H e raised a brow. "Are you kidding me? Penny texted and called me out on being an idiot and said someone was threatening you."

"She did?"

"Yeah."

That sounded like Penny. "So, you're here because she told you to come."

He frowned. "No, I'm here because she told me what was going on and I can't bear the thought of you in danger."

Okay, that was better. And she could understand that, but still . . .

Andy took her face in his and gave her a sweet kiss. "I've missed you."

She placed a hand on his chest and backed up. "Hold up with the kisses, Andy. You don't get to do that anymore." As much as she wanted to melt into his arms, there was too much wrong between them for that. "I'm not the one who went anywhere."

He closed his eyes. "I know. I know. You're right." He

glanced around. "Let's get you inside." He pushed the door open and allowed her to go first.

Holly stepped over the threshold and gave a low cry. Andy's hands came up to grip her shoulders. She simply stared at the red words spray-painted across her living room wall.

Leave town or die.

He moved her so her back was against the wall, then closed the door. "Call 911 and don't move from this spot."

While she fumbled for her phone, he pulled his gun and held it in front of him as he walked through her townhome.

"911. What's your emergency?"

"Someone broke into my home." She gave the address and clutched the phone to her ear. A surge of anger rose up hard and fast enough to nearly strangle her.

"Is the person still there?"

"I don't know. I have a friend who's a detective. He's checking the rooms now."

"Then stay still and wait for him to come back."

Holly had no trouble following that order. She wasn't sure her legs would work anyway. The ugly red words seemed to sear themselves onto her soul. Where was Andy? The townhome was small and wouldn't take but a few seconds to clear. Just as she was ready to go looking for him, he returned from her bedroom, his weapon holstered, but his face white. "It's clear."

Holly let out a slow breath. "The police are on the way."

He nodded.

"What's wrong?" she asked. "You found something else, didn't you?"

"In your bedroom, someone hung one of your dolls from the shelf and painted your name across the dress."

Holly darted from her spot by the door and headed to see for herself.

Andy caught her by the upper arm. "Don't go look. There's

no reason to, and you'll never be able to wipe the image from your brain once you see it."

She hesitated. "Which doll?"

"Not the one your dad brought back from Israel."

She almost wilted against him but pulled away at the last second and pressed a hand to her aching head. All the dolls in her collection were gifts from her father, but the one he'd brought her from Israel was special. "I'm scared," she whispered.

"I know. You can't stay here."

"I can stay at base." She'd never been so grateful for that home away from home. Her family when she needed them. And boy, did she need them now. "I can't believe this. What have I done to deserve this?"

"Hey, there's nothing you could have done to deserve this, so don't even think along those lines. But something sure has triggered someone."

"Yeah."

"And we're going to find out what."

She studied him. His eyes were narrowed and fierce, his jaw tight.

Officers arrived and processed her townhome, asking her questions until her head spun. Even the eight hundred milligrams of Motrin didn't completely stop the pain. Despite the nasty warning on the wall, she sat on the couch and simply just closed her eyes.

Andy finally escorted the last officer out of her home and shut the door. She opened her eyes as he turned to her. "You want me to pack a bag for you?" he asked.

"No, I'll do it in a bit." While he was here, she might as well see if he could answer all the questions she'd had bouncing around her head for the last two months. "Can you cover that up with a blanket then sit beside me?"

"Yeah, sure." It didn't take him long to hang a blanket over the spray-painted threat. "I'll get rid of the doll, too, for now. Until you decide if you want to have someone try to clean her up."

"Thanks."

Once those two items were done, Holly was able to finally pull in a deep breath.

She patted the cushion next to her. "Sit." He sank onto it and she took his hand. "Talk to me, Andy, please."

He sighed. "I've really been messed up, Holly. After Chris was killed, it sent me into a very dark place, and I haven't been able to come out of it." He looked at her. "Until now. When I heard you were in danger, it knocked me off my feet—and some sense into my head, I think."

"And so you came running."

"I did."

"Thank you for that. It means a lot." It didn't solve their problems, but it did let her know that he thought of her as a priority. At least when *she* needed him. But what about when *he* needed her?

"Yeah." He grabbed a blanket from the end of the couch and covered her up. She snuggled next to him. "See if you can sleep for a little bit, get the headache to ease. Then we'll pack your bag, get something to eat, and I'll take you to the hospital."

"We're finished talking?"

"For now." He squeezed her hand. "We'll talk more when you're feeling better."

"But—" At his tight features, she let it go. "Where will you stay tonight? You're not going home, are you?"

"No. I have enough vacation time built up that I don't have to be back for another two weeks. I'm not leaving until we find out who's responsible for this. As for where I'll stay, I'll get a room at the motel across the street from base."

"Okay." Relieved and feeling safe for the first time since the threats started, she let the fatigue settle over her and closed her eyes.

ANDY WATCHED Holly sleep for about an hour before he decided to be productive. He gently settled her against a pillow and pulled his phone from the clip on his side as he walked into the kitchen. From here, he could keep an eye on her and the front door but talk without waking her. He knew the evidence the officers had collected would be sent to the lab in Asheville. Thankfully, he knew Yasmine Forsythe, a lab tech, who worked there.

She answered on the second ring. "Hello, Andy."

"Hey Yasmine, thanks for picking up. I need a favor."

"Of course, what can I do for you?"

"Have you received the evidence from the break-in over here in Asheville? The victim is Holly Cooper."

"Um . . . not yet. Why?"

"When you get it, can you speed-process it?"

"Andy . . ."

"Come on, please?"

"She's special to you?"

"I've got the ring in my pocket."

She went silent, then sighed. "Oh. Well. I guess she is special. No promises other than to do my best to get it done ASAP."

"Thank you."

"Sure thing."

He hung up as Holly stirred and sat up. She rubbed her eyes, and he walked over to sit beside her once again. "How are you feeling?"

"Better. Hungry." She touched the area on her head and grimaced.

"How is it?" he asked.

"It's sore, but I think it was more of a glancing blow than a direct hit. At least the headache is basically gone."

"That's definitely a good sign. Want to head over to the hospital and grab something on the way? We can see if Penny and Raina need us to bring them anything."

She glanced at the clock. Just after lunchtime and she was starving. What a morning it had been. "Yes, sure." She packed a bag while he watched. The whole time she worked, he wanted to explain himself, beg her forgiveness, but this wasn't about him. He needed to be here for her, and when she was ready, maybe they could have a talk. A long-overdue, honest conversation.

Maybe . . .

Or should he try to set things straight while they were alone? But her body language shouted that she might not be super receptive to anything he had to say. So, he stayed quiet and determined just to be there for her for as long as she'd let him.

She followed him to his truck, and he helped her into the passenger seat. "You're sure you're okay?"

"I'm sure. For the moment."

"Let me know if that changes."

She placed a hand on his arm. "I'm okay, really."

He drew in a deep breath. "That shook me today. Not because I'm scared of the person doing this, but I'm terrified I won't be able to stop him from hurting you again."

Some of her stiffness relaxed and she dropped her hand into her lap. "Well, nothing to do but trust God and stay alert."

"Right." He paused, and his fingers spasmed where they rested on her arm. "I . . . I'm having a hard time with trusting him right now."

"I know." For a moment, her eyes were soft and kind, and he wanted to wrap her up and hold her close, protect her from every bad thing—and person—in the world. Then her gaze chilled once more and she shifted away from him.

He cleared his throat. "How about you trust him, and I help him out if presented with the opportunity?"

She gave a forced laugh, and his heart squeezed. What had he been thinking when he'd pushed this woman away? He should have leaned on her. And God. But Chris—

Andy shut off the "should haves."

He closed her door and walked around the truck to slide into the driver's seat. Seconds later, he pulled out of the town-home parking lot and headed for the highway that would lead them back to the hospital about ten minutes away. "One thing struck me about your break-in," he said.

"What?"

"There wasn't any forced entry. Did you leave the door unlocked?"

She frowned. "Of course not."

"Okay, then could Penny or Raina have given the key to someone?"

"Neither would do that. Not without clearing it with me first."

"Can you call Penny and ask her?"

She studied him for a moment, her frown deepening, then pulled out her phone and dialed Penny's number. She put the phone on speaker so he could listen in.

"Holly? I'm so glad you called. Are you okay?"

"Yes, I'm with Andy. We were heading back to the hospital. I'm going to stay at base tonight."

"Okay, why?"

"Someone broke into my house."

Her gasp echoed over the line. "Broke into your home! Are you okay?"

"Yes, I'm fine, but did you by any chance loan my key to anyone without telling me?"

"No way!"

"I didn't think so, but Andy insisted I ask."

"Holly, what's going on? First the attack in the supply closet and now this?

"I don't know, Penny. I really don't, but I'm working on figuring it out."

"Hold on a second. I'm going to check my purse."

Andy caught sight of the car behind him. It had been there awhile. He kept his eyes on the mirrors while he waited for Penny to return to the phone.

"Holly?" Penny's hushed voice finally came over the line. "The key is gone."

Andy's jaw tightened, and he spared a glance at Holly, who thanked her friend and hung up. She swallowed. "So, what does that mean?"

"We look for someone at the hospital who has a grudge against you."

"Dr. Mann is the first person who comes to mind."

"Dr. Mann."

He slowed to cross the bridge that would take them to the hospital exit and looked in the rearview mirror in time to see the sedan behind him slam into the back of his truck. The wheel spun beneath his fingers, Holly screamed, and he rammed into the side of the guardrail.

4

———————

Holly clutched the door handle and tried not to scream again while Andy yanked the wheel and got the tires back onto the road. In the side mirror, she could see the car coming back for another hit.

"Andy—"

"I see him." He waited until the last possible minute, and Holly braced herself for another crash.

Andy jerked the wheel to the right and pressed the gas to race up the exit ramp, escaping the second hit. The sedan's engine roared, but Andy whipped the wheel one more time, then slammed on his brakes to spin out of the oncoming sedan's path. The dark car roared past them and disappeared around the bend just ahead.

Andy muttered something under his breath as he shoved the truck into park.

"What?"

"The license plate number. I got it."

He grabbed a pen from his console and wrote on his palm. He tossed the pen down and grabbed his phone. After identifying himself, he started barking orders. "I need a plate run. Yes, now, please. The person nearly ran me off the road."

Breathe, Holly. Deep breath in . . . slow exhale. They were alive and the danger was over. As long as the person didn't come back. Andy hung up his phone. "Garrett Mann."

"What?"

"The car belonged to the doctor."

"Why doesn't that surprise me?" She pressed a hand to her head, thankful the incident hadn't triggered any more pain. "But, honestly, Andy, while Garrett is a flirt and a player who skates right up to the edge of sexual harassment, I'd never picture him doing something like this."

"Guess we're going to find out. Cops are looking for him as we speak." He hesitated. "As soon as they pick him up, they'll bring him in for questioning. Do you feel like going to the police station?"

Did she? "Yes, sure. Why not?"

He checked the damage to his truck and announced it minimal, then got them back on the road heading toward the police station. "You think they'll find Garrett today?" she asked.

"I would think so."

She bit her lip. "No, I've changed my mind. For now, I guess just take me to the motel across the street from the hospital. Assuming you can find him and pick him up, you can question him and tell me what happens. I don't need to see him—which means staying away from the hospital for the moment. Because if that was him in the car, he'll have to get back to work so he has an alibi. And if I'm at base . . ." She pressed a hand to her right temple. While her head wasn't hurting too much, she simply wanted to lie down.

"That's probably a good idea."

"Sorry I'm being such a wimp."

Andy reached over to snag her fingers in his. "You're not a

wimp, Holly, you're hurt and need to rest. I'm an idiot for forcing you to do too much too soon."

"You're not an idiot." She paused. "Well, not in this case anyway."

He barked a short laugh. "I'm working on it."

"Good."

Within minutes, he had her checked into the motel and inside her room. With a gentle finger, he stroked her cheek, looking like he wanted to kiss her, then backed off with a sigh. "Get some sleep. We'll talk when this is all over."

"You mean really talk?"

"Yeah. Really talk."

"Okay. Thanks."

He handed her the overnight bag, which she set on the floor beside her while she watched him leave. Once he was out of sight, Holly shut and bolted the door, went to the nearest bed, and sat on it with a groan. Her head ached, and she grabbed the Motrin from her purse and took another pill.

But finally, she was safe.

She would stay here tonight and make arrangements for the townhome to be painted and cleaned up as soon as possible. With that in mind, she called the pastor at her church and asked for a recommendation for someone to take care of the chores. Once she explained what happened, he told her he'd take care of it.

"But I don't expect—"

"I know you don't, Holly, but you've been a blessing and a help to more than one person in this church, myself included. Let us help you now."

So, she'd agreed with a grateful heart, checked in with her family—without telling them what happened, and turned on the television.

With the news playing in the background, she pulled her iPad from her bag. She planned to read while she waited to hear back from Andy, but soon, her lids grew heavy. She set the iPad aside and stretched out on the bed. Okay, so she'd sleep a little.

She'd just drifted off when her phone buzzed.

She grabbed it from the end table. Dr. Kirkpatrick. "Hello?"

"Holly, I just wanted to call and check on you."

"I'm doing okay. Headache has eased and, to be honest, I could have probably finished my shift."

"I'm so glad to hear you say that. Do you think you could come back in?"

She sat up. "Probably. Why?"

"We're short a nurse practitioner. Janine just got a call that her son has the flu, so she has to leave, and Hank is still on vacation."

"Um . . . yeah. Give me about thirty minutes to get there."

"Of course. Hopefully, we won't have a call before then."

"I'll shoot for twenty minutes."

"You're the best, Holly."

She hung up and texted Andy.

> Going in to work. I'll just have to avoid the ER and anywhere I might run into Garrett.

> I should have texted you. Mann is in custody. You should be safe for now.

Relief kept her rooted to the bed for a few seconds before she stood and headed for the shower. She probably still had blood in her hair and needed to freshen up. She glanced at the clock. She could do this—she just had to walk across the street to base. And she'd make sure she was walking with someone in the same direction, just to be safe.

"I'M TELLING YOU, you've got the wrong guy." Dr. Garrett Mann crossed his arms and leaned back in the chair.

Andy watched through the two-way mirror while the sheriff tried to wring a confession from the doctor. Only he wasn't budging. "Someone stole my car. And I was at the hospital during the time you say I was running that guy off the road."

"We're checking your alibi. Until we get some answers, you want to tell us about your relationship with Holly Cooper?"

"Relationship?" He snorted. "It's strictly professional."

"So, you've never asked her out?"

The doctor sighed. "Yes, I've asked her out. She said no, that she was in love with someone else. End of story."

Andy's heart flipped at the thought of Holly saying she loved him. She hadn't given up on him just because he'd acted like a jerk.

One of the deputies slipped into the conference room being used as the interrogation room and passed a note to the sheriff.

Sheriff Lewis read it and frowned. He looked up at the mirror. "Alibi is solid. And the stolen car report is there just like he said."

Dr. Mann stood. "Now, may I please leave and get back to work?"

"Yes. Thank you for your time."

He left, and Andy's heart chilled. "I need to get to back to Holly. If Mann's not the one we're after, the person threatening Holly is still out there."

The sheriff nodded. "You'd better give her a heads-up."

Andy headed for the exit, snagging his phone from his pocket. Still walking, he called Holly. When it went to voice mail, he texted her.

> Mann isn't the guy who's threatening you. Stay on guard. I'm heading to the hospital. You've got a bodyguard until all of this is resolved.

Her response was almost immediate.

> I'm headed for the chopper. We got a call. Will text when I'm back.

His adrenaline surge abated a fraction. As long as she was in the air, she was safe.

At least from someone who intentionally wanted to hurt her.

5

Reports of a multicar pileup on the interstate always sent dread through Holly. She sent up a silent prayer for those involved and buckled herself in. Penny sent them whirling into the air while Holly stayed in contact with the paramedic on the scene in order to be prepared for whatever emergency they were walking into.

"Three victims," Holly said, repeating the information. "The head trauma is ours."

Raina nodded, and five minutes later, Penny hovered over the area where she'd been cleared to land. Following the motions of the officer directing her, she touched down with barely a bump in the middle of the highway just a short distance from the collision. While Penny powered down the chopper, Raina and Holly beelined toward the scene.

"Over here!"

Holly followed the voice to find paramedics, Carl and Nadine, strapping the neck brace to the woman on the ground. Carl looked up. "Trauma dressing in place, you have two large bore IVs in the ACs, and 1000 ml of Normal Saline has been administered. She's lost a lot of blood, and it's possible she has a skull fracture, but she's stable for the moment. Let's get her on board."

They worked together to get the woman into the belly of the chopper and were soon back in the air heading toward the hospital. "I've got the doctor on the line," Raina said.

Holly commenced to give her report of the woman's condition. "Patient is a fifty-two-year-old female—"

"Holly, the bleeding isn't stopping."

"Administer LR, TXA, and two units of blood." TXA, a hemostatic agent commonly used to stop bleeding in severe trauma.

"On it."

They pushed fluids, and several seconds later, the woman's eyes blinked open. Panic flared. "What's going on?"

Holly took her hand. "You've been in a car accident, but you're going to be just fine." She took another look at the vital. Strong heartbeat, good breath sounds. Blood dripping into her veins to replenish what she'd lost. She was going to be fine. She reported the status to Dr. Mann.

"What's your name?" Holly asked her.

"Liza Hollister."

"Nice to meet you, Liza. Sorry it's under these circumstances."

Liza smiled then closed her eyes. "My head hurts," she whispered.

Because her brain was probably swelling. "We've got you covered. Raina, Decadron?" Decadron should reduce the brain swelling. She passed the woman the vial.

"On it." Raina pulled the meds and inserted them into the IV port.

Two minutes before they were to land, the woman went into cardiac arrest.

Holly reacted. "Grab the paddles!"

Raina was already moving. She placed the paddles on the

woman's chest. "Clear!"

Holly lifted her hands and watched the monitor. "Come on, come on, you can do this." Sinus rhythm appeared for a moment then went back into V-Fib. "Push one milligram of Epi. Follow with twenty of saline."

Raina inserted the needle into the IV port and administered the dose.

Two minutes after the first shock, Penny was landing on the tarmac. "Shock her again," Holly said.

Raina settled the paddles on the woman once more. "Clear."

The machine popped, and the woman bowed off the table before dropping back on it. A team met them at the chopper, ready to take over—Dr. Mann and Sylvia included. Thankfully, they were all business. Raina called out all the information, including the drugs and dosage amounts, while Holly did CPR until they could shock her again. "Get her in the trauma bay now," Dr. Mann said. Holly climbed on the gurney and continued the compressions all the way into the bay where the trauma team took over. They worked on her for the next thirty minutes before Garrett shook his head. All activity ceased, and the heart monitor squealed its tragic tone.

"Time of death, 6:04."

Raina closed her eyes and drew in a ragged breath. "I'm sorry."

"Yeah, me too."

Sylvia drew the sheet over the woman's face, and Holly pressed her fingers to quivering lips.

Her phone buzzed. The team was needed once more.

For the next three hours, Holly and the others worked nonstop. Once the last victim was rushed through the sliding glass doors, Holly, Raina, and Penny made their way to base. Holly fought exhaustion even while her mind was flipping through the events of the day.

When they stepped into the kitchen of the base, Holly shook her head. "I don't understand why she died."

Raina and Penny stopped and looked at her. "What?" Raina asked, a frown on her face.

"The woman with the head injury. We gave her blood, TXA, and fluids. Her vitals were starting to stabilize. I just don't understand what went wrong." She shook her head. "There was no reason for her to have arrested."

Raina bit her lip. "Well, there was something wrong, obviously. Maybe the paramedics on the ground missed it."

"No. Her heart rate was fine, and then all of a sudden she was in V-Fib."

"Come on, Holly," Penny said, "these things happen sometimes."

"Her husband was there. She had no history of heart issues. No allergies to drugs, nothing. She had a head injury and went into V-Fib. How does that make sense?"

Penny walked over and wrapped Holly in a hug. "You're upset because we lost her. It's understandable."

Holly sighed. It was more than that, but she wouldn't think about it for now. She checked her phone and found a message from Andy.

> Can we have dinner?

> Yes. What time?

> Whenever you can get away.

> I'm on duty, so has to be here.

As he well knew.

> Of course. Don't leave base without me. I want to meet you at the door and walk down with you.

He was worried she'd be attacked again. In the hospital where she'd always felt safe.

That's fine. I'll be here.

See you soon.

But what would she say to the man who'd ghosted her during one of the most painful events of his life?

While he appeared to regret that, could she ever trust him not to do it again?

And if Dr. Mann wasn't the person threatening her, who was?

ANDY WAITED for Holly to step through the door and join him in the hallway. She looked rough. Lovely, but... "Hard flight?"

"I can't even explain how hard."

He took her hand and led her to the hospital cafeteria, where they walked through the line then headed to their table in the corner. He slid onto the padded seat and over next to the wall, then waited for her to join him on the same side.

Only she put her tray on the table and took the opposite booth.

He raised a brow, his heart constricting, praying he didn't fumble his words. He cleared his throat. "So, I owe you an apology. An... explanation."

"No, you don't *owe* me anything. If you're going to explain, then do it because you *want* to, not because you believe you *owe* me something."

He paused and nodded. "Okay, fair enough." He drew in a steadying breath. "I . . . don't even know where to start. After Chris was killed, I just . . . reacted. I couldn't think. I didn't want to be around anyone." His eyes met hers. "Except you," he whispered.

She frowned. "Then why push me away?"

"Because I was afraid." He lifted a shoulder in a hesitant half-shrug.

"Afraid of what?"

"Of you seeing that side of me."

"What *side*? Please, Andy, don't make me drag this out of you."

He ran a hand down his face. "I'm not trying to make you do that." Clearing his throat, he took her hand. "You know that from the age of six, Jacob and I were in and out of the foster system."

"Yes."

"Well, when we got older, we ended up going back to live with our parents for a while. Shortly after Jacob and I were returned to our parents after the latest foster stay, my dad left. Just packed up his stuff and walked out the door without a backward glance."

"Oh, Andy, I'm so sorry."

"It was bad. So, then it was just my brother and Mom and me. Mom had to pick up another job, and I had to quit football and start working. It was a horrible, horrible season of life, and I spiraled real fast into a very dark hole. I suffered a debilitating bout of depression for about a year."

Her eyes were narrow, studying him. But not judging. They held sorrow and compassion and a love that nearly took his breath away. A love that he certainly didn't deserve.

"Why didn't you ever tell me this before?"

"Because it's ugly. It's not who I am. Not who I wanted to be. And I didn't want you to think it was."

A tear hovered on her lashes, and when she blinked, it rolled down her cheek. Andy lifted a thumb to brush it away.

"And you were afraid I'd judge you?" she asked. "Think bad

of you? Break up with you?"

He nodded. A slow dip of his head. "I don't know that I ever consciously thought that, but yes. I think, deep down, I was afraid if you saw me in the depths of grief—and yes, depression —you would walk away."

"But . . . why?"

He ran a hand over his face. "Probably because of Sharon, the girl I was dating when my dad left. She couldn't handle it. Didn't even want to. So, she left, too."

She blinked and her face stilled into a neutral expression he couldn't read. "And you thought I would be like this Sharon girl? Like a *teenager* who couldn't deal with your pain?" She pulled her hand from his and pinched the bridge of her nose, then swiped the tears from under her eyes.

"It sounds stupid when you say it like that." And it did.

"Like what, Andy? You compared our love, our commitment to one another, to some teenage puppy-love thing?" She shook her head. "I'm not saying that wasn't a traumatic experience, and I'm not belittling the pain I know that caused you, but I thought we had something that went deeper than—"

"We do, Holly, we do!" He kept his voice low but hoped she could feel the intensity behind the words. "I love you."

"And I love you, too, Andy." Tears welled in her eyes, and she looked away to breathe deeply. When she met his gaze once more, the tears were gone. "I honestly don't know what to think, but I've got to get back to work." She slid out of the booth and looked down at him. "I'm not walking away from you, from us. But I do need to process, to think."

"Holly—"

"Please, Andy, give me this time."

He'd blown it. He curled his fingers into fists on the table, but nodded. "All right."

She turned and walked away. He could only pray it wasn't forever.

6

Holly returned to base, her thoughts whirling, emotions sucker-punched once more. How many more hits could her heart take?

She opened the refrigerator and found a bottle of water.

Penny walked out of the bedroom, phone pressed to her ear. "I love you, too. Bye."

The words cut like shards of glass through Holly, and she had to work to keep the pain off her face even while she silently berated her reaction. She couldn't flinch every time she was around a happy couple.

"Can you toss me one of those waters?" Penny asked.

"Sure." Holly handed her the one she'd just retrieved and got herself another one while Penny took a seat on the couch in the living area.

"Any luck on figuring out who's out to get you?" Penny asked.

"No. I thought it was that creepy Dr. Mann, but they questioned him and it turns out it wasn't."

"Wow."

"I know."

"And now, feel free to spill the details on the status of you and Andy."

Raina swept through the doors and flopped onto the couch next to Penny. "Looks like I arrived just in time. I caught 'status of you and Andy.' I'm assuming there's an update?"

Holly bit back the sigh that wanted to escape. "I mean, he's apologized for ghosting me, and told me why he did, but I'm having a hard time wrapping my mind around it."

"You want to share that?" Raina asked. "And if you don't, that's okay."

"I know." Holly walked over to the recliner and sat, curling her legs beneath her. "It's fear."

Raina raised a brow. "Fear? Andy? I never got the impression that he's afraid of much of anything."

"Hm." Holly swigged her water. "Well, apparently, he allowed a bad experience from his past to influence him, and that's why he shut me out."

Penny wrinkled her nose. "Well, that stinks."

"No kidding. I mean, it's not that I don't understand. I can, on some level, if I look at it like some PTSD reaction to the situation. And, I mean, we all make mistakes."

"Then why do I get the feeling there's more going on here?" Raina leaned forward, eyes narrowed, hands clasped.

Holly studied her friends—women she was closer to than her own sister. "You know, I've had it pretty easy, all things considered. Life hasn't been a huge struggle for me like it has been for you guys."

"Don't sound like you feel guilty about that," Penny said. "That's a blessing."

"Oh, I know. I don't feel *guilty*, I just . . . I don't know what the word is . . . like, maybe I shouldn't vent or whine or complain when something rotten happens because it was bound to happen eventually, and I've been fortunate to avoid it up to this point?" She dropped her head in her hands. "I sound ridiculous, don't I?" They were silent, and Holly peered up through her fingers.

Raina shook her head. "Yes, completely crazy. And I mean that in the nicest way possible. Life hurts sometimes. Sometimes it hurts certain people more than others, but that doesn't mean you should trivialize your pain. Now, is there anything Penny or I can do?"

"No, I don't think so, but thank you for being my friends and letting me be sad and whine."

"It's not whining," Penny said. She and Raina enveloped Holly in a tight group hug before Penny stepped back. "Now, we need to figure out who attacked you in the supply closet, tried to run you off the road, and broke into your home. I'm assuming it's the same person."

"Yeah. I think it is, and so does Andy. I think it's the person who's done all this other stuff, and they're escalating."

"Well," Raina said, "if it's not Dr. Mann, who else could it be?"

Holly leaned back and stared at the ceiling. "I have absolutely no idea."

ANDY CHUGGED the first two cups of coffee, then slowly sipped the third. Thanks to a restless night in his motel room, he'd managed to watch hours of security footage that Sheriff Lewis had kindly shared with him.

He'd focused mostly on the hospital attack. Cameras had picked up Holly walking into the supply closet, but it was a busy area, and others had come and gone. No one looked suspicious—like they'd just attacked someone and were in a hurry to get away. Andy had also requested the footage from the ER because he knew Holly had spent some time there before going out on the call.

He saw Dr. Mann approach her in the ER and noted Holly's body language. Stiff shoulders, tight smile, cool eyes. She did *not* like the guy. Which meant Andy wanted to punch him for continuing to push his attentions on her. Or, at the very least, make it so she never had to see the man again.

Although after the interrogation at the police department, Andy had a feeling the doctor might be giving Holly a wide berth from now on.

At least something good had happened in the last twenty-four hours.

When the hospital footage hadn't enlightened him, he'd switched to her townhome complex and studied footage from different cameras with multiple angles. There, he'd found something he thought might be interesting. A car had pulled into the parking lot and sat there for an hour and fifteen minutes with the driver staying put. It was also in a good spot to see Holly's townhome door. Andy straightened when the driver finally got out of the car. Of course he had a hoodie on. He shoved his hands into the front pocket of the sweatshirt and hurried toward the residential building. Then bypassed Holly's door and disappeared around the corner of the building.

Andy sighed and kept going. Watching.

Until the same person reappeared, walked to Holly's door and opened it.

He had a key. Well, at least they knew what happened to Penny's key.

Five minutes later, the door opened, and the person reappeared, head down, face hidden. He shoved a can—which Andy figured was the red spray paint used to deface Holly's wall—into the front pocket of the hoodie, hurried to his vehicle, climbed in, and drove away.

Andy saved the clip of footage on his laptop, then went back to the shot of the vehicle and tried to get a plate. He was able to make it out and ran it.

Only to find it belonged to a black Mercedes, not the green Honda in the video. The guy had switched the plates. With a sigh, Andy shoved the laptop away and rose to pace. Then grabbed his jacket and headed out the door and across the street to the hospital.

7

Sitting at the kitchen table at the base, Holly studied the summary she'd written for her report while Raina worked in the kitchen. Penny's shift had ended, and she'd gone home to her husband. Maxine, one of the other pilots, had arrived and was going through the chopper checklist in hopes of finishing it before their next call.

Reading back through the report she'd written just reinforced her confusion about Liza Hollister's death. There was no medical reason for it—at least not that she could see. An autopsy would reveal the truth, but while motor vehicle accident deaths were ruled "unusual deaths," an autopsy wasn't done unless they *needed* to rule for cause of death.

She rubbed her eyes.

When she lowered her hand, her gaze fell on Andy, who'd just stepped through the glass doors. He had his hands in his pockets, and he looked so sad she wanted to run to him and throw her arms around him. Instead, she forced herself to stay put. "Hi."

"Hi." He cleared his throat. "I know you asked for space, but do you mind if I have a seat? I have some security footage from your townhome I think you should see."

"Oh. Okay. No, I don't mind."

He sat next to her and slid an iPad in front of her. "Tap the screen and watch."

She did so. The footage rolled, and she watched the person in the hoodie enter the townhome and leave again. Sickness curled in her belly, and she sucked in a deep breath. "Wow."

"Yeah."

"He definitely had Penny's key."

"Yeah."

"But . . . how? It has to be someone who has access to base lockers—which means it has to be someone I work with." She didn't want to believe that was possible, but with the evidence staring her in the face, what else was she supposed to think?

A knock sounded on the door, and she looked up to see Garrett Mann standing outside, eyes narrowed, jaw tight. "Great," she whispered.

"Want me to get rid of him?"

"No, I can handle him. If he thinks I need someone to run interference, he'll just keep pushing." She stood and went to open the door. "Dr. Mann."

"Holly." His eyes slid past her. "Detective."

From the corner of her eye, she saw Andy rise. "Did you find your car?"

"Yes. It was parked in the motel parking lot across the street."

"Interesting."

"And your keys?"

A flicker of uncertainty crossed his face and he frowned. "They showed back up in my desk."

"How convenient."

The doctor scowled and looked like he might be ready to lay into Andy, so Holly asked, "Can I help you?"

"There seems to be some concern about the way you handled one of the patients yesterday."

"What?" She blinked at him. "What are you talking about?"

"Liza Hollister."

"What about her?"

"It's been reported that you gave her the wrong medication, and that's why she died."

A cold chill swept over her. "That's not true. I did everything exactly the way it was supposed to be done. I followed *your* orders."

"But I wasn't there, so I don't know that, do I?"

"What is this?" Andy asked, stepping next to her. "Payback for giving you the brush-off? For the sheriff pulling you in yesterday?"

"Of course not." Garrett crossed his arms. "I'm just passing on information."

"That you got from where?" Andy asked.

"It's from an anonymous source."

"Well, that shouldn't come from you," Holly said. "That should come from Dr. Kirkpatrick. So unless you have anything else—"

Mann held up a hand. "I was just giving you a heads-up." He backed up and headed down the hallway.

Holly ran her hands down her face, then drew in a deep breath. She looked back at Andy. "I'm going to see Dr. Kirkpatrick."

"I'm right behind you."

～

"Do you want me to wait out here?" Andy asked her.

"No, you might as well hear everything firsthand. It will save me having to repeat it."

Holly knocked on her boss's office and entered when he said, "Come in."

The man was seated behind his desk. He looked up, and his eyes narrowed. "Holly. I was just about to ask you to come to my office. How'd you know I wanted to see you?"

"I didn't, but I figured it was coming. Garrett Mann said Morbidity and Mortality are looking into Liza Hollister's death."

Dr. Kirkpatrick huffed and leaned back in his chair. "How on earth did he know?"

"I guess the rumor mill is operating at warp speed." She raked a hand over her ponytail. "But this time, I'm stumped. I have no idea how anyone would know anything about what went on in the chopper. I only voiced my concerns to Penny and Raina. How did you come to hear about it?"

"I got a phone call from someone who said you had 'messed up'"—he used air quotes—"and that the patient shouldn't have died. And that the incident needed to be investigated."

"Well, shouldn't there be an autopsy first? To determine cause of death?"

"I've already asked the ME to make it a priority, but until we hear back from her, you just keep doing your job."

She studied him. "Are you sure?"

He sighed. "Look, this was an anonymous tip thing. I'm not a fan of those. If someone has information, proof, that you made a mistake, then they can bring it to my attention, tell me to my face. This is all hearsay, and I don't bench my players based on that."

Holly nodded, her relief evident, yet she was still concerned. "Will you face backlash because of this?"

"Did you do anything wrong?"

"No."

"Then I'm not worried about it."

She sighed. "At least not on purpose. I mean, I'm not

perfect, of course, but"—she twisted her fingers together, then straightened her shoulders and lifted her chin—"no. I did everything exactly how it should have been done, and I'd do everything the same if I had to do it all over again."

"Then, we won't worry about it until we have something to worry about."

She stood. "Thank you, Dr. Kirkpatrick."

"Sure."

She hesitated and glanced at Andy, then back to the doctor. "I didn't put this in my report because it's an opinion, not fact, but I think I'd like to run it by you."

The man raised a brow. "Okay."

Holly sat back down and walked him through the scenario on the helicopter. "I agree with your anonymous caller. I don't know what happened, but I don't think Liza Hollister should be dead, either."

Dr. Kirkpatrick frowned. "What do you mean?"

"I've been thinking about this, and I believe, before the chopper is used again, it needs a thorough inventory with everything checked. Including the meds. And—in light of the current accusations—it can't be me who goes through it."

He hesitated. "If we ground that chopper and someone needs it . . ."

"I know. I've thought of that, trust me, but I just keep going over and over everything that happened with Ms. Hollister and I can't help it. I don't understand why she died. Something's . . . not right. I don't know what, but . . . something."

He studied her a moment, and Andy thought he was going to refuse, then he gave a slow nod. "All right. I've never known you to overreact to anything. If you say something's off, I'll give you the benefit of the doubt." His phone pinged and he glanced at the screen. "Autopsy's in progress. We should know something shortly. I'll have someone start going over the chopper, but if we get a call, you'll have to go."

She nodded. "Okay. Thank you. I'm just going to head back to base."

"I'll be in touch as soon as I hear something."

Holly stood, and Andy led her out of the office. "That went well," he said."

"Better than I expected." She bit her lip. "Someone's out to get me, Andy. Someone wants me out of this hospital, and I don't know why."

8

H olly returned to base, her heart heavy with the current status of their relationship, while Andy said he was going to talk to the sheriff and see if the man had made any progress in the case.

What was she going to do?

Pray he'd learned something from the situation and that she could trust him again?

Or keep her heart under lock and key and possibly miss finding joy again in being with Andy?

"Ugh. Lord, tell me what to do, please," she whispered. "And if Andy and I are supposed to build a life together, give me the strength to overcome my doubts and hurt."

When she got no clear answer to her plea, she sighed. She'd just have to keep praying about it and listening. God would let her know. For now, though, she turned her focus back to the other thing that wouldn't stop bugging her.

Knowing a call could come in at any moment, Holly kept herself busy going back over every medical detail of what she'd done in flight. She even called the paramedics who'd worked on Liza Hollister and got their feedback and impressions of the woman's physical state. They were both shocked to learn she'd died.

"So, it's not just me," she muttered, hanging up.

"What's not just you?" Raina asked from her spot behind the stove.

So deep in her own musings, Holly hadn't noticed her enter. "I talked to Carl and Nadine. They both thought Liza Hollister would make it."

Raina stirred the spaghetti sauce then set the spoon aside. "Ever since you brought it up, I've been thinking about it. You're right. We gave her the meds. We got the bleeding stopped. She woke up and was lucid. You ordered the Decadron. Seconds later, she went into cardiac arrest. Could it be as simple as she was allergic?"

"Her husband said she didn't have any allergies."

"So, it was a new one."

"Yes. It's possible." Holly pursed her lips and shook her head. "It could have been anything, I guess. Maybe you and Penny are right and I just don't want to accept the loss."

"We've lost patients before," Raina said. "And it's hard, and we're always sad about it, but you're taking this harder than usual."

"Yeah. I am." She paused. "Well, going over and over it isn't helping, so I guess I just need to wait until we get the results of the autopsy."

"I noticed Andy was here earlier."

"He was."

"Are you going to forgive him?"

Holly paused. "Yes. I just don't know if I can trust him again. Just because I forgive him doesn't mean that I want to put myself back into the same situation."

Raina nodded. "I understand that."

"But I'm praying about it and working on finding peace no matter what the outcome is."

"And I'll join you in that prayer."

"Thank you, Raina." She had the best friends.

A knock on the door pulled her to her feet, and Dr. Kirkpatrick stepped inside. The frown on his face didn't bode well. "What is it?" she asked.

He waved a folder at her. "Got the autopsy report."

"And?"

"Cause of death is an overdose of epinephrine. Said no way was that an accident. I'm afraid I'm going to have to suspend you pending an investigation."

ANDY WAS SITTING across from the sheriff when his phone pinged with a message from Holly.

> Autopsy report came back. I'm suspended pending an investigation.

A groan slipped from him, and the sheriff looked up from the computer where he was watching the security footage from Holly's townhome. "What is it?"

"Holly was just suspended."

"For what?"

He read the next text. "The autopsy of Liza Hollister said she died from an overdose of epinephrine."

The sheriff frowned. "They think Holly did it on purpose?"

"I don't know what *they* think. *I* think someone's framing her. Trying to prove her incompetent."

"But . . . if that's the case," the sheriff said, his words slow and thoughtful, "whether the intention was for someone to die or not, someone did. And that's murder. Or at the very least manslaughter, depending on the circumstances."

"Yeah."

The sheriff eyed him. "If I were you, I wouldn't leave her alone right now. Someone wants her out of that hospital bad— and it doesn't look like they care if it's in a car or a coffin."

9

Holly dropped her packed bag on the floor of the locker room and turned to find Raina and Penny staring at her with sober faces and angry eyes. Angry on her behalf. "Stop," she said. "It'll be okay. The truth will come out." She frowned. "What are you doing here anyway? You're off shift."

"We're here for you, my friend," Penny said. "Just like you'd be for us."

Holly refused to cry over the love of her friends. Simply because if she started, she wouldn't stop. And that wouldn't help anyone. "Oh. Thank you."

"Where are you going?" Raina asked.

"Back to the motel. The sheriff called and said he doesn't want me going home until this has been resolved. I told him I would do that for the next couple of days, but after that, I wouldn't have a choice."

"And Andy? Where's he?"

"He was with the sheriff when he called, but he's on his way here. Said he wants to escort me to the motel."

"And then?"

She shrugged. "I don't know. I guess I'll just take it one day at a time."

"Well, you're not staying there by yourself," Raina said. "As soon as I'm off shift, I'm coming over."

"Yeah," Penny nodded. "Me too."

Holly stepped forward for a group hug. "Thanks, guys," she whispered.

After a tight squeeze, she let go and picked up her bag. She followed Raina and Penny back into the large living area only to see a dark-haired woman standing just inside the door.

"Hi," Penny said, "can we help you?"

"Yes, please. I'm looking for someone named Holly Cooper. I was told I could find her here."

Penny stepped in front of Holly from the right side while Raina did the same from the left. Closing in and protecting her.

"And who are you?" Penny asked.

"Victoria Mann."

Mann? As in Garrett Mann? A sister or cousin perhaps?

Holly wasn't about to let her friends put themselves in danger for her—should this woman be dangerous. She stepped around her self-appointed guardians. "I'm Holly." She set her bag on the floor but didn't move forward like she normally would. "What do you need?"

"I need you to stay away from my husband."

Penny gaped and Raina clasped Holly's bicep, obviously ready to yank her out of harm's way.

"And who is your husband?" Holly asked, knowing the answer without hearing it, but needing it confirmed.

"Garrett Mann."

She knew it, but she still gasped. When she snapped her lips shut, she couldn't help but stare. "I'm sorry, what? Garrett Mann is *married*?"

The woman scoffed and crossed her arms. "Are you saying you didn't know?"

"Of course I didn't know. Not that it would matter, because I'm not interested in the man."

"Then why is your picture all over his phone?"

Holly blinked. "Again, I'm completely at a loss. I have no idea why he'd have my picture."

The woman pulled her phone from her purse, tapped the screen and then held the device out to Holly. "This is my phone. When he was in the shower yesterday morning, I AirDropped the pictures from his phone to mine. Look. Nothing but you."

Raina snatched the phone before Holly could move and passed it over to her. Holly raised a brow at her friend. "Thanks." Then she glanced at the screen and sucked in a breath. Swipe after swipe revealed pictures she had no idea had been taken. A tremor swept through her. "No." She shook her head. "I don't know why he has these, but if you look closely, you can see they were taken when I wasn't looking at the camera."

A flicker of uncertainty flashed in Mrs. Mann's eyes. "Even so, it's obvious he's obsessed with you."

Holly passed the phone back to the woman. "But I'm not with him. In fact, it looks like he's stalking me."

Her quiet words hovered in the air between them, then with a huff, Mrs. Mann spun and darted out the door.

"You need to tell the sheriff about this," Raina said. "I know that they cleared Dr. Mann as being the one after you, but what if they're wrong? What if someone is working with him and he just reported his car stolen so he had that out?"

Holly bit her lip and nodded. "I'll call the sheriff."

"And Andy," Penny said.

"Yes. And Andy."

ANDY HAD his finger over the button that would send the call to Holly's phone when her call came in. He answered. "Hey. I was just getting ready to call you."

"Well, I've finished packing up my stuff and am ready to head to the motel whenever you can take me. But, first, I wanted to tell you about an interesting encounter I had with Mrs. Garrett Mann."

"*Mrs.?* The man's married?"

"Very."

"Oh boy. Does he know she knows that he's been . . . um . . . ?"

"Unfaithful? I have no idea. She went searching on his phone and found a bunch of pictures of me. He's been stalking me, Andy, but I don't know what to think about setting me up to be suspended. Or fired. What would he have to gain from that?"

"Revenge?"

She sighed. "Maybe. I don't know. I just know I'm tired and want to go home."

"No, don't go home. Not yet."

"I'm not, I promise."

"Perfect. And honestly, this suspension might be a blessing in disguise. I don't know that you're safe at the hospital base."

"Or maybe someone just wants me to get away from the base so they have easier access to me?"

He blinked. "Or that. We'll just have to be super careful. I'll come get you and take you to the motel, so just hang tight and I'll be there shortly. The sheriff plans to pick up Mann and dig a little deeper into his previous story. He's still our number one pick for the one causing all of your problems."

"Fine. I'm going down to the lobby. I'll wait for you there?"

"No, go to the ER entrance. I'll park in the police spot and come in and get you."

"Fine. See you in a little bit."

10

H olly sighed. Her head was aching, and she wanted to have a good cry. But that would just aggravate her headache. She walked to the elevator with Raina and Penny on either side of her. The three rode the elevator down to the ER floor and walked the hallway toward the ER. "I feel like I have my own personal protection unit."

"You do," Penny said. "For now."

"Until this guy is caught," Raina said with a nod.

". . . really think I wouldn't find out?" The screech came from the direction of the ER and Holly paused, then hurried toward the commotion.

Dr. Mann stood in the hallway, hand outstretched toward his wife. "Come on, Vicki, you know you're the one I love. I just flirt. It's harmless."

"Pictures, Garrett. Many, many pictures."

"I didn't take those!"

"Then how did they get on your phone? Hidden away in a little album labeled Holly Cooper? Huh? You think I'm too stupid to figure out technology?"

"No, of course not, but I'm telling you, I didn't put those there."

"Well, someone knew they were there, because someone left me a note under my windshield wiper telling me to go take a look."

Holly's gaze bounced between the husband and wife while everyone else stood staring in shock.

"What's going on here?" Dr. Nick Israel appeared and walked toward the dueling couple. "Garrett?"

"A personal issue, Nick. I'm sorry. We were just getting ready to leave and take this to a more private area."

"Good idea. Why don't you do that?" He clapped his hands, then waved them in a shooing motion. "All right, children, the show is over. Back to work."

"No need to take this somewhere more private," Victoria said, her voice icy enough to send a cold front through the Mojave Desert in the dead of summer. "We're done." She tugged at the collar of her coat. "And I do mean *done* in every way imaginable."

Rachel stepped up beside Holly. "What in the world?"

Holly shook her head, her heart aching for the shattered wife and the apparent end to a marriage. "So sad," she whispered. She placed a hand on Rachel's bicep. "Stay away from Dr. Mann. He's nothing but heartbreak waiting to happen."

Rachel shot her a dark look but nodded her head. "Unbelievable," she muttered.

Victoria Mann swept out of the ER area with a toss of her head and a glare at them all. Garrett Mann looked up, saw everyone watching, and scowled. His gaze landed on Holly and his expression morphed into a smirk. "Well, my marriage is over. Guess you could go out with me now?"

Rachel gasped. "Seriously?"

Holly could see the deep pain in his eyes in spite of his poor attempt at a joke. "I'm sorry, Garrett," she said, "very, very sorry for you and Victoria."

"Yeah." The man sighed, lifted his iPad and headed for the nearest patient room.

Rachel followed him, and Holly checked the time. Andy and the sheriff would be there soon. Andy, to take her to the motel, and the sheriff to take Garrett back into custody.

The doctor didn't know it, but his day was getting ready to go from bad to worse.

ANDY PULLED to a stop in one of the reserved law enforcement spaces in front of the ER entrance. The sheriff parked behind him and climbed out to join him on the sidewalk. "I'll go after Mann. You get Holly to the motel."

"You really think he's our guy?"

"I don't know, but I'm going to press a little harder this time to find out. I think he's connected in some way, for sure, since it was his car that was supposedly stolen."

"Right."

Andy rushed inside to find Holly in a huddle with Raina and Penny just outside the double doors of the emergency room entrance. She looked up, and his gaze collided with hers while his heart thudded with regret at the choices he made and prayers that she would offer him another chance.

"Everything okay?" he asked.

"It's been an exciting couple of hours," Holly said. "I'll explain on the way to the motel."

He frowned and nodded.

"Holly?"

Holly turned, and Andy thought he recognized the woman approaching. Rachel?

"Are you leaving?" Rachel asked.

"I am."

"But . . . why? Aren't you still on shift?"

"I've been suspended," Holly said, her eyes flashing. "But I'll be back once the investigation is over."

"Oh no! What happened?"

"It's a long story. Ask Garrett if you're still speaking to him."

Surprise flickered across Rachel's face and Holly sighed. "I'm sorry. That was petty." She paused. "Did you know he was married?"

"No." Rachel's features tightened, and a fist curled at her side. "I can't believe I was such an idiot."

"Oh, honey, you weren't an idiot. Just deceived by a very good deceiver."

Rachel shook her head. "I've got to get back to work."

She hurried away, and Holly nodded to Andy. "I'm ready, I guess."

Andy escorted her to his car while the sheriff went in search of Dr. Mann.

The trip to the motel took all of three minutes, and soon he was standing inside her door while she set her bag on the bed. The fact that she insisted on getting it herself, refusing to let him carry it for her, spoke volumes. "Holly, can we please talk?"

"I'm still processing, Andy."

He sighed and dropped his chin to his chest. "All right." He turned to go.

When his hand landed on the knob, she covered it with hers. "Wait."

"What?"

"I'm not being fair to you. If you want to talk, then we should talk."

His burden shifted. "I would really appreciate it."

She gestured to the small table in the corner. "Have a seat."

He did, and she lowered herself into the chair opposite him.

"Andy, I love you. If I didn't, I would have just walked away from you. But I don't do that with people I love."

"Like I did?"

"Yeah, pretty much."

He nodded. "I know. But thank you for sticking with me."

"I'm going to be honest. I'm having trust issues."

"I know. And all I can do is promise to never do that to you again." He cleared his throat. "My therapist is helping me understand that my childhood has had a big impact on who I am as an adult. And . . . I have trust issues of my own."

"Of course you do. Who wouldn't?"

"But that's just it. I thought I'd gotten past all that. I met you—as an adult—and it was everything I'd dreamed of for years. Being with you, loving you, . . . it changed me. In a good way."

She bit her lip, and tears flooded her eyes. "I'm glad to hear that."

"And then Chris was killed, and it nearly killed *me*. All my life, I've handled my problems on my own because I had to. My counselor pointed out that I simply don't know how to lean on someone else for emotional support." He frowned. "And I guess I have to admit that's true. But," he took her hands, "I want to learn. And I want that person to be you."

She sniffed and nodded. "I do too, Andy."

"Then we can try again? Will you give me a second chance?"

She smiled. "I want to."

"I want you to."

"We just have to be able to talk through the bad times. And the good, of course, but most especially, the bad. And . . . this is a really good start."

Thank you, Lord.

He stood and pulled her up with him. "Can I kiss you?"

She laughed. "Yes."

Just as his lips settled over hers, his phone buzzed. He

ignored it and let it go to voice mail while he relished the feel of Holly in his arms once more.

When it buzzed again, he groaned and lifted his head. "I guess I should see who it is."

"Probably."

He pulled the phone from his pocket. "It's the sheriff." He swiped the screen. "Hello?"

"Hey, are you with Holly?"

"I am."

"Is she safe?"

"She's in a motel room. Why?"

"I really think we got our guy. You should see the stuff on his computer. Obsessed doesn't even come close to describing his interest in her. And the pictures on his phone are only a few of the thousands he has of her. I don't know where his wife thought he was when he wasn't at the hospital because he sure wasn't at home. He was too busy stalking Holly."

"You have him in custody?"

"We do. His wife—soon to be 'ex' according to her—came by and gave us more incriminating evidence against him. Said she found more pictures in his desk at his house."

"Is she still there?"

"Yes, I think so. Why?"

Something didn't sit right with Andy. "Do you mind if I come by and have a chat with her? And maybe Garrett as well?"

The sheriff paused. "Why? You think I'm wrong?"

"No, not at all. I just think there's more going on here than we're seeing, and I've got a few questions I'd like to run by them both."

"Then come on over. I'll have her waiting for you." The sheriff gave him a description of the woman and Andy hung up. He turned back to Holly. "You heard my side and put two and two together?"

"Yes."

"Will you be all right while I go talk to the Manns again?"

"What do you think we missed?"

He rubbed a hand over his chin and shook his head. "I don't know, but I have questions, so don't go home just yet, okay?"

"Yeah. Okay, sure. I guess while you do that, I'm going to take a nap and then start preparing my statement for the board."

Still, he hesitated. "I don't want to leave you alone."

"Raina and Penny are coming by in a couple of hours. I'll be fine. Go."

He kissed her again, then stroked a hand over her cheek, marveling at the softness. And at the love in her eyes. "Okay, I'll be back soon."

"I'll be here."

Andy shut the door and heard the deadbolt engage. He took a deep breath then reassured himself that he was only going to be three minutes away. The police station was just around the corner from the hospital. He could be back fast if he had to be. But if he thought he would need to do that, should he leave her?

The door opened. "Go, Andy, I'll be fine. Mann is in custody, and I'm going to sleep a bit, then work."

He sighed and nodded. "Okay, see you in a little while."

He hurried to the sheriff's office and walked inside to find a woman matching the sheriff's description sitting in the lobby. It could only be Victoria Mann. "Mrs. Mann?"

She stood. "You're the man the sheriff said wanted to talk to me?"

"If you don't mind. I just had a few questions that were nagging at me—about Garrett."

"Okay, if it helps me make sure I get my fair share in the divorce, then I'm happy to answer."

"Right." He cleared his throat. "So, the pictures that you

found on Garrett's phone. You said you got a tip that they were there."

"Yes, someone left a note under my windshield wiper and said they hated to be the bearer of bad news, but that I needed to find a time to check his phone, that he had a girlfriend." She spread her hands, then clasped them at her waist. "And the person was right. Obviously."

"And the pictures in his desk?"

"Some of the same." She swallowed hard. "I'm very angry with Garrett because of this whole stalking thing, but I honestly don't see him as someone who'd do the other stuff that they're accusing him of."

"What other stuff?"

"They're saying he switched the drugs in the chopper. Drugs that killed a woman. The sheriff asked me if I'd noticed anything at home—drug vials and whatnot. So before you ask, the answer is no. Why would he bring that stuff home when he was at the hospital?"

"So, drugs were switched?"

"Yes, while I was talking to Garrett, the sheriff came in and said the report had come back that epinephrine was found in a Decadron bottle. They suspect that someone switched them out, and as a result, the nurse, Holly, had inadvertently given the patient a lethal dose of the epinephrine." She frowned. "I think I remembered all that correctly."

"Oh no."

"That's not all. There were other medications that had been tampered with as well. According to the sheriff, someone was going to die in that chopper—and soon. If it hadn't been the Decadron and epinephrine tragedy, it would have been something else."

Then this was a premeditated murder, not just a crime of opportunity.

"But," she went on, "like I said, I just can't see Garrett having any part of that. He loves being a doctor." She clicked her tongue. "Much more than he loves being a husband, obviously. As much as I don't want to defend the two-timing jerk, I have to admit he'd never do anything to jeopardize his career."

Andy processed the words. "When did you find out about Holly? That he was obsessed with her?"

She frowned. "This morning when I found the note."

"Do you still have the note?"

"No, I threw it away."

"Okay, then—"

The sheriff stepped out of the interrogation room. "Andy, a word?"

"Of course."

Andy stepped over to the sheriff, out of earshot of Mrs. Mann. "Dr. Mann decided to talk a little more," the sheriff said. "I'll fill you in on that in just a minute, but I also just got word that one of the forensics guys said while the photos were real, they were all uploaded at the same time to the cloud from the hospital coffee shop. Of course, I wanted to know who did the uploading, and hospital security checked the date and time and sent me three pictures of the people in there using a laptop. And two using their phones." He turned his iPad around and showed Andy the pictures.

Andy lifted his gaze. "You're kidding me. Her?"

"I called and she clocked out about two minutes ago."

"She's going after Holly. She was in the ER lobby when we left. What if she followed us to the motel?"

Together, they raced for Sheriff Lewis's cruiser, and Andy slung himself into the passenger seat even while he dialed Holly's cell phone number.

When it went to voice mail, his heart thundered in his ears. "Hurry."

The sheriff turned on the lights and siren, and they

screamed down the road toward the motel where he'd left Holly.

Alone.

Unprotected.

He tried her number again. Voice mail.

Please God, take care of her.

"She could be in the shower," the sheriff said. "Or sleeping."

"True." But he didn't believe it.

11

A knock on the door woke her. A quick glance at the clock said an hour and a half had passed since Andy had dropped her at the motel. Was he back already?

She glanced through the peephole and opened the door. "Hi. What are you doing here?"

The figure raised her right arm, and Holly found herself staring down the barrel of a wicked-looking gun. "Come with me."

Holly stumbled back, and the woman shoved her way in. "What are you doing?"

"Now. Or I shoot you and go back and find that man who seems to care so much for you."

Heart thudding, Holly straightened with her hands held so the woman could see them. "I thought we were friends, Rachel."

"Not in this lifetime."

"It was you? You set me up?"

"With pleasure. Although, if you remember, at first, I did try to simply get you to leave. I didn't want to hurt you."

"But you hurt Liza Hollister."

"No, you did."

"What?"

A cruel smile curved Rachel's lips. "Just because there's a label on the bottle, doesn't mean that's what's inside it."

It didn't take a genius to figure out what she meant. "You switched the drugs? Then reported my mistake anonymously." It made sense now.

"It was the only thing I could think of to get you to leave!"

"But I've been suspended. Your plan worked. Why all this?"

"But for how long? Eventually, it'll be proven that it wasn't your fault. Even I know that. It's only a matter of time. But right now, it all looks hopeless, doesn't it?"

"Hopeless? What are you—" It hit her. Suicide. Rachel planned to make Holly's death look like a suicide. Cold fear curled in her midsection.

"Yes," the woman spat. "Hopeless. Poor little Holly caved when the pressure hit. Now come on, or I'm going to take my chances and just shoot you right here."

Holly decided she'd have a better chance of escape outside the motel room than in it. She stepped out and let the door shut behind her, then, with the gun pressed in her lower back, she walked toward the car her kidnapper indicated. "Get in."

"Why are you doing this? I don't understand. What did I do to make you hate me so much?"

"You made him fall in love with you! And he'll never see me again until you and that stupid wife of his are gone. Victoria saw the pictures I uploaded and is talking divorce, so that's one problem taken care of. Now you. Garrett Mann is mine—or he will be soon."

"But I don't want him," Holly cried. "I told him I wasn't interested and refused to go out with him. You know all this. You were there for a lot of it. And then today? With that awful confrontation in the ER? You really still want him?"

Rachel didn't move the gun. All Holly could do was just pray the woman didn't accidentally pull the trigger.

"I'm done talking. Just get in the car. Climb in the passenger side and slide over."

"Where are you taking me?" Holly's hand shook when she opened the car door. Fear pounded through her, and she was afraid she'd stop thinking clearly.

"It doesn't matter," Rachel said. "I just need you gone."

"So I'll leave."

"I already tried to warn you away, but you just wouldn't go!"

"I will!" Where was everyone? Holly looked around for help, but the place was empty, deserted. Most of the people who stayed at the extended-stay motel worked at the hospital. Those who weren't at work were probably sleeping.

But she didn't dare call for someone to help her in fear that Rachel would shoot them.

Sirens in the distance caused the woman to jerk. "You're driving. If you stall a minute longer, I'll shoot you and deal with the consequences."

Holly lowered herself into the car and slid across to the driver's side. Rachel didn't take her eyes from Holly as she slipped into the passenger seat. She shut the door. As Holly had hoped, Rachel reached for the seatbelt, and for just a moment, her attention fell away from Holly when she automatically looked down to clip her seatbelt into place. Holly struck out with her right hand against the inside of Rachel's wrist and the gun tumbled to the floorboard.

With Rachel's scream of fury echoing in her ears while the woman scrambled for the gun, Holly threw open the driver's door and shot out of the vehicle. She fell to the ground and rolled. A gunshot sounded, and the bullet whizzed over her head.

Police vehicles pulled into the parking lot, lights flashing, sirens wailing. Holly rolled to her feet and heard someone call her name. Thinking it was Rachel, she raced away from the vehicle.

A hard hand clamped onto her upper left bicep, and she spun with a cry, ready to fight once more.

And saw that it was Andy.

She fell into his arms, and he pulled her to the ground as another crack split the air.

"Police! Put the weapon down! Drop the gun! Hands in the air!"

The officers' commands came one after the other. Holly turned to see Rachel freeze. She held the gun as though unsure what to do with it.

"Drop it," Holly whispered. "Drop it." Even with all the grief Rachel had caused her, she didn't want the woman to die.

With a sob, Rachel let the gun drop from her fingers. It clattered to the ground. Officers rushed in, and then it was over.

Andy pulled her into a lung-crushing hug. "I love you, Holly. I love you."

Holly dissolved into sobs as his precious words washed over her. She pulled back and then kissed him. "I love you, too, Andy. I have for a long time." She looked back at Rachel as the officers led her away and shuddered. "How did you know I was in trouble?"

"Dr. Mann finally confessed that Rachel had been acting strange. She'd been harassing him about getting back together."

"I knew she had a crush on him and was hurt when he called things off, but from what I understand, that's usually the way things worked with him."

"The sheriff told him about the message on your wall, and he said Rachel had come to work late with red paint on her hands. But the clincher was the footage of the café where she uploaded all those pictures to his cloud account. She'd gotten his password from when they'd been together, and he never changed it. When we finally put it all together . . ."

". . . you rushed over here."

"Absolutely." Andy pulled her away to his vehicle. "And I don't want to wait another minute. Will you marry me?"

Tears leaked again. This time happy tears. She sniffed and nodded. "I'll marry you."

"I didn't plan on asking you this way."

"I don't care how you ask, just that you asked."

He kissed her again then leaned back and cupped her face. "I didn't realize."

"What?"

"How hard it must have been for you to let me pull away and wallow in my misery."

"I didn't want to. You gave me no choice."

"And I regret that with every fiber of my being. I won't do it again, I promise. If you had pushed me away—more so than you did—while all this was going on with you, I would have been a crazy person."

"I know. I'm glad you were here."

"And I will be from now on."

She nodded. "From now on, we're a team."

"A winning team." He pulled her back into his arms, and she knew there was no other place she'd rather be.

EPILOGUE

Holly let the door shut behind her and carried the bag of groceries into the kitchen. Her spotless, newly painted kitchen. When the pastor said he had volunteers who wanted to paint and would she please pick out her favorite color for the project, she hadn't realized he meant they intended to paint her entire place.

But she loved it.

It had been two weeks since Rachel had been caught, and Holly was working hard to put it behind her. Which meant having her home filled with love and laughter. Right now Raina, Andy, Penny, and Holt, were on their way to hang out with her.

Knuckles rapped on the door. "Come in!"

It felt weird to leave her door unlocked, but she was trying not to believe every person on the other side of it had ill intentions.

Andy stepped inside. "I'm early."

"No, you have perfect timing. Wanna fire up the grill?"

He grinned. "I thought you might need me for something."

She walked over to him and wrapped her arms around his

neck. He dipped his head and pressed a kiss to her lips. "Mm, now that's worth being early for."

"The grill, my sweet man, the grill." She stepped back and he caught her hand.

"Have I told you that I love you today?"

"A few times."

"I do, Holly."

"I know." She hugged him. "I have good news."

"I already know it."

She stepped back with a frown. "You do?"

"Yes. You said you'd marry me."

"No, silly. Dr. Kirkpatrick called. I've been cleared in every way and am free to resume my duties on the chopper."

He turned serious. "Aw, that's great, Holly. I'm happy for you."

Emotion wanted to choke her, but she swallowed it. "Thanks. I'm thrilled. I'm still so sad about Mrs. Hollister, but so relieved it wasn't anything I did that caused her death. No mistake or—"

He pressed a finger to her lips. "It's a tragedy that we'll think about forever, but we can pray for her family."

"Absolutely. I'm so glad you and God are back on good terms."

He laughed. "Yeah. It feels good. One more kiss, then I'm going to play with fire."

"I'd say you do that on a regular basis," Holt drawled from the open door.

Holly giggled, and her friends crowded into her living area and kitchen. "Time to light the grill."

"Not without my kiss," Andy said. "They don't get to take that from me."

She kissed him. A long, lingering cling to his lips that left her wanting to call the pastor and have him perform the ceremony immediately. Instead, she stepped away and gave him a light shove toward the small patio that held the grill. "Go."

"I'm going, but I'll be back."

A gagging noise behind her spun her around. Holt was clutching his throat, but the grin on his face said he wasn't in trouble. Medical trouble anyway. "Keep it up, Satterfield, and your steak might get more crispy than you'd like."

The threat worked, and he immediately put on an innocent face. "Y'all are just the cutest couple ever."

"That's better. Now, you can go join Andy. My girls and I have a wedding to plan."

Available Now

Extreme Measures Series

Coming August 2023

www.lynetteeason.com

LYNETTE EASON'S BIO:

Lynette Eason is the best-selling, award-winning author of over sixty books including the Extreme Measure Series. Her books have appeared on the CBA, ECPA, and Parable bestseller lists. She has won several awards including the Carol Award, the Selah, the Golden Scroll and more. Her novel, *Her Stolen Past* was made into a movie for the Lifetime Movie Network. Lynette teaches at writing conferences all over the country. She is a member of American Christian Fiction Writers (ACFW), Mystery Writers of America (MWA), International Thriller Writers (ITW), and Faith, Hope, and Love. Lynette always loves to hear from her readers. You can reach out at her website. www.lynetteeason.com.

ACKNOWLEDGMENTS

It's always a team effort to bring a book into the world—even one as short as a novella.

First and foremost, I have to give a huge THANK YOU to friend and paramedic, Teresa Harris. She was an amazing help with the scene in the chopper and I'm so proud of how it turned out. So, thank you, Teresa, for answering my questions and basically rewriting the scene for me! You did FABULOUS. On a side note, it's really funny/interesting how Teresa and I met (via Facebook regarding a photography post!), but sometimes God just knows the people He needs to put in your life. Teresa, and her husband, Jeff, are two such people. You guys are the best and I thank you for all you do day in and day out.

Thank you to my fellow anthology contributors: Lynn, Lisa and Beth. Y'all are so incredibly talented! I count myself blessed to know you and have my name on the cover with you.

Thank you to my family. Jack, Lauryn, Will, Mom, Dad, my in-laws (Bill and Diane), Lane, Molly, Shelby and Thomas. You all make me feel so loved and supported. I couldn't do this without you.

And last, but never least, thank you to my Lord and Savior, Jesus. Thank you for letting me do what I do and thank you for keeping your hand on the stories.

Dear Reader,

Thank you so much for joining me on Holly and Andy's journey to reconciliation. If you've read Life Flight, then you met Holly in that story. When I was creating the Extreme Measures series, I knew that I wanted to explore Holly's character further so when Lynn, Lisa, Beth and I decided to put together this anthology, I thought she would be the perfect heroine. Besides, I was really curious about her and how she came to be a part of the team. Now we know! LOL.

Next up in the series is Crossfire. I do hope you'll keep an eye out for that book. It follows Life Flight and is Julianna and Clay's story. It releases August 2022 and then book 3 is Critical Threat with Grace and Sam's story. Book 4 is Raina and Vincent's story It doesn't have a title yet, but I hope to have one soon.

Again, thank you for taking time to read the book. I hope you've fallen in love with the characters and are ready for more! I know I am!

If you'd like to follow me on social media, you can find me on Facebook at www.facebook.com/lynette.eason and on Twitter at @lynetteeason.

My website is www.lynetteeason.com and you can always send me a message through the contact page.

Thank you again and happy reading!

God Bless,

Lynette

DAWN'S HIDDEN THREAT

ELIZABETH GODDARD

SOUTHEAST ALASKA, FEBRUARY

1

Angie Greenwood stared into the killer's eyes. Her back was to the precipice, the snow up to her knees, and a biting arctic gust seized her breath. A storm was definitely on the way. But a stone-cold one faced her now. Terror ignited—how had it come to this? Finger on the trigger, she had the advantage as she looked straight down the barrel of the Glock 19 9mm that she gripped tightly in both hands. She couldn't afford the emotion that surged and took her hostage.

Don't make me do this.

His eyes grew darker, and he leaned forward as if daring her to shoot.

The snow beneath her feet shuddered, and the ground suddenly dropped out from under her. Her stomach clenched, and a scream tore from her throat. Free-falling, she flailed helplessly, staring up at the gray clouds.

He stared down at her as she fell. Her terror shifted away from the killer as realization dawned—she was going to die.

∾

F*OLLOWING* *Thunder is going to get me killed one day.*

"Thunder, get back here." Ridge Ledger called his avalanche-rescue dog. Thunder was a golden retriever and loved to chase the wildlife. In turn, Ridge was now chasing Thunder.

"We need to get off this mountain!" With the storm warning, Ridge had been pushing his luck to stay this long, but he'd been determined to finish mapping the mountain and testing out the new drone software from Hanstech before the forecasted record snowfall hit.

Equally determined, Thunder had his own plans. On the ski patrol team at Mammoth Mountain alongside Ridge, Thunder had been the best avalanche dog, but when he wasn't working, he liked to play.

The wind intensified, and Ridge glanced up at the low-hanging gray clouds. This weather system was expected to dump at least fifteen inches of snow on them. He'd wanted to map the mountain beforehand so they could more easily predict the avalanche risk, especially after the deadly avalanches last week—the reason he'd left Mammoth Mountain in California and returned to Shadow Gap in Southeast Alaska. He needed to protect his sister and nephew.

Thunder barked, drawing his attention back to the trail. Ridge wasn't wearing snowshoes and was already sinking to his knees, which made the trek more strenuous. Not good since Thunder was leading Ridge up the mountain.

"Thunder, come!" Ridge gave him the vital and basic command that could save Thunder's life, and he chose not to listen.

The dog disappeared through the trees, and his bark now sounded muffled. *Great.* Ridge had no choice but to follow, and he came to a rocky incline. Somehow Thunder had found a way to scramble up. Fortunately, the trees kept much of the incline free from slick ice or too much snow. Ridge climbed until he reached the ledge but still couldn't see Thunder.

He could hear him, though—again his bark sounded muffled. "Thunder?"

He glanced around at the incredible view—the Lewis Inlet, the Goldrock River, and he even caught a glimpse of the small town of Shadow Gap. He shifted back to the mountain, and that's when he saw it.

A tangle of tree limbs aching with their burden of snow mostly blocked his view of the ledge, but he spotted a dark recess. He pushed through the limbs to get a better look. Could it be? Ridge had grown up in Shadow Gap. He'd trekked the mountain trail and knew the geography well. But he'd never noticed the opening cocooned by the rock wall here. Thunder's bark echoed out from the cave.

I hope he didn't disturb a hibernating bear.

Ridge carried a .44 Magnum—the minimum caliber needed to face off with a charging bear. But he also carried bear spray, which he grabbed along with his flashlight. Approaching the entrance to the cave, he crouched, entered, and shined the light inside it. Creeping forward, he moved farther and was able to stand up a few yards from the opening. Thunder sniffed and nudged a lump on the ground.

Before checking out Thunder's discovery, Ridge shined the light deeper into the cave. He couldn't see all the way back and really didn't want to disturb whatever wildlife might have taken up residence here. He turned his attention to the lump.

"What have you got here, boy?" A dear carcass?

He aimed the light at the mound and peered closely.

A body? His chest tightened. Thunder wasn't a cadaver dog. He'd been trained to dig for survivors under the snow, which was an entirely different scent than human remains. He continued forward, watching Thunder lick a face hidden by thick matted hair that spilled out from under a black knit cap. The woman groaned.

Alive! Relief rushed through him. Ridge dropped to his knees and tried to assess her injuries.

"You're going to be okay." At least he hoped so. He couldn't get a read on the extent of the damage.

Blood caked her head to go with a nasty bump. He couldn't see any broken bones, but spinal, neck, or internal injuries were still a possibility.

He shouldn't risk moving her.

"I have to make a call for help, and I'll be right back." He headed back to the cave's entrance, then exited and used his radio to call for emergency services, explaining that he needed assistance in getting an injured person down. As a SAR—search and rescue—volunteer, he was trained for this scenario, but special equipment was needed to safely transport the woman out of here.

He sensed a subtle shift in the atmosphere and instinctively whirled around. A fist landed in his face. Pain ignited along with surprise, as he stumbled back and almost fell from the ledge. "Hey! What are you doing?"

He stared into blue irises and recognition slammed into him.

Angie?

She took another swipe, but he dodged it, and she swayed and stumbled, her knees buckling. He caught her before she collapsed. She mumbled unintelligibly and closed her eyes. Unconscious again? What had happened to her?

A ferocious growl from deep inside the cave jarred him to the bones. Thunder's bark had shifted to a warning. They were in imminent danger. He hadn't wanted to take Angie down to his snow machine without assistance. But . . .

We just woke a hibernating grizzly.

2

A t the entrance to the cave, dizziness swept over her, and she squeezed her eyes shut. Then when she opened them, everything swayed again, and nausea erupted. She might have tumbled completely off the snowy ledge if the man hadn't caught her. His grip on her was firm but gentle, and his voice was smooth and reassuring. Why had she thought that he'd attacked her?

Uncertainty corded her insides. One thing for sure—she must have a concussion.

A large creature grumbled from deep inside the cave, and the man held her closer. Tighter. "I don't know why you struck me. I'm here to help you. I'm going to have to carry you out of here or else face off with the bear. Do you understand?"

His words shot through her brain and ignited more pounding. Waves of nausea hit her. No way was she walking out of this. She was coherent enough to admit that she needed his help and would have to trust this stranger.

"Yes. Just . . . go . . ."

He gently lifted her in his arms. "Thunder, come!"

She gripped his sleeve and pressed her face against his coat as he carried her away from the cave, the path rocky and uneven. The pain was overwhelming, but she tried to remain conscious. The grizzly's roar echoed in the cave, shuddering through her core.

"Get. Us. Out."

"Hold on. We have to wait for assistance. I can't get you down without help."

She lifted her head to see what he meant. A steep, rocky grade lay ahead. Could she make that slope? Could she last for a few moments? The roar grew louder. "I don't think we have a choice. Let's try."

"No way you can get down with your head injury, and if you fall again . . ."

The impact might cause further damage or kill her. "But can we hide from a grizzly?"

"We *are* hiding. But you're right. Bears have an incredible sense of smell. If he comes out of that cave, I'll take care of him."

"No." She whispered.

"I have nonlethal methods of sending him back into the cave." He gently placed her against the snow. Frosted pine needles hung over her.

Darkness edged her vision.

SHE WOKE to the jarring antiseptic scent of a sterile hospital room. Wary of opening her eyes to bright lights that could ignite the pain again, she kept them shut for now. She reached up to touch her head and felt a bandage.

"You're awake," a man said.

His words startled her, and she opened her eyes. Fortunately, the lights had been dimmed and she didn't experience the rush of discomfort she'd expected. A man in a white coat stood to her right and smiled down at her. To the left, the window revealed it was dark outside. She knew she was in a hospital, but where? Her pulse stuttered as panic began snaking around her throat.

"I'm Dr. Combs. We were concerned about you."

She blinked up at the forty-something physician. "How long have I been here?"

"They brought you down from the mountain a few hours ago."

"They?"

"A rescue team."

Dr. Combs took out a flashlight and shined it in her eyes.

She squeezed them shut and turned her head away.

"I didn't mean to cause you pain. Just testing for light sensitivity. Can you tell me your name?"

Her pulse jumped. She kept her eyes closed and concentrated. Realization hit her in the chest.

My name, my name, my name . . . What's my name?

She could hear the rapid beeping of a monitor as she felt her heart race. They'd put a heart monitor on her? Not the most important issue right now. She should know her name. This couldn't be happening.

For now, she would make one up. "Angie." The name sounded right. But what was the rest? She'd already blown it. She could tell by the look on Dr. Comb's face.

"Do you know where you are?" he asked.

"Yes. It's . . . I'm . . . in a hospital." Maybe she should have been completely honest with him, but wariness filled her.

He nodded. "I'll check back with you in a bit." He turned to walk away.

"Wait. What about the guy with the dog?"

"You mean Ridge Ledger and Thunder?"

"Did I hear my name?" The guy who'd rescued her from the cave peeked into the room.

Dr. Combs arched a brow and glanced at her.

"He can come in," she said.

"Oh, before I go. The chief wanted me to let her know as soon as you woke up," Dr. Combs said. "She has some questions for you, and she'll be checking in soon, just to give you a heads-up."

How was she supposed to answer questions? "The chief?"

"Shadow Gap Police Chief Autumn Long."

Shadow Gap. That told her she was in Shadow Gap, Alaska, but she didn't know why. *Is this a dream or a nightmare?* Amnesia happened only in movies and novels, didn't it?

"Well, I'll leave you two to chat." Dr. Combs exited the room.

The man who'd found her and rescued her from the cave, and whom she'd punched in the face, stood at the edge of the bed. His nose appeared a little swollen and he had subtle dark circles around his eyes. Thinking about his injuries caused her head to throb, but the pain wasn't nearly as bad as when she'd woken up in the cave. She hadn't gotten a good look at her rescuer before but now took in his appearance. Strong, scruffy jaw. Thick wheat-colored hair that stopped just above his shoulders. His hazel eyes looked thoughtful and caring.

He gave her a strange look. "I didn't mean to intrude, I just wanted to check on you."

"I'm sorry I punched you." She'd thought he was there to hurt her, but she wasn't sure why—just a feeling. At least she remembered those events. "Thanks for getting me out of that cave before the bear got to me."

"We both owe Thunder. He's the one that found you. I wasn't anywhere near that cave. I didn't even know it existed."

A woman in a police uniform knocked lightly on the door

then stepped into the room with a smile. "I'm Police Chief Autumn Long. I hope you don't mind if I ask a few questions."

"Well, I should get going." Ridge gave her a brief smile, then turned and walked out of the room.

Angie kind of wish he'd stayed—he was the only person she knew right now. Knew in the sense that he'd saved her life, at least—and that counted for something.

"No. I don't mind if you ask." Of course, asking didn't mean that Angie could answer.

"We couldn't find identification on you or any emergency contact information. Is there someone we can call on your behalf?"

Angie squeezed her eyes shut again and composed herself. She wouldn't lose it in front of the chief. Why was it so hard to process? "I'm sorry. I don't have anyone that you can contact."

She opened her eyes to read the chief's reaction.

Chief Long's lips flattened. "I understand. I want you to know that you're in a safe place and we'll take care of you."

The chief sounded like she suspected Angie had been the victim of violence. Human trafficking? Something. She couldn't remember what had landed her here, but the sense of peril pressed in on her.

"Can you tell me what happened? Why were you in the cave?"

Why was she there? She had to remember something.

A man with dark eyes stared at me.

Air rushed behind me.

The slightest nuance of memory blew through her, confirming that sense of danger closing in. She had to get out of here.

She couldn't breathe. The chief pressed the button next to her bed, and a nurse rushed in and took her vitals.

"You need to calm down and just breathe, honey."

Dr. Combs entered the room again.

And now was her chance. "When can I get out of here?"

He looked at the heart monitor. "As soon as you're stable."

She slowed her breathing and her heat rate dropped. "I'm fine. Just have a headache. I can rest at home."

"And where is home?" the chief asked.

Angie wasn't so stubborn or stupid to believe that she could manage on her own. Not until she knew more.

"I don't know why I was in the cave. I don't know where home is. I don't know if my name is really Angie."

But she remembered that menacing face and knew she was in survival mode.

THE NEXT MORNING, Angie dressed and waited for discharge papers, though she wasn't sure why she shouldn't just walk out. In the clothes they'd placed in a plastic bag, she found a waist holster *and* an ankle holster. That had surprised her. Had the hospital confiscated the guns that belonged in the holsters? Or had Chief Long taken them? Using the serial numbers, the chief could begin the search for the owner as a means of finding out who Angie really was, though it would take time. Hopefully before then, she would have her memory back.

Dr. Combs entered, smiled, and took a seat. He had gentle eyes, and Angie decided she liked him, but she didn't like the frown lines that formed between his brows.

"Does Mammoth Mountain sound familiar to you?"

Angie angled her head. "I mean . . . not personally, no. But I know it's in California and there's a ski resort there. Why should it be familiar?"

"Chief Long is still searching for more information and can tell you. But we believe your name is Angie Harris and you lived in Mammoth Mountain. You're not on any missing persons database, and your face doesn't appear on any searches or social media that we could find. You aren't showing up in vital statistics records in California. Maybe by the time we learn more, you'll have your memory back. My point is that we're working to find out who you are so that you can reconnect with your family and friends. Leave that to us, while you heal."

"But why can't I remember?" That was obvious, given her injuries, but she wanted to understand more.

"We know you've had a concussion, and I believe you're out of danger now. Concussions can lead to confusion and memory issues with new information but usually no lasting effects of amnesia. Generally, you can remember who you are and where you're from, so I'm concerned. I didn't want to say more last night until I'd spoken with a neurologist friend in Seattle."

Her throat constricted. She needed her memory back. Not more bad news. "No neurologists in Shadow Gap, I'm guessing."

He smiled and shook his head. "There's another type of amnesia. It's rare, though. It's called dissociative or psychogenic amnesia."

That meant she was the kind of person to beat the stats. "Well, that sounds promising."

He held up his hand. "I'm not saying that's what's going on here. But"—again that concerned frown—"it stems from emotional shock or trauma."

So her memories had been scared out of her? "Like?"

He cleared his throat. "It can happen to victims of a violent crime."

Dr. Combs and Chief Long suspected she was a victim of a violent crime and was repressing memories? Of course, the concussion served as a complicating factor.

Images flashed in her mind . . . an evil, gloating face . . . the sensation of falling . . . her insides lurching . . . "What's my prognosis?"

His smile was warm. "No matter the kind of amnesia suffered, memories usually return quickly."

But not quickly enough. Intuition told her that she had to get out of here if she wanted to live.

One thing she *did* remember—her instincts were never wrong.

3

"Uncle Ridge! Uncle Ridge!" Tommy raced toward him.

Lifting Tommy in the air, Ridge swung him around to a chorus of giggles before releasing the little guy on the floor. When his feet touched the ground, he was like a wound-up car. The five-year-old raced away and finally dropped to his knees to finish building his *Star Wars* A-wing Starfighter Lego set. If only Ridge had that much energy.

Arms crossed, his sister, Steph, stared at him, her blue-green eyes just like Tommy's. Her hair was bright blond while Tommy's was brown like his father's. "You don't have to do this, you know. You don't have to be here. Will they even let you go back?"

Ridge had left Mammoth Mountain Ski Resort in the middle of the season, and his boss hadn't been happy. He had no idea if he could go back, but it didn't matter. "I'm here because I want to be."

He'd come to Shadow Gap, a small community nestled in a fjord in Southeast Alaska, on the heels of the deadliest avalanche season in the history of the region. Haines, Skagway, and Shadow Gap had all been hit hard, and over twenty people had died—that death toll was far too high. He hoped he could protect Steph and Tommy and work to help prevent future disasters.

Steph's eyes shimmered with unshed tears. "You're here out of some sense of . . ." She let the words trail off and wiped her nose. "I'm sorry."

Out of some sense of guilt. That's what she'd started to say. But he didn't want to argue in front of Tommy or make Steph more upset. Still, the accusation stung, and Ridge felt a sudden lump in his throat. He would never recover from the fact that her husband, Manny, had been working with Ridge to monitor avalanches when he'd been crushed by one. That had been just over two years ago. Ridge had returned to that tragic day a thousand times in his mind. He'd been the more experienced of the two and should have seen the warning signs—the whole purpose of his job back then as an avalanche specialist had been to predict and warn. Yet, he'd allowed his brother-in-law to get caught. They'd been pushing the limits as they'd moved in too close to a cornice. At the memory, grief shot through him once again.

He might never get over it, but Steph and Tommy were the ones to suffer the most. She'd lost a husband. Tommy, his father.

Ridge caught her studying him, gauging him.

"I'm here because I love you." He didn't know what more he could say or do. He only knew that he should never have taken that job on the ski patrol at Mammoth two years ago, leaving Steph and Tommy behind. He might as well have been a million miles away. But at the time, she'd blamed him, and he needed to escape. That was on him. He could at least admit that he'd made a mistake when he left.

But he was back now. Maybe for good. "And I want to protect you."

With the half smile emerging in her face, relief swelled in his heart.

"I know you do, but don't forget you wanted to test that drone mapping technology, too," she teased, and headed to the kitchen where she started cutting the potatoes resting on the counter. "Do you think that's going to work?"

"We'll see."

He'd agreed to help his friend Cade Warren, an avalanche specialist out of Mountain Cove, by testing the avalanche mapping technology for Hanstech. The company out of Montana was a drone software company that had branched out from gathering data to forecast wildfire activity, to gathering avalanche data to create a prediction model. The avalanche center guys usually flew out in a helicopter to check on the mountains, but Shadow Gap had no such team of specialists or even a group like a ski patrol. This new drone technology could be a game changer, he hoped, but he still had his work cut out for him. He needed to continue to map the mountains nearest Shadow Gap even through the storm.

"Whatever the reason you're back, I'm glad you're here, and so is Tommy." She turned from the counter to smile at him. "And I know that woman you saved in the cave yesterday is glad you're here too. She might still be there if not for you and Thunder."

If she was still in the cave, she would probably be dead. He hadn't told Steph the person he'd found was Angie, the woman who broke his heart back in Mammoth. The other reason he'd headed to Shadow Gap. Mammoth only reminded him of Angie, and he was still trying to figure out why he'd found her wounded in Alaska. He told Chief Long what he knew about her—and in the telling, he realized he knew far too little. Did she have family or an emergency contact? Where had she lived before Mammoth?

The biggest question of all was why she was here in Shadow Gap. He could think of only one reason—she'd come here for him, but she didn't remember him and suffered from amnesia. He'd overheard Dr. Combs mention it to Angie's nurse, right after Ridge had given the nurse his number in case Angie wanted to call him. That is, if her memory returned. Man, this was messed up.

He approached his sister at the counter. "I need to run to town and check on something."

"In this storm? Why not drive?"

"Ha. Funny. I'll be back. You need anything?"

"Just be back for dinner. I'm making elk stew and home-made bread."

He could already smell the bread baking. "I wouldn't miss it."

He kissed her on the cheek. Tommy remained engrossed in his Lego set, and Ridge wouldn't disturb him.

He donned his coat and cap and considered Angie's phone call. She'd contacted him from the hospital and asked to see him. But he could tell with the way she stumbled with her words that she hadn't gotten her memory back.

She didn't have a clue who he was to her.

IN THE SMALL HOSPITAL LOBBY, Angie waited in a corner behind a fake corn plant and stared out the window, watching the sky dump layers of snowfall on downtown Shadow Gap. A snow-plow pushed dirty snow off the street as it passed the hospital. Really, this was nothing more than a clinic by comparison to any other hospital she'd known. Funny—she could remember hospitals, but not her name and who she was or why she was even here. Her life before. Family. Friends.

Who am I?

Her pulse spiked. She blinked back the sudden surge of tears. A few deep breaths and the knot in her stomach finally began to unwind. *I'll get there if I give it some time.*

The fact that she possessed two holsters led her to believe she might have been in law enforcement. At least she hoped that was the reason, but she had no badge or credentials or identification on her, according to the chief.

The chill permeated the glass, and a shiver pushed her to slip into her insulated jacket while she waited.

Come on, Ridge. How long does it take?

Maybe she'd been asking too much to get him out in this storm. But she needed to learn if he'd found anything else besides her in that cave. Like her guns. The hospital didn't have them—she'd discreetly asked the nurse who'd been assigned to her when she'd been brought in with the head injury.

Maybe Ridge has them.

If not, would he be willing to take her up the mountain to the cave? Unfortunately, this storm could very well bury the guns forever—or at least until spring breakup.

Dr. Combs had arranged for her to stay at the Lively Moose until she could go back to where she'd come from. *Wherever that is.* She puffed out a sigh. No memory. No cash or credit cards.

No Plan B.

Her stomach churned. She tried not to glance over her shoulder every five seconds, or fidget. But there was nothing she could do about the tightening in her chest.

Stop. Take a deep breath. The full memory of the assault would come back to her. Sooner rather than later, she hoped. Dr. Combs had kind eyes, and Chief Long seemed trustworthy, but if she had to trust one person, Ridge Ledger was that person. Never mind she could still remember the feel of his muscles, his strength when he'd helped her out of the cave. At the unbidden thought, Angie rubbed her arms. She sensed that she was a strong, independent person, and she obviously knew how to land a punch.

What does that say about me? She just had to be patient and give her brain time to rest so she could remember more than her attacker's face.

He looked like he wanted to kill me. Why?

Once again, she considered the man's face. He watched her as she fell, and she sensed the evil coming off him along with her desire to end him, then . . . The rush of air behind her. Arms flailing. Her fear, the certainty she would die. But she'd survived the fall. *Was it cushioned by the snow?* She guessed her head had hit a rock. *Or did he hit me in the head and think I was dead?*

In survival mode, she must have crawled into the cave.

The snowfall angled in the driving wind. She rubbed her neck and released a heavy exhale.

Ridge isn't going to make it.

But she'd been asking too much. She should have simply talked to him over the phone about the guns. Before she turned away, she noticed a bundled figure, a man with purposeful strides walking down the sidewalk, and hope surged.

Ridge? She started to rush out the doors but caught a glimpse of his face as he turned briefly to look at the hospital.

The man from the cliff!

Her pulse raced. *Deep breath. Slow, long exhale.* She pressed back into the shadows and tried to calm her pounding heart. She'd come close to rushing outside and into harm's way. *Well, that was a lesson.* She would have to stay hidden as much as possible until she was herself again.

Still, one thing was clear.

He's still after me.

If she could find out the man's identity, then she could find out who *she* was and why he wanted to kill her. Or maybe she had it all wrong. *Maybe I'm the villain!*

And she simply couldn't remember. Could that actually be a thing?

4

Ridge strode down the short hallways of the small hospital. He'd looked everywhere he'd been allowed to search but couldn't find her anywhere. Strange. She'd called and said she would meet him in the lobby. When she hadn't been waiting, he went to the small cafe and then the vending machines. But no Angie.

He approached the information desk. "Hey, Nancy. I'm looking for a woman that was supposed to meet me here. She's about five foot five, with thick brown hair and the most amazing blue eyes. Pretty." He might have shared more than he should have.

Nancy quirked a grin. "Come to think of it, I saw her. It's not like we've had a lot of activity today, though I expect that to change." She gestured toward the glass doors and the snowstorm outside.

"Well, do you know where she went?"

"She had that look about her—like she was lost. She was waiting on someone, now I know that was you. I kind of felt sorry for her. She didn't tell me where she was going, but I saw her slip out the front doors about five minutes ago."

"In this storm?"

"Well, you're out in it. But I get your point." She leaned closer and whispered, "I heard she can't remember anything, but it's not my business."

"Can you tell me where she's staying?"

"I believe Dr. Combs made arrangements for her, but he didn't tell me the details. If you want, I can try to find out."

"No need." He shoved off the counter and headed back into the storm. The only place he could think the doctor would arrange for her would be the local Eagle Bluff motel. He stepped along the recently shoveled sidewalk, which would need more shoveling within a few minutes. At the Eagle Bluff, he pushed through the entrance and a bell jingled. He stomped the snow off his feet by the door.

Clair Tompkins, one of Steph's friends, looked up at him from behind the counter. "Hey Ridge. What are you doing here? You don't plan to stay in town tonight to ride out the storm, do you?"

Steph's place was only three miles out of town. "No. I'm looking for a woman named Angie. Dr. Combs might have made arrangements for her to stay here."

Clair started shaking her head before he even finished. "We're all booked up, but Dr. Combs never contacted me. Sorry." Steph had tried to set them up a few years back, but Clair was married now. "You could check the Lively Moose."

"It's not a lodge."

"But they have the extra rooms upstairs. I've known Dr. Combs to work with the chief and arrange with the Livelys at least once."

That made sense since the Livelys were Chief Long's grandparents. He could try there next, but it would be getting dark soon, and that stew was calling to him. Steph wouldn't be happy if he missed dinner. But concern for Angie wouldn't let him leave until he knew she was safe in a room somewhere and he found out what she wanted from him. He hadn't so quickly forgotten the pain of their breakup and her sudden disappearance two months ago—it was fresh on his mind and heart. But she needed his help.

He crossed the street and walked a few blocks. Across from the small Shadow Gap police station, he pushed through the doors of the Lively Moose and took in the lofted ceilings, mounted wildlife, and rich woodwork. Ridge searched for Pearl Lively, who preferred to be called Birdy, and instead found Ike, her husband, behind the counter.

"Hey, Ike."

"Ridge Ledger. I heard you were back in town."

"Yep. I'm here for a bit, trying to help with the avalanche season."

"Glad to hear it. What can I do for you? You don't act like you're here for an early dinner."

Ridge smiled. "Nah. Steph is making stew, so I'd better not. But . . ." Ridge leaned closer so the couple a few seats away couldn't hear. "Someone said that Dr. Combs might have arranged for a woman, um . . . she lost her memory . . . to stay in one of your extra rooms upstairs. Her name is Angie." Angie Harris.

Chief Long had asked Ridge questions about how he found her, and if he was telling the truth or had been the one to cause Angie's injuries. The chief didn't believe Ridge was responsible, but she had to ask. At least that had been her explanation. She indicated she would find out more about Angie and try to find someone—besides Ridge—who could care for Angie until she recovered. In the meantime, he got the distinct impression that the police chief wanted him to keep his distance. All well and good, but he'd left his number with the nurse in case Angie had asked for him. And Angie had called him, after all.

Ike nodded, curiosity evident in his gaze. "The good doctor made the arrangement, yes."

Ridge blew out a relief-filled breath. At least she'd found her way here safe and sound. "I'm glad to know she's not out in the weather. Can you let her know I'm here? She wanted to see me."

"But that's just it, Ridge. She isn't here. She never showed up. Autumn—er, the chief—seemed pretty upset."

This wasn't good news. Not at all. Ridge flattened his hands against the counter. He would try to look on the bright side. "Well at least Chief Long is out there looking for her too."

That knowledge should make him feel better, but instead unease crawled over him. "Well, thanks, Ike. If she shows up, give me a call."

"Will do. You heading home now?"

"Not exactly."

In the meantime, he could pray. *Lord, please keep her safe out there. Help her to remember. Help her find her way. And if you're willing, help me locate her to learn what she wanted.* He wasn't sure what to say or how to talk to her in this situation. *And please, please give me the right words.*

He had a feeling she was in trouble, though with the way she'd punched him dead on, he suspected she could very well take care of herself.

Once she remembered.

5

A ngie hadn't gone to the Lively Moose because that's where the doctor had sent her.

The man after her might find that out. Nor would she check in at the local motel—the only one—because that was a logical choice. He would find her there too. Angie couldn't afford to take the obvious next steps.

She'd wanted Ridge to help her locate her guns and nothing more, but that opportunity had passed. He'd probably gone to the hospital and, when he learned that she'd gone, simply returned home. She could call him—she still had his number in her pocket—but she didn't have a cell phone yet.

Ugh. I hate feeling so helpless!

Telling Chief Long about the man after her was also logical —then again, she would wait until she knew more. The doctor had said she would most likely recover in a few days. In the meantime, she was in a foreign place surrounded by strangers.

So she was Angie Harris—that meant she had at least remembered something. A good sign. But her name meant nothing if she didn't remember who she was. She'd had no reaction to the doctor's mention of Mammoth Mountain. None.

What did that mean? She would do her own search on the internet as soon she got settled with a phone. Without funds, she was trapped.

Instead of checking in at the Lively Moose or the local motel, she found herself looking at the thermal parkas at the local outfitters store while she made a plan. The place was open for only another hour. And then what?

Lord, . . . where do I go? What do I do? Who am I?

She might not know about herself beyond a name, but she remembered God. She had a relationship with him. He was all she had, and she'd just have to trust him to protect her and lead her.

God, I'm in trouble.

The wind gusted through the store along with thick snowflakes as a couple men pushed through the doors. She hunkered behind the rack and, to make sure neither of them was the man after her, peered at them over the coats in bright shades of turquoise, blue, pink, and orange.

The doors whooshed open again. More cold air, and—her heart leapt to her throat—*he* was entering the store! Surely her labored breathing and slamming pulse could be heard across the room.

Staying hidden, she grabbed a turquoise parka off the rack and weaved around thick jackets and waterproof pants— heading discreetly for the changing room at the back. She slipped inside, praying he hadn't seen her.

"Can I help you?" the store clerk asked.

"Yeah, I'm just looking for my wife. I dropped her off earlier to grab a few things." His voice was deep and rough, and she didn't recognize it any more than she recognized him. He couldn't be her husband. Could he? Was it possible? No, he was too old. She couldn't fathom marrying someone twice her age.

"Well, friend, I haven't seen you around here before. What's your wife look like?"

The man described Angie exactly. He almost sounded as if he knew more about her than she did about herself. Her breathing hitched up so loud she was sure everyone in the store could hear. She couldn't rush out of the room and out of the store—he'd see her, and he might try to grab her. Her head remained tender and achy, so she wasn't running anywhere.

But she knew one thing. If he opened the door to the changing room, she would definitely hurt him. She remembered she knew defensive moves, and that made her smile. Muscle memory, but all the same, it could mean her amnesia was subsiding. Slowly, but surely.

"I saw her earlier," the clerk said, "but she must have left. I don't see her now."

His response surprised her, but maybe he hadn't seen her go into the changing room. The store was packed with enough stuff a person could get lost.

"Take care out there," the clerk called.

Cold air circled through the store and hit her even in the changing room at the back. So he'd left. Relief filled her. She waited a few moments. She was about to exit the changing room when she heard the door open again and felt the cold. She slipped out of the coat she had on and tried on the new one to see if it fit, and she was instantly warm. This jacket was much better than the one she'd been wearing. If only she had money to buy it.

"I'm looking for a woman."

She stiffened. Again?

"Don't tell me. You lost your wife."

"What? Why would you say that?"

The clerk chuckled. "Just kidding, Ridge. Another man came in a few minutes ago looking for his wife."

Angie decided to wait and hear what response Ridge would give.

"Who are you looking for?"

"Oh, she's about yay tall. A head of thick brown hair that hangs just below her shoulders. The prettiest blue eyes."

The way he described her warmed her as much as the coat.

"Sounds like you're looking for that other man's wife."

Ridge remained quiet a few breaths before asking, "Can you describe him?"

"Well, he was about average height. In his fifties, I'd say. Black hair with gray at the temples. Brown eyes. Nothing really stood out. But he had that look about him, you know, that said you don't want to mess with him."

"Yeah. I know that look." Ridge blew out a breath. "Well, thanks."

"I hope you find her."

Footfalls sounded as Ridge headed away.

"Wait!" She exited the changing room in a rush that started up the pounding in her head again. But she didn't care. "Ridge . . . wait."

He whirled. "Angie?"

"Hey, aren't you the wife? Wait a minute, are you two—"

"No!" They said simultaneously to the store clerk.

"I'm nobody's wife." But could she be sure? Maybe the man had been her husband and she'd been a victim of violence and so traumatized she couldn't remember.

A pang shot through her chest, and her insides squeezed. No . . . no, that couldn't be it. She glanced at her ring finger. No ring.

"Come on, then," Ridge held his hand out.

"Wait a minute. Are you going to pay for that?"

Angie froze and stared down at the beautiful parka she'd slipped into while in the changing rom. "I'm sorry . . . I . . ." She quickly removed it.

"Here you go." Ridge yanked his wallet out and laid a few bills on the counter.

"No, you don't need to do that." She set the coat on the counter in front of the clerk. "It's a beautiful parka, by the way."

"And warm." Ridge grabbed a thick white Columbia snow beanie, a bright pink scarf, and black gloves from the nearby racks.

He pressed the cap onto her head then held out the new coat for her to slip into.

"I told you, no, thank you."

"I already paid for this stuff, so come on." He winked, then gave a look she couldn't read, but then it dawned on her that he meant to change her clothes so her so-called husband couldn't so easily recognize her if he was looking for her in certain attire.

After she was fully dressed in the new digs, Ridge laid the price tags on the counter. He glanced up to the clerk. "Does that cover it?"

The store clerk smiled and slapped his hand over the bills and counted them. "Yep. I'll get your change."

"Keep it." Ridge gently ushered her toward the front of the store.

Her pulse raced. Was she making a mistake to go with him? Rethinking her choice, she hesitated and stepped back from the exit door.

Ridge stopped and looked at her with those gentle hazel eyes that peered into her soul.

"I remembered something." *Wait. Does he know I have amnesia? Why would he? She should explain.* "Ridge . . ." She lowered her voice to a whisper. "I can't remember anything. I have amnesia."

He held her gaze, a tenuous smile in his face. "I know. It's going to be okay. But what is it? What do you remember?" His expression was hopeful, expectant.

"That I'm usually completely independent." She sounded

less convincing than she'd wanted, but she needed him to know she could take care of herself. Um, . . . normally.

"I have no doubt. You punched me in the nose."

"Again, I'm sorry about that."

His smile produced dimples on each cheek, which she found endearing.

He leaned in. "Let's get out of here. My sister makes a mean elk stew, and we don't want to be late for dinner. At her house, you can rest and heal and tell me about this man who claims he's your husband." Ridge's eyes flicked to the remnants of the bruise on her head.

If only she could. "I don't want to put her in danger."

"You won't. Stay at our house tonight and we'll figure something else out for tomorrow if you prefer. We can also let Chief Long know about this man who's going around looking for his wife. People in this town band together. He won't last long."

Maybe her memory would come back by morning. Dawn couldn't come soon enough. If not, at least she would be with Ridge, and he could help her find her guns—protection against this hidden threat. Because she had no idea why that man was after her.

6

_____

Darkness descended on Shadow Gap, and the heavy snow filled Ridge's windshield as he focused on the short but intense drive home. Angie kept to herself, and he didn't press her to talk. Dr. Combs had probably instructed her to continue to rest in the room at the Lively Moose, but she hadn't followed those instructions. He couldn't imagine what she was going through.

He should contact Chief Long to let her know that Angie was staying with them at Steph's house. The chief was welcome to check on Angie tonight. He assumed the chief had told her that Ridge had known her before, and that's how they even knew her name. But Ridge had not shared that he and Angie had been in a relationship and that Angie had broken things off with him. Dr. Combs and Chief Long weren't entirely sure that Ridge hadn't been the source of Angie's physical trauma and the resulting loss of memory. Telling them that they'd dated, and she'd broken off with him would only add to their suspicions. Not telling them, of course, also added to the mix.

Common sense told him that learning about their relationship could be pivotal in helping Angie get her memory back, but on the other hand, the situation was volatile, depending on whether Angie saw Ridge as a threat or a friend. So Ridge would let Angie bring up that conversation. He was only trying to help her, but he still felt awkward. He had no idea how to approach the topic under such strange circumstances.

His heart thumped unevenly with the stressful thoughts.

Regardless of how the truth came out, she would be hurt and angry with him for not telling her the moment he learned of her amnesia, and he hated being in this predicament. But he wanted to do the right thing—whatever was best for her. Right now, he wasn't sure what that was.

He only knew that with that creep out there looking for her, and her belief that she was in danger, Ridge would keep her safe until someone else took over.

Their shared past skated through his mind, jabbing the vulnerable places.

"I'm sorry, Ridge, I can't do this anymore. It was a good time while it lasted. I'm leaving Mammoth Mountain."

At the time, he'd struggled to accept that it was truly over. Whatever. Right now, he had to push their last encounter out of his mind. He steered up the road in the Dodge Ram that used to be Manny's, then turned into the drive and parked behind his sister's red Ford Explorer.

Angie turned to him, shadows under her eyes. She definitely needed to rest. "Are you sure your sister is okay with this?"

"Don't worry. She'll be fine, and you'll like her. Steph will make you feel right at home." *I hope.* He opened the door and went around to help her, but she had already climbed out. She appeared perfectly capable of hiking through the deep snow. He'd have to shovel the sidewalk at least once before bed.

Steph might be fine with Angie staying, but Ridge wasn't exactly sure he would be. Guilt settled in his gut, and he made the decision to tell her everything tonight, after all.

He hiked next to her through the snow to the front door, glad for the light on the porch to guide their path. Southeast Alaska didn't experience as much darkness as mainland Alaska, but dusk still fell early. In the light of the porch, he took in her shadowed profile.

Would she remember everything by dawn? His gut tightened at the thought, and he hoped she wouldn't hate him.

He'd done a little of his own research about amnesia and found the most sensational stories, which left him disturbed. Most of the stories ended well, but others were tragic. Apparently, real-life amnesia stories were bizarre compared to even those stories told in movies and novels.

Just like this current real-life situation was hard to believe. Angie Harris—a woman he thought he'd never see again—was staying in Steph's house tonight. He'd loved her, and now she was so close and yet so far.

God, . . . please help her remember.

Ridge opened the door and let her enter ahead of him. But just inside the threshold, she hesitated—a look of panic crossing her face. He placed his hand at the small of her back and gently guided her into the kitchen. "Steph! I brought a guest to dinner."

Tommy rushed around his mother. "Uncle Ridge! Who's she? She's pretty!"

Warmth spread through him. Tommy was right.

Thunder barked and ran through the house, panting as he came up to Angie. She bent to pet him and let him lick her cheeks. Ridge held his breath—could Thunder jog her memory? Regardless, Ridge's heart thrummed at the sight. Angie Harris was a real heartbreaker. But he could put aside the pain and focus on what was important—her recovery, and the fact she was in trouble.

His sister smiled and thrust her hand forward. "I'm Steph. We're so glad you could join us. I'll just set another place."

"And I'm Angie." Angie glanced between Steph and Ridge. "I don't mean to intrude. Ridge said it would be all right if I stayed."

"Stayed?" Steph hesitated, then, "Well, sure. Of course. I'll just make sure the extra room has everything you need."

When she turned and moved to the counter, he caught the surprised look she'd barely managed to hide from Angie. What could he say? He owed his sister. He'd explain everything later.

He texted the chief about Angie's location and set his cell aside. Chief Long might think he was some kind of weird stalker who had pursued Angie and brought her here to try to woo her or something. A small wave of nausea hit him at the thought—this wasn't like that at all. The chief needed to know that someone was out there looking for Angie to cause her harm, and that someone was not Ridge.

With the fire stoked in the fireplace and the snow coming down hard outside, they sat at the small round table and ate stew out of handmade ceramic bowls, the fresh-baked bread a perfect complement. Steph had loved being a wife and mom, and he had to hand it to her—she hadn't crushed under the loss and had remained a good mother for Tommy.

"So, tell me about yourself, Angie. Where are you from? What brought you to Shadow Gap?"

Ridge dropped his spoon against the bowl. Angie, to her credit, kept her composure. She stared at her stew and cleared her throat.

Ridge started to speak, but she interrupted him.

"I wish I could answer that, but I have amnesia from a concussion." A nervous chuckle escaped. "I'm told my memory will return soon."

"Oh." Steph pressed her hand against her chest. "I'm so sorry."

Angie lifted her incredible eyes and smiled—that beautiful smile he remembered and . . . loved. "You didn't know. Please, it's not a problem. Why don't you tell me about your life here in Shadow Gap?"

"Uh, well." Steph glanced at Ridge. "Tommy and I make our home here in Shadow Gap, but Ridge only recently came back to help with the avalanche season. We've had a rough one. Why don't I let you tell *your* story, Ridge?"

Why did Steph have to turn the focus to him? But maybe if he shared, it would help Angie remember her life. He should have done this to begin with. "Thunder works with me as a search-and-rescue avalanche dog. We worked at Mammoth Mountain on the ski patrol. Nothing much to tell."

He stared into her beautiful blue eyes and searched for recognition. *Come on, Angie. Remember? You worked at the lodge. We were together.*

He didn't care that she broke it off. He wanted only for her to be herself again, and to be safe.

And right now, zero recognition lit her eyes.

"That's admirable of you. Impressive." She set her spoon on her empty bowl. "I take it you were the one to inform Chief Long of my identity."

He nodded. "I thought you knew."

"No. Chief Long didn't share that, but I should have asked. I didn't even think of it."

"That's understandable." How could she think clearly to ask the right questions until her brain healed?

"Would you like some more?" Steph offered.

"No, I'm good. The stew was wonderful, and the bread practically melted in my mouth. Thank you so much for including an unexpected guest." Angie flashed a beautiful smile.

And his heart bounced around against his chest all over again. He ignored the rising emotions—clearly, Angie hadn't felt the same way about him.

"You're welcome." Steph started removing the dishes.

Angie got up, but Ridge stopped her and Steph. "I'll get the dishes."

"Not tonight you won't. You have to shovel the sidewalk so we can at least get out tomorrow."

"I'll help." Angie pushed from the table.

"I got it," he said. "Your head will get better faster, and you'll get your memories back sooner, if you give yourself a chance to heal." He headed for the door.

As he exited, he got a text from the chief that she wanted to speak with Angie. He heard Steph's cell ring and stepped back inside to listen.

The chief had called his sister. "Sure, she's right here. Angie, Chief Long wants to talk to you."

Angie took the cell. "Hello? Yes, I'm fine, thanks. No, not yet. I . . . I'm good here. Okay. I'll see you in the morning."

Leave it to Chief Long to make good and sure that Angie was safe and that Ridge Ledger wasn't the man who'd knocked her out up in that cave. Though if the chief truly believed that, she wouldn't allow Angie to stay here. At least he could find some measure of relief in the thought.

Outside, he grabbed the shovel and started in on the layers, glad for the escape. She would probably remember who she was by tomorrow and then she would be gone from his life again.

Still, he couldn't ignore the fact she'd shown up here. Shadow Gap wasn't the kind of place a person fell into accidentally. You had to be deliberate about finding your way here.

7
_____

Angie appreciated the comfy room and the privacy. The snow muted the night sounds. She peered out the window and, with the security light out front, could see the huge flakes. At least for now, she felt safe. No one had followed them from town, and it wasn't likely the man after her could figure out she stayed with a random guy at his sister's house.

But he's not so random, is he?

He'd worked at Mammoth Mountain—the place Dr. Combs told her she lived. When Ridge had mentioned it, Angie had held back her gasp of surprise.

What does it all mean?

She hadn't had much time to figure it out. Steph had brought her some more comfortable clothes to slip into and offered to launder her dirty ones, which she declined. She remembered how to do laundry, after all, and would do her own. She gathered up the layered clothing she'd been wearing when she'd been attacked or fallen or both. Out of habit she dug in her pockets and found a wrapped candy from O'Daire's.

Images flashed across her mind, and she slumped onto the

bed. She was at a table with friends. No, wait. Not friends. Who were they? A man and a woman. Loud music around them. The image felt wrong and distasteful.

Oh, Lord, . . . who was I before? Why is this happening to me?

She gathered her clothes and took them to the laundry room. She would press Ridge for details on what he knew about her at Mammoth Mountain, borrow a laptop so she could search the internet for clues about her life, then get him to help her find her guns. She put her clothes in the washing machine, adding some detergent and warm water before dropping the lid. Steph and Tommy were already in bed, and she didn't know where Ridge was at the moment—probably in bed too. He'd already shoveled the snow, and that had to be exhausting.

She couldn't sleep, so she eased onto the cushy sofa in front of the fire. Thunder was lying on the rug and his tail thumped. She pulled a beautiful blue-and-white afghan over her, curled up with the pillow under her head, and watched the fire as she thought about what she knew.

She might be law enforcement. City, state, or federal? Why didn't she have identification on her? She knew defensive moves, and for some reason she couldn't fathom, she barely survived a fall after facing off with a man who was looking for her around town. The last person's face she'd seen before the fall. A man she suspected wanted to kill her, to harm her.

Which meant eventually he would find her here.

Angie couldn't stay. Tomorrow she could remember more. She would leave this house, regardless. She hoped she hadn't put this family in danger, but this place felt safe, and she'd needed that feeling—if only for one night.

Ridge had been a godsend. He'd saved her life, after all.

She let the fire mesmerize her and dozed off.

～

ANGIE TRIED to shift her position, but a heavy form prevented her from moving. She woke up and found Thunder next to her on the sofa. Practically on top of her.

A feeling gusted through her.

Déjà vu.

Thunder sleeping against her on the sofa in front of the fire. This . . . felt familiar.

She remained next to the dog for a few moments and closed her eyes. Memories? Or was she losing reality? She gently nudged Thunder off her, then noticed Ridge slept in the recliner across from her.

Thunder crept over to the fire and curled up again. She knew the dog. Yep. She remembered Thunder. So did that mean she also knew Ridge in a more personal way? She quietly rose and snuck over. Grabbed his cell phone resting on the stand next to his chair then moved back to the sofa. He shifted but didn't wake up.

She swiped the screen, relieved that it opened without requiring a passcode or fingerprint. She might be overstepping and intruding on his privacy, but she needed answers. Angie found the photos app and scrolled through, almost wishing she hadn't.

The images stunned her. Nausea erupted inside.

RIDGE WOKE UP WITH A START. Cold air rushed over him, and snowflakes swirled into the room and landed on his face and arms. He bolted from the old recliner and grabbed his gun in one fluid motion, then whipped around to stop the threat. He'd been dreaming about the man after Angie.

Her stalker wasn't standing in the doorway, but instead Angie stood with her back to the now-closed door and glared at him. He had the distinct impression that she'd opened and slammed the door to wake him up.

"What happened? What's going on? Is he out there?" He asked the questions even as realization dawned—the look on her face told him everything.

She marched forward and jabbed her finger into his chest. "You didn't say a word. You didn't tell me about *us*. Why didn't you? And your answer had better be good."

I would if you'd calm down and give me a chance. He bit back the words, understanding they would make things only worse.

Angie thrust a cell phone at him—*his* cell phone—and on the screen were images of Ridge and Angie together at Mammoth Mountain. Smiling, wrapped in each other's arms, the snowy scenery behind them. Lots and lots of pictures he'd never shared on social media.

He groaned inside. Scraped a hand down his face. "Look, Angie, I had planned to tell you. I wanted to tell you."

Turning from her, he paced the small space, then finally eased onto the sofa. When Thunder approached and whined, he buried his hands in the dog's thick winter coat.

"You're the reason they had a name for me. I get that. But why hold back the rest?" She cast a suspicious look at him.

"How do you tell someone who they are, that you knew them before, especially since I could be the person you don't want to see again or hear from?"

"I don't get it. Why would I never want to see you again? The pictures show us together, and I'm in Shadow Gap for a reason. I have to assume that reason is you."

"I wish . . . I wish you could remember." The awkwardness squeezed his insides, but he kept his gaze on her, kept the emotions buried deep. "We were together until you broke things off and left."

She moved to the recliner and sat, her hands between her knees. "Chief Long could have told me, then. Or maybe the police chief wanted to look into my past first and make sure I wasn't a threat to the community."

He scraped a hand through his hair. This just kept getting more complicated. "She didn't know we were together. I . . . I didn't tell her about the breakup. I think she already viewed me as a potential threat to you. I found you injured, but for all she knows, I could have caused the injury. I knew you before, and then you showed up here. You see how that looks. I know it sounds bad. I should have told you, and I was going to tonight. But the embarrassing part of it is that even though we were together, I don't know much about you. I only knew you while you worked at Mammoth, but beyond that—your life before— you never told me." So how serious could Angie have been about Ridge to have kept so much of herself from him?

She lifted her gaze to him. "Tell me about myself. About . . . us."

"You can't remember anything about working at the lodge?"

"No. Mammoth Mountain doesn't sound right to me. Doesn't feel right. I have had a few memories, and they don't feel right. That makes no sense at all. Then tonight I woke up with Thunder next to me on the sofa. I *remembered* him. I realized I must have known you pretty well. You were not just an acquaintance from Mammoth." She handed over his cell phone. "Those images . . . you and me . . ."

A deep ache cut across his heart. "They don't feel right?"

"I wasn't going to say that. But something about us doesn't feel right."

Okay, now that hurt like she was breaking up with him all over again, but he wouldn't let the pain go deeper. "I don't understand enough about amnesia to know what feeling one way or another has to do with anything."

"Honestly, neither do I. But it would help if you told me what you know about me."

"Everything?"

"Yes."

He hung his head. *God, give me the right words.*

"You don't need to be nervous. Just tell me the truth as you see it, and if you lie about anything, I'll eventually find out."

He lifted his head at that and found her smiling.

"I'm only teasing. I obviously trust you, Ridge, or I wouldn't be here. Maybe that says something about our relationship." Hurt flickered through her eyes.

Did she still care, in some strange, weird way, even though she couldn't remember him?

"Look. I need to remember. You can help me get the process started. Earlier, I found a candy wrapper from a place called O'Daire's. A few memories came back. I don't remember what they're about. It was just a flash. And a feeling."

"The place isn't familiar, no, but it could be from somewhere besides Mammoth Mountain."

"What do you mean?"

He blew out a breath. "As you already know, I was on ski patrol and I worked with Thunder. You worked at the lodge. That's how we met, and we hung out a lot. And eventually got very close."

"I saw the pictures." Her tone was caring and gentle. "I get that we were close. The pictures don't lie. So what happened?"

"That's just it. I don't know. About two months ago, early December, you suddenly broke things off and you'd quit your job, and you just . . . left . . ." *Me with a broken heart.* She had enough on her plate without him giving her a guilt trip. "Our relationship isn't important here. Finding out who you are and who is after you is."

"Why am I here, Ridge? Do you know?"

"When I told Chief Long about you, I realized just how much I don't know about you. I don't know where you're from or about your family. Nothing." Except how much he cared . . . loved her, really . . . and how amazing she was. "But when I saw you, I thought the only reason you could have come to Shadow Gap was to find me."

She held his gaze. "And why would I do that if I broke up with you?"

Exactly.

8

She had a feeling about Ridge. A good, positive feeling. As she stared into his deep hazel eyes, she thought she might just remember him. More than anything she *wanted* to remember this man, Ridge Ledger. Why would she have broken things off with him and left him behind? He was a great guy with strong moral character who volunteered on a SAR team. But relationships could be so complicated, even when everything was going the right way.

A man was after her and wanted to kill her, and she'd come to Shadow Gap for Ridge. She could think of several possible scenarios that might have brought her here, but only one pushed forward and raced through her mind.

So that Ridge could protect her? No, that didn't feel right. So she could protect him? To warn him?

Her throat tightened. "Are you sure that's all you can tell me?"

He stood from the sofa and approached her, standing much too close. Ridge pressed the back of his hand lightly against her cheek, and she saw the hurt behind his eyes. She'd broken his heart—she knew that now.

"I hope you can forgive me for not telling you sooner. I feared that I wasn't the right person, anyway, given we have a history, and hearing it from me might be the wrong thing for you. But like I said, I had planned to tell you tonight, but I found you asleep on the sofa."

Her breath hitched at his touch. Clearly, she still had feelings for this man. They were buried in her memories, but her heart . . . her heart remembered. "I was furious that you hadn't told me. But I get it now. It's okay, Ridge."

He dropped his hand, and she instantly felt the disconnection. "I'm going to bed now, and since I had the memory with Thunder, I'm hoping that I'll wake up and know everything. Remember everything." Including why she would dare to break things off with this guy she clearly still cared deeply about.

She headed to her room as the heat rushed to her cheeks. If he kissed her, how many more memories might rush back? Was it worth a try? Maybe tomorrow if she hadn't fully recovered, she would see about that. And then she would need to leave to protect him and his family. This time, she could at least tell him why.

She hoped that daybreak would bring more memories and expose the hidden dangers.

RIDGE WAS UP WELL before sunrise, and he went ahead and made breakfast so Steph could sleep in, though the noise might wake her up. Angie had woken him with her demand for answers after viewing the images on his phone of them together. Understandable. What did it say about him that he hadn't deleted them? He hadn't been able to let go and move on so quickly? But he was the farthest thing from Angie's heart. After all, she'd remembered Thunder. He wasn't sure if he should be insulted those memories of his dog came back to her first. He could almost chuckle at that, but the situation was far too serious. At least bits of her past, her life, were coming back to her. He couldn't begin to imagine how completely vulnerable a person would feel to not know themselves, their past, their family or friends. *Who could she trust?*

He determined to be the man Angie could depend on. Last night, he'd desperately wanted to kiss her. But what he'd had with her was over even if she couldn't remember she wanted it to be over. He couldn't do that to her now. She was much too vulnerable.

He was so relieved to have finally shared the truth with Angie, though learning they had a past together didn't help jog her memory. Regardless, after their conversation, he'd spent the rest of the night formulating a plan.

With someone after her, someone she obviously feared, he couldn't let her stay with his family. What if the man caught up to her here? No. He'd take her someplace safe until she remembered more about her life and what had brought her to his town.

He still didn't understand why she'd come searching for him, and he wasn't sure he wanted to know. Then again, had she wanted to put things back together with him? Nah. That was only wishful thinking. With a man after her, she could have been seeking refuge, a safe place to hide, and believed Ridge would help her. She had been right.

Hair disheveled, Angie emerged from the hall and yawned. "Why are you up so early?"

"I didn't mean to wake you."

She plopped into a chair and rubbed her eyes. "No. I think you did. You want me out of your sister's house, and I don't blame you. Come on, bacon and eggs and coffee? Who could sleep through that noise?"

"You mean those smells."

"Whatever." She grinned.

He loved it when she grinned, but he didn't give himself away. "Want some coffee?"

"I mean . . . if you're offering."

"I am." He poured a large mug, then added some sugar and cream. "No specialty coffees here, I'm afraid, but I'll do my best to imitate what you drank."

"At Mammoth?"

"Yes." He handed the mug off and studied her. Had she remembered anything?

She sipped the coffee and closed her eyes, savoring it. Watching her sent memories rushing through him . . . Weaving his fingers through her luscious hair, and maybe grabbing a few kisses along her neck. He closed his eyes and tried to calm his heart, which beat entirely too fast.

He wished she would—

"I remembered something."

He opened his eyes and sat at the table across from her with his own cup of coffee. He'd already had three.

"And?" Had she remembered her life? Did he factor into her memories at all?

She stared at her cup. "I remember handing my badge in. That's it. I don't know what it means other than"—she lifted her gaze to him—"I think I was a DEA Special Agent."

9

She knew those words must have hit him hard, because after all, according to Ridge, she had worked at the lodge at Mammoth Mountain Ski Resort. Dr. Combs and Chief Long based all their intel off what Ridge had told them. The fact that he believed that about her, but she remembered something else entirely, was disturbing.

Confusing.

Or it was telling.

"How can that be? You worked at the lodge. I know you did. Sure, I saw the holster on you in the cave when I assessed your injuries, and I thought you'd lost your gun. People in Alaska, in the mountains anywhere, carry guns." His deep frown caused a pang to shoot through her.

Yep. In her heart, she knew that she still cared deeply for this man she'd hurt. She apparently was heaping more hurt on him because she must have lied to him.

Ridge was sharp. He could put two and two together. If she was a DEA Special Agent, while "working at the lodge" she must have been undercover. She'd give him time to process the news and figure it out. Shoot, she needed time to process and figure it out, too.

An ache pounded at the back of her head, reminding her of the concussion. Squeezing her eyes shut, she rubbed her temples. She was so done with the pain, with the fear, with the not knowing who she was. But she was getting there.

God, . . . please. Just help me.

Working undercover for the DEA—if it wasn't just some figment of her imagination or something she'd seen in the movies that was masquerading as her memories—meant she'd dealt with some serious bad guys. The nausea erupting in her stomach was becoming an unwelcome but familiar sensation.

Breathe in. Breathe out. She opened her eyes.

Ridge was staring into his mug, clearly lost in his own morbid thoughts—like what had he gotten himself into? Why had he been dating an undercover agent? He slowly lifted his gaze to meet hers and held it.

She could almost read his mind—he was thinking what she was thinking. What could all of it mean?

I don't know . . . maybe that danger is knocking at your door? She held back that answer to his silent question.

If she was working undercover, her name might not be Angie Harris, after all.

The smoke alarm went off, and Ridge bolted from the chair. He moved the smoking pan off the burner. "Well, there goes the bacon."

Steph entered the kitchen, hands on her hips. "Are you trying to burn the house down?"

"I'm sorry. I just got distracted."

"Well, that's not hard to figure out." Her tone was teasing and filled with love as she grabbed his arms and ushered him over to the table. Then she kissed him on the cheek as he took a seat. "Thank you, big brother, for trying to make breakfast. I love you. Now, let me finish for you while you focus on the nice lady."

Her words elicited a laugh from Angie and Ridge as well, and he glanced up at her and then back to his coffee. Then he cleared his throat. Was he . . . blushing? She didn't think that guys blushed, but wow was that endearing. If she still had her own phone, would she find all those same pictures of them together?

Oh no!

Her phone with all the pictures. If someone found it, or if her cover had been blown, Ridge and his family could be in danger. That had to be it. Maybe that's why she was here to begin with. For the life of her, she wished that she could think of another reason that she would have come to Shadow Gap. *Any* other reason than Ridge was in danger because of her.

Heart pounding, she tried to compose her emotions. She needed to warn him, protect him, and get out of here.

"I don't like burned bacon." Tommy climbed up in a chair.

"I'm making more." Steph set a glass of orange juice in front of the little guy and brushed her hand over his hair.

What an adorable family. Angie had brought danger to their door simply by getting too close. Now that she remembered she'd had the DEA badge and had been returning it—as in, quitting the job—she could contact them, and they could find information about her true identity.

Still, she'd handed in her badge. Why? Could the man after her be wrapped up in her DEA identity or her undercover identity? She couldn't call the agency yet, not until she knew more.

They quickly ate their breakfast, Steph and Tommy filling the silence with small talk.

Steph looked out the window. "We're all snowed in. I heard from the district there's no school today, kiddo."

"Yippee!"

"I can work from home today and grade papers. But did you ever get the information transmitted to the avalanche center?"

"Yes. I need to check with them on the results. Plus, I probably need to go back and use the drone to get more data." He glanced across at Angie. "I was using the new drone tech when Thunder took off after wildlife. I think that's how he ended up finding you in the cave."

"How exactly does the drone help predict avalanches?"

"The drones don't do the predicting, but they're used to gather the data. I only have one drone, but it flies back and forth and builds an image of the slope, and then with each layer of snow the images overlap. Algorithms use the data points to look at the load on the slopes and how the terrain affects it."

She smiled. "Impressive."

"It's more complicated than that, but I'm just the drone guy, not the brains behind the software."

"But you said you worked on the ski patrol, and part of their job is to measure the avalanche risk. So you're more than just the drone guy."

He looked uncomfortable with that line of questioning— was it because she should already know about his job?

"Yes, that's part of my job. As for using drones, technology can assist us in predicting avalanches, and we hope to save more lives." His last words came out as if he was in pain and he hung his head.

Angie knew she'd overstepped. There was something behind this. Something she was missing. "Since you made breakfast, I'll clean up the dishes."

"I burned breakfast. I'll clean them up." Ridge sent her an apologetic look. She suspected he was eager to continue their conversation and to explain, but now wasn't the time.

Hands on her hips, Steph glanced between them. "I'll do the dishes. You two have things to figure out. I know that."

"Thanks, sis." Ridge gestured toward the living room.

Angie realized that Steph might have been suddenly woken up, but she looked put together. Angie quickly finger-combed her hair as she glanced down at the T-shirt and sweats she'd slept in.

"You look fine. We need to talk." Ridge had obviously read her thoughts. He headed to the living area and stoked the fire. She followed him and plopped on the floor next to Thunder so she could pet him. "You're such a good boy. Yes, you are."

He laid his head across her legs and gave a happy-dog sigh. She smiled and ran her hands through his fur. *God, I want my memories back.* She'd had a good thing with Ridge—and Thunder, too. She wanted to believe that she'd broken things off with him for a reason that had nothing at all to do with how she felt about him.

He sat on the edge of the chair near the fire and kept his tone hushed. "You're DEA, and that means back at the lodge . . ."

"I was working undercover. It makes sense. I can't think of another scenario, can you?"

He shook his head. "And the guy after you? The one who said he was your husband?"

"Is not my husband. That was just his way of getting information. My guess is that he's probably a really bad guy."

"But this is good news. You can talk to the DEA and get your life back. Find out where you live. The works."

Yeah. She'd been thinking about that. "Not so fast. First, my name could be something other than Angie Harris if I was working undercover, and the information might not be something searchable. Contacting a DEA agency with an undercover name could be the wrong way to go. The thing is, I remember turning my badge in, but I don't remember why."

"Are you saying you can't trust your people?"

"I think I can. I hope I can. But right now, I don't know. It sounds logical to contact them and get information, but there are too many questions. Things aren't adding up, so I need to wait and see if I get my full memory back. It's coming back slowly, in bits and pieces." Leaving her with missing pieces of this big, dangerous puzzle.

A few moments of silence lapsed. The fire crackled. Thunder shifted to a new position.

"What's your plan then?" Ridge asked.

"If you're going back to the mountain to map it, I'm going too. I can find my guns."

He chuckled. "You're not going to find them until the spring. But you don't need them. If you turned in your badge, that means you turned in your department-issued guns. You must have had personal guns on you instead. I have weapons you can use until this is over."

She reached across the short distance and pressed her hand over his. "Thanks, Ridge, but I shouldn't take them. I don't know what's going to happen. I do know that I can't stay here anymore."

He peered at her, his eyes intense. "I know."

10

Angie—if that was her real name—couldn't stay here with his family. He couldn't let her bring to them the kind of danger presented with this scenario.

"But this doesn't mean you'll be alone."

"What are you saying?"

"I'll go with you somewhere safe. We're in this together until we're not."

"I can't let you do that." Angie held his gaze.

"I'm already in this. Besides . . . I know the area. I have the required gear. And I come with guns." He offered a half-smile to bring levity, and he hoped to win her over.

She returned his grin. "Well, when you put it like that."

Thought so.

Ridge left her to pace while he gathered everything he needed.

An hour later, he'd packed all the gear he thought they could possibly need in case they had no choice but to go completely off-grid. He'd grabbed a burner phone he'd purchased just yesterday, thinking he might give her a phone since she'd lost that along with her identification and guns.

She'd taken the phone and thanked him, and now rode in the truck next to him. Fortunately, the truck had a plow on the front end, and he plowed the drive for Steph on his way out.

Concern rippled through him. He didn't want to leave Steph and Tommy unprotected, but Steph had assured him that she knew how to protect herself. Of course, she reminded him that she and Tommy had been alone for the two years since Manny had died and Ridge had left. He just hoped he hadn't led Angie's stalker here to the house. No one could have followed last night without him seeing, and he'd been watching. If it weren't for the risk to Steph and Tommy, the house would be a good place to sit tight while Ridge and Angie figured things out. But the best thing he could do for them now was to draw the potential danger away.

Still, first things first. "Before we head to the mountain so I can use the drone, we should stop by the police station and tell Chief Long."

"Um . . . I don't know."

Her reply surprised Ridge. "You can trust her. Once you explain everything, she'll understand that adding in another agency or police department could be dangerous."

"What good would her knowing do right now?"

"She could dig into your files through her police channels."

"Without tipping anyone off that I'm here? I don't know. It's too risky."

Angie remained overly wary, in his opinion. But he hadn't worked undercover, and maybe she was right to move forward with all caution. Still . . . "Someone already knows that you're here."

"I'm saying if there was someone on my task force, my undercover team, that I couldn't trust—the whole reason that I turned in my badge—then I don't want them to know where I am."

"Exactly why Chief Long can help."

"I don't know. If she starts digging, depending on the level of sophistication of whoever wants to take me down, she could alert them and give up my location, adding to the stalker already here." She blew out a breath.

"Look, if you say no, then we won't bring her in. On the other hand, the faster we get this person to show his face, the faster he can be taken down. To do that, we need Chief Long in this with us, and you need to trust at least one more person." The whole town of Shadow Gap would have Angie's back, if she would let them. "So what do you say?"

"You're right. I can't hide away forever afraid of every shadow. I . . . can't believe I'm saying this, but let's inform the police chief. Once she knows about the man who tried to kill me and that he's still in town, then she can help bring him into custody. I guess I just figured it would be best if I remembered who he is and then face off with him alone."

And that worked so well for you last time . . .

He kept the thought to himself. He didn't know the details of the incident that left her in the cave. And neither did she.

Lord, please lead us. Guide us. Please restore her memory.

WARINESS GRIPPED her as they slowly drove along the snow-packed street that led right through downtown Shadow Gap. The snowplow was *behind* them, clearing the street. Of course. That underscored how she felt the moment she'd woken up in the cave—behind the curve on everything pertaining to the life she couldn't remember.

If only she could spot the man searching for her. Could he somehow have learned that she'd lost her memory? She hoped not, because he might try to use that against her. Still, she remembered his face. She at least had that going for her.

She almost wanted to knock herself in the head again.

Maybe that would jar something loose. Wasn't she supposed to have remembered everything by now? Maybe after seeing the chief, they could stop in and talk to Dr. Combs.

Ridge carefully turned down a plowed alley next to the police station where he parked.

"You ready?" His gaze was pensive, but still compassionate. Understanding. And another emotion mingled there as well, so strong her breath hitched. The depth of his feelings for her stunned her, and she wished she could return them.

"Thank you for sticking with me, even though I apparently lied to you about my identity. I'm sorry about everything."

"You must have had your reasons. Apology accepted."

She followed Ridge into the Shadow Gap Police Department, which had to be the smallest police station she'd ever seen. Before she entered, she glanced over her shoulder at the sidewalk someone had shoveled on this side of the berm. Was he watching her, even now?

All the better. Bring it on. She was ready to face him. With that thought, she felt some of her old self returning. But she had probably been ready before and still he'd almost taken her out.

Ridge held the door for her and motioned her to go inside first. Angie entered and stopped at the front counter, where a black-haired woman clicked away at the keyboard in front of her. Tanya—according to the nameplate fastened on her lapel —stopped typing and stared up at them. "The chief is expecting you. Go on to her office."

Angie glanced at Ridge.

So he'd already informed the police chief they were coming? *Why was he so sure I'd agree to this?*

She wanted to be angry, but then again, he'd done nothing wrong, and in the end, she'd agreed to go. Ridge took a few steps down the hall, then opened an office door and stuck his head in before motioning for Angie to step into the small space ahead of him.

Two chairs sat across from Chief Long's desk.

She smiled and nodded. "Ridge, it's good to see you. You too, Angie. Why don't you have a seat?"

Tension rolled through Angie, and though she knew she should feel comfortable in a law enforcement office, her insides spasmed as she sat. Maybe her reaction had everything to do with the fact that she still didn't know who she was, and she feared talking to Chief Long because, really . . . could Angie be a dirty cop? Could she have been asked to resign or had she faced a reprimand? That didn't feel right to her, but she couldn't rely on feelings alone.

Chief Long looked at Angie. "Ridge said that you've remembered something but not everything."

She nodded. "He also convinced me that we could trust you."

The chief narrowed her eyes briefly. "Yes. Of course, you can trust me."

Angie explained about facing off with a man intending to harm her. "I think a he shoved me off the cliff, and that's when I fell and hit my head. I remember his face. I'm guessing I crawled into the cave before I collapsed. Since I got out of the hospital, I've seen him around town and he's searching for me." She glanced at Ridge. "And I know that Ridge and I were a couple at Mammoth Mountain because he told me. I saw the pictures of us together on his phone. But I left. I've also remembered that I turned in my DEA badge."

Chief Long's eyes widened.

She leaned back in her chair. "Anything else?"

"Nothing that I remember with clarity, but I've reasoned that I must have been working undercover at the lodge. It's probable that my name isn't Angie Harris, as Ridge thought." She sent him an apologetic look.

"I see." Chief Long studied Angie and her scrutiny made Angie a little uncomfortable. "What can I do to help?"

"Can you find out more about who I am but please be discreet?" She might as well lay it all out there. "I don't know who I can trust. I don't know if I was a dirty cop or ..."

Being here in this office sitting in front of Chief Long shook her to her core. A feeling washed over her, through her.

"What is it?" Ridge asked.

Images flashed through her heart and mind, and she sucked in a sharp breath.

"I remember!" Angie pressed her hand against her mouth. Pain surged behind her eyes, but she held the tears back. She'd been tough before, she knew that, and she remained tough now. "One of my task force partners was murdered. I was warned away by ... by ..."

Angie rushed out of the office. She had to get fresh air. She headed out the front door and stopped at the berm of dirty snow. Pressing her hands against her thighs, she bent over, nausea roiling inside.

She'd been warned. He'd warned her he would stop her if she tried to turn in the evidence she'd gathered of his drug and human trafficking ring. Of course, she'd ignored the warning and had been on her way to hand off video-recorded conversations when she'd been T-boned and her passenger, Richard Hatfield, had been killed. But she couldn't let her DEA partner's death be in vain. She delivered the evidence and federal agents had shut everything down.

But the man heading up the trafficking operation had escaped.

She'd been sent a warning that those she loved would be part of his new endeavor. There was only one person she loved, so she'd come to Shadow Gap to warn Ridge.

He rushed out the door and approached from behind. "Angie ..."

Concern edged his tone. She'd broken his heart, and her heart too. She knew that now. But she'd done that to protect him. It hadn't mattered.

Angie stood and faced him to deliver the news. She'd come for Ridge, but now his family was in danger too. Ridge had texted her images of Steph and Tommy the week before she broke things off. Those had been on the phone the man had stolen along with her ID.

"Ridge. You're in danger. I came here to warn you, and . . . to protect you. But now your family. Your sister and Tommy. They're in danger." They'd suspected that could be the case, but they hadn't known the extent of the deadly threat.

11

B ile rose in his throat to go with the fear spreading through his chest.

Ridge gripped Angie. "What are you talking about?"

"They need to go into protective custody *now*." She shrugged out of his grip and raced back inside, presumably to inform Chief Long. He wanted to climb in his truck and drive home, but he couldn't do that yet. Instead, he texted Stephanie.

> Lock the doors. Stay away from the windows.
> I'll be home soon.

After sending the text, he entered the police station again and hurried past the counter to stand in the doorjamb, where he heard the rest of Angie's plea. "They're in danger. It's all my fault. Please, do you have a place for them to stay until we get him?"

"Officer Ross Miller and I will go to the house and get them. We'll make the arrangements. And this man after you? We'll try to find and capture him. In the meantime, let's notify federal agents of his whereabouts."

"All good. I need to head home now." Ridge didn't wait for an answer.

Angie rushed after him and hopped into the truck. Fear could paralyze him. Steph hadn't returned his text, so while he drove, he tried calling her.

"I'm so sorry, Ridge. I hope you can forgive me. And when we get to the house, I'll take those guns you mentioned."

"There's nothing to forgive. And the guns are in the gear I packed. You can grab them when we get home." The call finally went to voice mail, and he squeezed the steering wheel, anger pulsing through him. "No answer. Why wouldn't she answer?"

"She said she would be working from home today, grading papers. She could be outside shoveling snow. A lot of reasons that she didn't hear your call or text."

He repeated the call, and the sound of the cell ringing filled the cab of the truck. "Answer the phone, Steph!" The truck swerved. Fortunately, he was able to correct the vehicle and stay on the road.

"Easy, now. If you want to make it to your sister's, then you need to concentrate on the road. I know you're upset. And there's nothing I can say to make it better. But like you said, we're in this together. I'm here to help you protect them. I'm sorry for all the trouble I've caused you."

"You didn't intend for this to happen." Wrapping his mind around the fact he'd fallen in love with an undercover DEA agent would take some time, especially since she'd come to Shadow Gap and brought danger to the people most precious to him. His and Steph's father had been an Alaska State Trooper, and a man he'd put away came looking for him at the house after he'd been released from prison. Dad had been shot and killed protecting his family.

So Ridge and Steph had subsequently chosen safer career paths. Mom had died a few years ago, but their family had been broken by Dad's death. And now to find himself in love with someone who'd brought danger to them was unfathomable.

He pushed the morbid thoughts away. He had to find them and keep them safe, and Angie would leave Shadow Gap once this was all over. Once again, he would lose her.

At the edge of town, he floored the accelerator—trusting the winter tires would keep the truck on the road. Behind him, Chief Long and Officer Miller followed in a Ford Interceptor, lights flashing and sirens blaring. The chief passed him on the road, and he appreciated how she took this danger seriously.

Chief Long stopped short of plowing into his house before exiting her vehicle. He was right behind her. He raced to the door and pushed by her as he rushed into the unlocked house.

"Stephanie! Steph. Tommy?"

No one was home.

A bark came from the back of the house. He rushed through the kitchen and into the hall, then opened the bathroom door. Thunder rushed out, whining and barking, clearly upset.

A fear he'd never known gripped Ridge as he shared a look with Angie. Neither Steph nor Tommy would have locked Thunder in the bathroom.

THE FEAR and panic in Ridge's eyes—maybe even accusation—ripped through her. Angie wanted to collapse onto her knees, but she had to hold strong and see this through.

Why couldn't I have remembered that I came here to warn him, protect him and his family, before it was too late?

Ridge rushed out the door and started calling out his sister's name as if she and Tommy had gone out to play in the snow.

His desperate cries echoed back to her as he disappeared into the woods, and Angie fled the house to go help him search.

The sounds of his panic knifed through her, sending additional adrenaline pouring through her body. Chief Long had remained behind in the house—presumably to search for clues to the whereabouts of Ridge's family. A note perhaps? They might have seen tracks in the snow, but it had started up again a half hour ago—thick and heavy and enough to disguise any prints Steph and Tommy—or their abductors—may have made.

Angie searched the area well but came up empty, and her hopes were quickly fading. She headed back.

Chief Long stepped out of the house as Angie approached. "I have your guns. I had planned to return them today." The chief waved Angie over to her vehicle where she handed off Angie's Glock and Sig pistols.

The guns felt right in her hands. "Thanks."

Chief Long followed Angie to Ridge's truck. "What more can you tell me about this man who came for you? If Steph and Tommy aren't in the woods or out with friends, where would he have taken them?"

Angie found and secured her waist and ankle holsters, then placed the loaded guns in them. "I don't know where he'd go. I would think he'd lie low. Taking a woman and her child would only put more heat on his back." She grabbed the burner phone that Ridge had gotten her. "I'm calling my superior to let him know what's happened and that we need backup."

"You know he won't get here in time to be much help. I've contacted the Alaska State Troopers," Chief Long said. "But we can't wait for them to get here, either. In the meantime, I'm closing off his only means of escape." The police chief got on her own cell.

Right. He could leave Shadow Gap only by air or the Alaska Marine Highway. The roads didn't connect Shadow Gap to the outside world. The town was landlocked like Juneau. You had to go through Haines or Skagway if you wanted to drive from

the Panhandle into mainland Alaska or Canada. The big question—was he savvy enough about all things Alaska to have
planned for that?

Ridge tromped back to the house.

He hung his head, and she feared he might fall to his knees.
"I can't lose them."

The sight squeezed her insides so hard that she couldn't
breathe. How did she comfort Ridge? She had no idea. *God, help
me to do something!*

If the killer had taken Steph and Tommy, he was only using
them to get to her. Yes, he'd threatened to use them in his oper-
ations, and she didn't want to think about what that could
mean, but in the end, he wanted *her*—the DEA Special Agent
who had taken him down. He'd already tried to kill her.

In Chief Long's office, her memories had rushed back with
a force that could have knocked her over, but some information
still trickled in. Like . . .

His email.

"Ridge, can I have your cell? I need a smartphone."

"Huh?" Agony carved deep lines in his forehead and
between his brows.

"I have an idea that could help us find them."

"And what is that?"

"I'll explain later. This is related to my work. Please."

He tossed his cell to her, then made his way into the house.
Ignoring the pain slashing at her heart, she swiped the screen,
found her mail server, and logged into her email. Then she
typed in the subject line.

Me for them

IN THE BODY of the email she sent the burner phone number
where he could text her since this wasn't her phone, and she'd
have to return it.

She held her breath. Was this still his email? She knew he preferred satellite phones, so connection shouldn't be a problem. But would he even respond? *Please, please let him respond.*

Seconds ticked by, and she stood on the sidewalk in need of more shoveling, the chill creeping into her bones. The muted sound of falling snow was the only sound.

Finally, a text came through, rather than an email, with his reply.

What took you so long?

Angie was done playing games with the man who had destroyed her family, leaving her with no one.

I'm coming for you, Uncle Felix.

12

Inside the house, Ridge paced the room and listened to Chief Long talking to her officers and other law enforcement agencies around the state. She'd closed down Shadow Gap. No one was getting out unless they hiked out in this storm.

All Ridge could do was pray hard. He didn't know what else to do. He should have stayed and defended his sister and nephew, but he'd let them down. He didn't want to blame Angie, but how had her attempt to warn him, to protect him, twisted into this nightmare?

"Ridge, we'll find them." Chief Long sounded confident.

Was that for his benefit?

He turned around to face her, searching for reassurance in her eyes.

"He can't get out of Shadow Gap. I've shut transportation down."

"Unless he fled beforehand."

"That's true, but my officers are talking to everyone and will confirm one way or another. Ross left in my Interceptor, so I'm here with you for the time being, but he'll return shortly. Your sister's house is the command center at the moment. Shadow Gap has been put on alert. Everyone loves your sister and nephew. Those who can do so are out searching for them."

"I don't want anyone else to get hurt because of . . . this . . . this . . ."

"Take a deep breath, Ridge. Steph and Tommy need you."

"You're right. I'll be okay." Then it hit him . . . "Where's Angie?"

At the thought of her, his throat tightened, and he struggled to swallow.

"Special Agent Greenwood is on the job."

"Greenwood. That's her name?"

Chief Long nodded. "Angie Greenwood. So she remembered at least her first name."

"She handed in her badge so she's not an agent anymore."

"When I spoke with her superior, he told me he hadn't accepted her resignation. Also, I found her guns in the snow when searching for clues about what happened. I chose not to say anything until I knew more about the person I was dealing with. I've returned them. They aren't her department-issued, and she has no badge, but this is all related to her operation."

"And she needs backup."

"We're here to assist."

Ridge didn't know what to think. This undercover agent wasn't the Angie he knew and loved. Had their relationship even been real, or had it instead been part of her ruse? He could figure that out later.

Ridge headed for the door. "I can't stand here and do nothing. I'm taking the snow machine out and searching. If this guy can't get out of town, he's out there somewhere."

"I'll go with you."

"Someone needs to stay here at the house in case they return." Ridge grabbed his satellite communicator charging on the counter. In the backcountry, he would need it.

"Ross will be back before we leave. Have you got two snow machines?"

"We have three. I'll get them ready."

"I'll tell Ross to hurry."

Ridge stomped outside, hiked through the deepening snow, and squinted on his way to the garage. Inside, he found only one snow machine.

Had Steph and Tommy gone out for a joyride? With Thunder locked in the bathroom, he didn't think so. Someone had taken them. Then he spotted the necklace on the ground— Manny had given it to her. Steph leaving him a message? With or without the necklace, he knew that his sister and nephew were in trouble.

Ridge would take the one snow machine left and find them. He grabbed the loaded backpack and secured it, then climbed on, started the engine, and eased out of the garage.

Angie stepped in front of him. "I'm sorry, but I going to need that snow machine, Ridge."

"Not without me, you won't."

A PANG SHOT through her heart. "I'm sorry . . . I can't allow that."

"What's this about?" Distrust surged in his eyes.

"I know where they are, and I'm the one he wants. So I'm taking the snow machine now. If you want to see them again, you'll get off and hand it over."

He stared at her. Measuring her words? "Go ahead and take it, but I'm going with you. In fact, climb on and let's go get my sister."

"I don't want to put you in more danger. I've already done enough." This was her fault, after all. She never should have gotten involved with him at that lodge. Then no one would have come to Shadow Gap to use Ridge's family against her.

"Then you owe me the courtesy of letting me finish this with you. Right now, you're wasting our time."

He was right, and she knew he wasn't going to back down. She rushed around and climbed on behind him.

He revved the engine, then shouted over his shoulder. "Where are we going?"

She held his smartphone so he could see the pin on the map. She'd received the coordinates via the text but had to use the smartphone for the map. "Do you know the place?"

"Of course. It's up close to the river—three miles from here. What's the plan?"

"He wants me in exchange for them."

"Angie, I can't let you do that."

"You can and you will. Now go. Time is running out!"

"I . . . can't."

"Ridge. You don't understand. This is my moment to face off with the man I blame for my parents' death."

"What?"

"Please . . . we have only a few minutes to get there."

"Or what?"

"You don't want to find out." She couldn't be sure that he would kill them because he trusted her to exchange herself, but she had to convince Ridge that the threat was real.

But then what would Felix do once he got his hands on her? The evidence she'd gathered had already been turned over to law enforcement, and Felix's criminal organization—his trafficking rings—had been taken down. He wouldn't soon recover from that even if he continued to evade authorities.

But she was DEA, and she would be the one to face him and end the chaos. This time, she wouldn't fail.

The memory shot through her again of his staring her down on that ledge.

Don't make me do this.

The cruel expression on his face had only deepened. Felix

hadn't thought Angie would shoot him. If she'd taken that shot, then Steph and poor, sweet Tommy wouldn't be in danger now.

She had to remember that if she had no other choice, shooting Felix would save lives.

Ridge accelerated on the snow machine, and she wrapped her arms around his waist and held on tight. The vehicle raced across the white landscape into the woods and away from the house. The engine roared, and she glanced over her shoulder in time to spot Chief Long stepping out of the house. She hadn't told the chief about her text with Felix Grendel because she didn't want to be shut down. Going to meet him was the only way to end this.

Once and for all.

She tightened her arms around Ridge's midsection, feeling his strong core even through his coat. His skill with the snow machine—"snowmobile" to her—far exceeded hers. The driving snow whipped over her face and stuck to her lashes, froze her cheeks. She wished for a mouth covering and goggles, but there'd been no time to suit up for this endeavor that she hoped would end soon.

Either in her death, or Felix's capture.

Her supervisory special agent was sending in local DEA out of Anchorage, but like Chief Long had already stated, backup wouldn't arrive in time—it would take far too many hours for them to get here.

This was all on her and, unfortunately, Ridge.

The man she loved.

13

Ridge stopped the vehicle. "Get off."

"What are you doing? Are we here? I don't see the place."

"I'm getting off the snow machine, and you need to get off first."

"Okay." She hopped off but stayed near. He assumed she didn't trust that he wouldn't take off without her, so he climbed off the machine and explained. "They'll hear us coming. We're going to hike in the rest of the way."

"Can we get there in time? The snow is deep."

"Snowshoes are in the pack, but only one pair. You can take them. But no way I'm letting you give yourself up. We'll do this together."

"Ridge, this man who has Steph and Tommy is a man from my past."

Ridge stumbled back in the thigh-deep snow. "I don't understand."

"When I was a kid, my dad had a close friend whom I considered an uncle. He promised to take care of me if anything happened to them, kind of like a godfather. Turned out he had criminal connections and that got my parents killed. I ran away or he would have tried to take me in. I grew up in foster homes. After college, I joined the DEA, and a few years into that, an opportunity opened for me to work undercover on a trafficking ring investigation. Turned out the ringleader, Felix Grendel, was my dad's friend—only he'd changed his name. He was never connected to my family or their deaths, nor did I tell the DEA. Now that he was heading up his own organized crime ring, I was determined to take him down. So I worked undercover at the lodge."

"But how did you do that? He would know you."

"He hadn't seen me in twenty-five years, and I went by another name in an obscure lodge. That said, the day I told you goodbye and left was the day he showed up at the lodge, and I couldn't take the risk he would recognize me. I had to get out of there and work on the investigation behind the scenes. I'd gotten the information I needed to take him down. Only he got away. I feared he would come after you, so I traveled here to warn you."

Angie put on the snowshoes.

Ridge had a sinking feeling he knew what came next. "And you want to face off with him now, all by yourself. You're glad it's happening here and now because there's no one around to help you."

"That's . . . no, you make me sound irresponsible. I remember now what really happened the last time we met. He got the advantage and abducted me. Stripped me of my phone, weapons and ID. I figured he planned to traffic me. But I escaped, grabbed my guns, but couldn't find the ID. In the end, he caught up to me. But he didn't push me off the cliff. I was going to shoot him, but I hesitated, and the snow shifted beneath me. Turned out it wasn't solid, and I fell. He found me at the bottom where the snow had cushioned my fall. I tried to use the gun in my ankle holster, but it misfired. He kicked the gun away and bashed my head with a rock. I guess he thought I was as good as dead, lying unconscious in the snow, so he left me. I don't remember crawling into the cave, but I must have." She stared at the frosted landscape. "Obviously, he learned that I hadn't died, after all, and was rescued. I should have taken the shot when I had the chance." She studied the map on the cell that had now lost its signal then she started hiking. "This time, I'll take the shot."

"You're going the wrong direction. Follow me. You're determined to do this, and I know I'm not going to stop you. While you're distracting him, I'll get Steph and Tommy to safety." He turned and gripped her. "In case I don't get a chance to tell you what I never told you before . . . I love you. I don't know how you felt about me then, or if you even remember me."

She leaned closer. "I remember you, Ridge. I love you too. I loved you enough to leave you, but I would have come back. Now, let's go save your sister and nephew."

They continued forward, Ridge leading the way until he made out the cabin near the Goldrock River, which was iced over along the banks. Someone had shoveled the snow around the structure. Two snow machines he recognized sat out front —Steph's and Manny's—but two more sat next to them.

He leaned on the wide trunk of a Sitka spruce. "He's not alone."

She blew out a breath. "I didn't think he would be."

"But how are we going to save them? Save you?"

She thumped a gloved finger against her lips, her cheeks red with cold. "I need to create a diversion and draw them out. Then we can take them down, quietly."

"That sounds too dangerous."

"We get Felix alone, then the situation is more manageable. Me for Steph and Tommy. That was the deal I sent him."

"He'll just kill you."

"Maybe. But I think he has other plans for me."

Ridge didn't want to spend one second imagining what those plans might by. She'd mentioned human trafficking. How could anyone be that vile?

"Now, you sit tight here while I make my move."

He watched her creep over to a snow machine, start it up, and send it into the river—where it cracked the ice and sank. Who was this woman he'd fallen in love with?

Two burly men came out of the house loaded for bear. Fear for his family, fear for Angie could choke him.

God, . . . please let the good guys win today!

ANGIE WAS ready and waiting when the first gunman came around the corner. She slammed the back of his head with the butt of her Glock 19, and he dropped face first into the snow. With no idea how long he would be out, she went to work quickly. She was in position near the house behind a bush piled high with snow when the other man came to check on his buddy. This one had taken the time to put on snowshoes. He turned his partner-in-crime over in the snow and bent to check for a pulse, aiming his 9mm into the woods. But Angie assaulted him from behind, using the same technique on him as she had on his buddy.

Only he didn't drop in the snow.

Instead, he whipped around, leading with his gun. Acting on instinct, she shoved his arm up and the gunshot went high. She took that split second to step out of his reach and aim at his chest point-blank. "DEA Special Agent Greenwood. Put your gun down now."

Unlike Felix, this guy believed she would shoot him, and without hesitation he dropped his gun into the snow.

"Lift your hands above your head, then get on your stomach."

"What? The snow's too deep."

"Your knees then. Do it now." She barked her demands. She couldn't afford to waste time on him.

He followed her instructions precisely. Aiming the Glock, she moved in and strapped plastic ties she found in Steph's garage on his wrists and ankles. "You move and I'll shoot you."

"You can't just leave me here."

Ignoring him, she moved to the other man and secured him as well.

She figured one more guy was still inside with Felix, who had to be feeling nervous by now. Nervous and even more dangerous. She crept around the corner. Suddenly, thick arms grabbed her from behind and yanked the gun out of her hands. The man lifted her up in the air, then tossed her to the ground and fired rounds at her. She rolled in the snow, then pulled the Sig P365 from her ankle and fired twice at his chest.

Gunman number three dropped. Too bad for him that he'd lost the advantage, and that had cost him his life.

Now to slip in through a back door or window. She glanced at the woods and couldn't see Ridge. Probably he'd used her distraction to attempt to free his family. She ran around the back and found the window already open.

Heart pounding, she climbed through it and hoped Ridge didn't make things worse. He wasn't trained in law enforcement techniques. Angie gripped the Glock she'd retrieved from the snow, ready to face what came next. Felix would have heard the gunfire, so he was now expecting a different kind of entrance.

She paused in the small, stuffy bedroom, deliberately slowing her breathing.

God, show me what to do. Help me save them.

"Angie, I know you're in the house. Come out now and I won't kill them."

Rolling her head forward, she squeezed her eyes shut. Not what she'd wanted to hear, but what had she expected?

How can I change it up and throw him off?

Nothing like the direct approach. She raised her voice to deliver the words. "All your men outside are incapacitated." One of them was dead, but she didn't want to accelerate the lethal aspect of this scenario.

"Time to give it up, Angie."

"Let them go. This is between you and me and no one else."

"Then you shouldn't have involved them."

Angie wasn't a crier, but right now, she felt the tears surge. This was all on her.

"I told you on the mountain I didn't want to shoot you. I'm begging you now, don't make me do this."

Where was Ridge? Was he being held hostage as well? Felix would let none of them go.

A gunshot cracked the air, and a silent scream rent her soul. She marched into the living room, leading with her gun. No negotiation.

He held a gun to Steph's temple, and Tommy stood in front of him—a human shield. So he hadn't shot anyone, but used the gunfire to draw her out.

Angie's finger rested on the trigger. *Don't make me do this.*

Another shot rang out, and Felix dropped to the side, releasing Steph and Tommy. Steph screamed and pulled Tommy to her, and Ridge rushed from the kitchen and grabbed them up in his arms.

Ridge . . . He'd known she would hesitate to shoot this man she'd once called "uncle." She moved to Felix, checked for a pulse, and found it thready. She located the gunshot wound and applied pressure. Suddenly, snow machines roared outside. She stiffened and glanced at Ridge.

"I texted Chief Long to send help." He gestured at the satellite communicator in his hand that looked like a walkie talkie, a necessity so far out.

She nodded. "Thank you." The words croaked out of her.

It was over. Finally, over. But did that mean she and Ridge were also finally over?

14

Ridge directed the drone to finish up on the mountain and brought it home. No matter that he'd almost lost Steph and Tommy—the work still had to be done. He'd come here to save lives, after all.

And instead he'd almost cost them theirs.

He struggled to forgive himself for letting things get out of hand again. He'd already cost his brother-in-law his life. He'd forgiven himself for making that mistake, but he couldn't afford another one. That's why he hadn't been able to let Angie risk herself.

Thunder barked next to him.

"Oh, no you don't!" He snatched up the dog's leash. "I'm not letting you take off again. Last time you found trouble."

Along with that woman he'd fallen for at the ski lodge. Angie was in town today, debriefing with her DEA agency—those who'd come to take Felix Grendel into custody. After all that had happened, the guy would live. Just as well—he could pay for his crimes in prison instead of taking the easy way out by dying.

Ridge landed the drone and bent to pick it up while

hanging onto Thunder's leash. In his peripheral vision he saw long, slender legs sinking almost a foot into the snow and coming his way. *Angie . . .*

Her smile was tenuous as she approached. "Steph told me I could find you here."

He handed off the leash, and she took it, then crouched to let Thunder lick her face, laughing through it all. He loved that laugh, but he didn't know if he could take his heart getting broken again. He lifted the drone and started hiking back toward where he'd parked the truck. She followed along, Thunder bounding around them until the leash limited his reach.

"I guess you're heading back—you never told me who you are, really. Where you're from." He stopped at his truck and packed the drone and controller into the big plastic box before shutting the tailgate.

Angie smiled and thrust her hand out. "Hi, I'm Angie Greenwood. I'm originally from Colorado, but I've been working out of the Dallas, Texas, DEA field office—that is, when I'm not working undercover."

She angled her head and squinted. The clouds had cleared, and the sky was blue, making the snow entirely too bright.

"So what's next for you, Angie? Is it back to the great state of Texas?"

She crossed her arms. "I know I hurt you, Ridge. I hurt myself too. I hope you understand now why I left."

"I think I do, yes. But what now?"

She stepped closer and pressed her hand against his chest. He could feel the heat, the electricity surge even through his jacket. "I still feel the same about you. So you're the one who needs to answer that question."

"What do you mean?"

"What's next for me . . . will depend on you."

Seriously? "I haven't stopped loving you, but I don't know

how to do a long-distance relationship. And I can't leave Steph and Tommy again."

She pressed her fingers over his lips. "And you don't have to. I'm out of the undercover business. I'm done with traffickers. Chief Long offered me a job here as one of her officers if I want it."

"And would you be happy? Is that what you really want to do?"

"What I really want to do is get to know the man I love better, and for him to get to know the real me. So what do you say?"

Let me think . . . "Are you sure about this? I mean, is there anything about us that you don't remember from before? Anything that's fuzzy?"

She squinted up at the sky, then looked back at him, amusement dancing in her beautiful blue eyes. "I don't remember what it feels like to kiss you."

His pulse raced at her words, the memories. "Then I guess I'd better remedy that." Ridge stepped forward and pulled her into his arms, kissing her thoroughly. When they were both breathless, he released her. "Does that answer your question about whether you should stay?"

"I'm staying. Definitely staying."

In the distance, Thunder barked and took off.

"Oh, no. I let him go while you were kissing me." She laughed.

And he joined her. "I think we're off to a great start."

"Thunder, come back!" Ridge and Angie chased after the dog together.

DEAR READER:

Thank you so much for reading *Dawn's Hidden Threat*! If you enjoyed the story, please consider leaving a review.

Dawn's Hidden Threat is the prequel novella to my *Missing in Alaska* series. Book 1, *Cold Light of Day*, will release early 2023! In the meantime, you don't want to miss my action -packed adventure romance series Rocky Mountain Courage. In *Dawn's Hidden Threat*, Ridge is using drones from a company you can read about in *Critical Alliance* (Book 3 in Rocky Mountain Courage!)

In *Critical Alliance,* Diplomatic Security Services special agent Alex Knight is back home in Montana to decompress from a mission gone wrong. But even as he's trying to relax, he's drawn into another mystery, complete with suspicious deaths, lethal threats, and whispers of espionage that all have one thing in common--a beautiful cybersecurity expert with a dark past.

To learn more about upcoming releases, sign up for my newsletter at my website—ElizabethGoddard.com

MORE ABOUT ROCKY MOUNTAIN COURAGE

With the breathtaking Montana landscape as a backdrop, each story in the series includes characters who are connected by a past tragedy that face challenges of the heart, mind and body to ultimately prove they have rocky mountain courage.

In *Present Danger*, a special agent's investigation into archaeological crimes leads to her own family's buried secrets.

In *Deadly Target,* a crime psychologist turned podcaster agrees to assist a county detective in finding the answers to a cold case that has suddenly grown warm.

In *Critical Alliance*, a troubled Diplomatic Security Services special agent teams up with a criminal hacker turned college professor in order to save lives.

Rocky Mountain Courage

 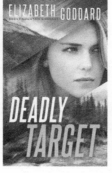 

https://elizabethgoddard.com/

ELIZABETH GODDARD BIO:

Elizabeth Goddard is the *USA Today* bestselling and award-winning author of more than 50 novels, including *Present Danger*, *Deadly Target*, and the Uncommon Justice series. Her books have sold over 1 million copies. She is a Carol Award winner and a Daphne du Maurier Award finalist. When she's not writing, she loves spending time with her family, traveling to find inspiration for her next book, and serving with her husband in ministry. For more information about her books, visit her website at www.elizabethgoddard.com.

To learn about Elizabeth's other books visit:
https://elizabethgoddard.com

POINT BLANK

LISA HARRIS

1

Nikki Boyd Grant held on to the edge of the open cargo door of the Black Hawk helicopter, working to steady the adrenaline pumping through her as they flew toward their target. It wasn't the first time she'd plunged off the edge of an overhang, but today was different. Today she wasn't rappelling the sandstone cliffs of one of her favorite spots near the Obed River east of Nashville. Today, she was waiting for the signal to fast-rope out of the helo in front of their four-man tactical team, in order to rescue an injured hostage.

The scenario they'd been given was clear. They were to breach the target building, neutralize any threats, and secure the hostage. The exercise was the culmination of a week's training, and while they wouldn't be using live fire today, a hit by one of the non-lethal rounds still packed a fiery punch she wanted to avoid. Body armor, ear protection, and headgear had been mandatory. So was communication and trust. Gaining this kind of experience would translate to them staying alive in the real world where there were no fake targets and the bullets shot at them were deadly.

The familiar image of Tyler with his military haircut and brown eyes tried to push into her thoughts, but she couldn't allow herself to think about how distant her husband had been these last few days. Or the test results she was waiting for from the doctor. No. She had to keep her private life buried in the back of her mind. A distraction, no matter how small, could mean a compromised mission or injury—something none of them could afford.

She glanced behind, ensuring her team was in place while she anticipated the go signal through her earpiece. Jack Spencer had retired from the military before transitioning into life as a police officer and eventually joining her team as part of the Tennessee Missing Persons Special Task Force. Over the years, they'd worked together as partners and he'd become someone she trusted with her life. Ryan Bailey was a new member of their task force, but after six months of working with him, she'd found him to be focused and completely capable of pulling his weight. The only team member she hadn't worked with before was Madison James. They'd all been brought here to train under Jonas Quinn, a Deputy US Marshal who taught live-fire and tactical training to officers from different regional agencies.

The brisk order came through. They were a go.

Nikki heaved the thick coiled rope out the cargo door, then grasped hold of it with her leather gloves. Her pulse raced as she pushed off from the helo and slid down the rope. Seconds later, her feet touched the ground, and she moved quickly to clear out of the way for her teammates descending directly above her.

Weapon out in front of her, Nikki felt the hairs on her neck prickle as she headed toward the predetermined rendezvous at the entrance of the target building. Their detailed plan was to explosively breach the exterior door with a coiled flex linear charge Jack carried in his leg pouch. From there, they would quickly clear the rooms one by one until they found their hostage. While the plan was straight-forward in theory, she knew they had to be prepared for the unexpected.

The four of them arrived at the house, and Jack motioned for them to take cover as he prepared to set off the charge at the entrance. The door blew open, and Nikki could feel the heat from the blast. Smoke filled her lungs, but she signaled her team forward, ignoring the burning in her chest. Inside the first room, she caught movement, aimed her firearm, and shot one of the hostiles lunging toward them. Orange paint splattered across his torso before he could fire a shot in return. The man went down. Room cleared, they kept moving. Hallways and corners equaled blind spots that could easily turn into an ambush situation, but years of experience, complemented by this week's training, kept her from hesitating. It was a game of cat and mouse where one wrong move could risk taking a bullet. And it was a game she was determined not to lose. They filed down the hallway systematically, flushing out hostile targets with well-aimed shots, until they got to the opposite side of the house.

Nikki halted. The house was clear, but they still hadn't met their objective. They hadn't found the hostage.

Where was he?

A quick glimpse outside the south window answered her question. A figure sat tied to a chair on a concrete slab. Head down and blindfolded. Nikki searched the perimeter of the property. To get to the hostage meant no cover and would expose them to possible shooters hiding behind the thick tree line a hundred feet beyond the house.

But if they were to save his life, they didn't have a choice.

Nikki signaled for her team to cover them while she and Jack prepared to pull the injured man to safety back inside the shelter of the building. Heart racing, she counted to three, then swung open the outside door. She and Jack rushed toward the man, staying low, while her team fired shots toward the perimeter. She slashed the rope off the man's wrists and he managed to stand up, then stumbled toward them. Her team fired off additional shots, fighting to give them the cover they needed until they could get the hostage inside.

A rally of shots fired back from the tree line. A bullet struck the brick wall behind her, splattering yellow paint. She shouted for her team to get back inside the building, but as she turned, a sharp sting shot through her. She bit the side of her lip and glanced down at her side. She'd been hit.

A groan shifted her attention. She backed toward the open door where they'd just exited, helping Jack get the hostage to cover, but the groan wasn't coming from their rescued man. Ryan, who had been giving them cover, had dropped to the ground. She signaled for Jack to get inside. While injury was still possible with non-lethal bullets, they weren't supposed to incapacitate someone.

Nikki turned to Ryan. They needed to move quickly before they got pinned down. "Ryan?"

He wasn't moving.

"Ryan. . .talk to me."

She crouched down beside him while bullets smashed into the wall just above her, then found what wasn't possible right below his vest. A pool of sticky red blood.

She shouted into her comm. "Man down. I repeat, man down. Hold your fire."

Ryan groaned and tried to push her away.

"Ryan, don't move."

Nikki fought past the confusion of what had just happened. It couldn't have been a lethal bullet that had struck Ryan. Too many strict precautions had been set in place to avoid this very scenario. Everyone involved in the simulation used their own firearms with conversion kits, allowing the training to replicate the effects of live fire without the danger of a stray or ricochet bullet. So how could this have happened, when every weapon had been checked and every safety protocol put into place?

She pulled a bandana from her pocket and pressed it against Ryan's side. Jonas started barking orders through the comm system, putting their emergency protocol put into place.

How had this happened?

The routine prior to the start of an exercise was strict. Beyond a check of their weapons, a thorough inspection was made of the building for any safety issues. Every room was checked to ensure that no unauthorized personnel was present. The building had been constructed with ballistic rubber on the walls, ensuring no ricocheting or bullet splatter. This clearly had not been a part of the set-up scenario. Something had gone wrong. The only other option was that someone else—someone who wasn't a part of the tactical team—had taken the shot.

Movement caught her attention south of the shoot house, just inside the thick row of trees.

"Jack," she said, getting to her feet as he and Jonas approached. "I need you to come with me."

Jonas glanced at Jack, then back at Nikki. "Where are you going?"

"The shooter's out there."

It was the only thing that made sense. Her team had been with her the whole time. The second four-man team had been inside the house, playing the part of hostiles, while a third four-man team was placed along the eastern edge of the open space, to pose as the enemy. But someone had shot Ryan with a real bullet. And if her theory was right, that someone was still out there.

"Can you account for the perimeter tactical team?" she asked Jonas.

"They were straight ahead and to your left along the ridge," he said. "I've ordered them all to come in."

Her assessment was correct. That was where the first volley
of enemy fire had come from. But the bullet that had hit Ryan
came from the right.

"We'll search the south end of the property," Nikki said.

"Copy that," Jonas said. "We've got an ambulance on the
way."

Her heart raced as she and Jack headed down the perimeter
of the property toward the field they'd used as a parking lot.
This time they weren't looking for hostile actors playing a role.
They were looking for someone who could shoot back with a
real bullet. Someone who'd just shot one of her teammates.

A car was leaving the property on the far, south side of the
building. One she didn't recognize. One she was sure hadn't
been there this morning.

"That's got to be them," Jack said.

She jumped into the driver's seat of a jeep and grabbed the
keys from the visor where she'd seen the driver put them. Her
own car keys and personal items were locked up in the trunk of
Jonas's vehicle along with everyone else's.

"They just took a left out of the parking lot," Jack said, grabbing on to the arm rest.

She pressed on the accelerator and sped down the dirt road.
The shoot house where they'd been training was set on a large
plot of land, giving them a 360-degree view of the property and
located in a place where they didn't have to worry about noise.

Her mind raced through the possible scenarios. "Whoever
shot Ryan must have managed to slip through our perimeter,
dressed in camo."

"Agreed. This was well thought out and planned."

"But how?"

She pressed her foot against the accelerator and took the
next curve. The car they were chasing was at least three
hundred yards ahead of them and gaining ground. Up ahead
was another sharp curve. She slowed down to take the turn.

Jack grabbed the dash. "Where are they?"

"I don't know." Her earpiece crackled. "Go ahead."

"Have you found them?" It was Jonas.

"We just lost visual of the vehicle."

Which didn't make sense. Nikki scanned the forested terrain. How could they have just disappeared?

"What about Ryan?" she asked, still searching for a possible turnoff the other car could have taken.

There was a long pause before Jonas replied. "I'm sorry, but he didn't make it."

2

The hot summer Nashville sun beat down on Jonas Quinn as he hurried outside the shoot house toward one of the other buildings on the property where he and the two instructors working with him did their after-action reviews. As a deputy US Marshal, part of his job was training other law enforcement agencies across the country in both classroom and hands-on tactical instruction. The results of the augmented training had been a huge success, equipping local officers with additional skills and resources.

But losing someone in the process wasn't acceptable.

He walked across the dirt path to the building, trying to calm his simmering agitation. While he preferred hands-on observation and real-time guidance from the catwalk, this location had closed-circuit cameras that recorded the training scenarios so they could review the exercises. Today, they were having to use the equipment to search for a murderer.

Madison James was leaning against the building in the shade of the awning. Until this moment, Jonas hadn't thought about how little he knew her on a personal level. Although she wasn't as experienced as the other members of her team, he wouldn't have known it by her technical abilities or her reaction to the simulations she'd been put through. She was one of the best officers he'd ever trained. She'd been a last-minute addition to his training class, but she'd quickly risen to the top. She was focused, absorbing everything he taught her like a sponge, and could shoot as well or better than he could. Which said a lot.

He started to head inside the building, then stopped. "Are you okay?"

"I'm fine, I just. . .I needed some air."

He glanced down at her black T-shirt covered with blood. "Are you sure?"

"It's not my blood."

She didn't have to say anything more. He knew she wasn't really okay. The moment Nikki and Jack had left to chase down their shooter, she'd taken over trying to stabilize Ryan, and in the process had watched him bleed out.

"Thank you for stepping up," he said.

"It wasn't enough," she said finally, looking up at him.

Her haunted expression captured the pain he knew she was feeling. The same pain that gnawed on him every time he lost someone to this job.

"The paramedics told me you did exactly what you should have done," Jonas said. "They think the bullet hit an artery from the amount of blood that was lost. There's nothing any of us could have done."

She folded her arms across her chest. "Maybe, but that doesn't make me feel any better."

"Did you know Ryan?" he asked.

"Just from the training here. I know he was getting married. He showed us a photo of his fiancée, but now. . ." She shook her head. "I go to work every day not knowing if I'm going to come home. Not knowing what's going to happen on every call. I didn't expect it here, in a training exercise."

"We're going to find out who did this," Jonas said.

"I know, and I'm sorry." She pushed back her shoulders. "I'm not usually so emotional. It's not the first time I've seen someone die, and I know in our line of work, it won't be my last."

"It's a very human reaction, and you have nothing to apologize for. I hope you're never in this field so long you stop caring."

She looked up at him. "Thank you."

Her reaction surprised him. It was as if she hadn't expected to see the softer side of him. And maybe there was validity to her reaction. While he was fair with his people, he knew that showing softness could get someone killed.

"The sheriff is here and is bringing in the Training Division's Chief Inspector. They're going to want to interview each of us."

"Of course. I'll be inside in a minute."

"Take your time."

Jonas slipped inside the building. Although he felt the urgency of finding Ryan's killer, he also knew he couldn't dismiss the mental health concerns of the teams he'd been working with. Trauma effected people in different ways, but just because his people dealt with it on a day-to-day basis didn't mean they were immune to the effects. He knew that firsthand.

Straight ahead was a conference room used for debriefing and where the teams had gathered. He'd need to talk with each of them, but for now, he stopped in the room they used to tape the training exercises for feedback.

"Tony's in with the teams." Bill Peterson sat in front of the row of monitors, going through taped footage.

"Have you found anything?" Jonas asked.

"I might have," Bill said, turning his chair toward him. "Look at this."

Jonas had instructed him to go through the video footage,

knowing that the sooner they could ID their suspect the sooner they could get a detailed BOLO out that would in turn help local law enforcement hunt down their suspect.

Jonas sat down in the chair next to Bill, who rewound the footage, pushed pause, then let it play forward.

"Nikki said the shot came from the right. She saw movement and believes it was the shooter." Bill paused the footage again, then pointed at the screen. "You can see the team spread out here. . .but then if I scroll to the right, you can see a fifth figure."

"Can you get a clearer image?"

"The footage is too grainy," Bill said, shaking his head. "But I can account for everyone else. There was definitely an intruder."

Jonas stood up and ran his fingers through his hair. Nikki and Jack had lost the suspect, so he'd told them to return to the shoot house. But the more time that passed, the harder it was going to be to track down their suspect. It had to have been someone who knew what was going on at the property. Someone who had inside access to their schedule and routine. And someone who had the ability to bypass their security measures.

"We need to know how this happened," Jonas said, his voice rising. "This never should have happened."

"I agree, but—"

"I'm sorry." Jonas lowered his tone a notch, trying to reel back his frustration. "This isn't your fault."

"Don't worry. I want to find them as much as you do. I've got one more camera to check. I'm hoping it'll pick up a different angle of the parking lot."

"Keep looking and let me know if you find anything else." Jonas looked out the window as three squad cars pulled up to the building. He let out a sharp breath. It was time to face the music.

Chief Inspector Jeremiah Velasquez and three other suits had just arrived in the training room when Jonas got there. A long rectangular table filled the room as well as more than a dozen chairs, most of which were already filled with the tactical teams he'd been training.

"Chief Inspector Velasquez. It's good to see you again," Jonas said, shaking the older man's hand."

"I'm sorry for the intrusion, but it was decided that we do the interviews here, on site, while my team processes the house."

"Not a problem, sir."

"Any updates?" the chief inspector asked.

"We still don't know exactly what happened, but we have identified there was an intruder on the property south of team three when the shooting occurred."

"And he—or she—managed to get in the shot that killed Officer Bailey?"

"Yes, sir."

"Are you certain that the shot didn't come from one of your teams' weapons?"

Jonas frowned, but it was a question he'd expected. "You know we take every safety precaution we can by checking every weapon thoroughly. Everyone was accounted for and the trajectory of the shot corroborates our theory."

"An intruder who killed one of your team members on your watch."

Nausea swirled in Jonas's gut. "Yes, sir."

"Who was in charge of Ryan Bailey's team?"

"Nikki Grant."

"I'll start with her. Have her meet me in the smaller conference room. The others will give their statements to the rest of the team I brought with me."

"Yes, sir."

Five minutes later, Jonas stood in the corner of the room

listening to the conversation, trying to curb the growing irritation he wasn't out looking for their suspect. They might be following protocol, but he'd just spent a week with these officers, and he knew they were clean. Which meant they were wasting time.

But that wasn't his call to make.

"Special Agent Nikki Grant," the chief inspector said, sliding into the chair across from her.

"Yes, sir."

Jonas folded his arms across his chest and listened to the routine questions the chief inspector asked. He and Nikki had worked briefly together a couple of years ago on a joint task force that had ended up rescuing twenty-one endangered children in the Nashville area. She'd made a name for herself across the state for her role in leading the bureau's missing persons division.

"I need you to tell me what happened this morning," Velasquez said.

Nikki nodded. "We'd just stepped outside the shoot house to extract the hostage. I had two of my team covering Jack and me while we pulled the hostage inside."

"When did you notice Bailey was down?"

"There was a rally of shots from the tree line when we stepped outside. I was hit as we pulled the hostage toward the door. I heard someone groan, looked down, and Ryan was lying on the ground, bleeding. I sent Jack inside with the hostage and went to examine him."

"That's when you saw he'd been hit with a lethal bullet?"

Nikki nodded, but while her stoic expression didn't change, it was clear that Madison wasn't the only one affected by Ryan's death.

"The team members' weapons?" Velasquez asked. "Is it possible that someone's missed the inspection?"

"Impossible," Nikki said. "They were all checked. Every weapon was converted according to protocol."

The chief inspector glanced down at his notes. "You have an impressive record working with the missing persons task force in Nashville."

"Thank you, sir."

He looked up again. "You were behind the capture of the Angel Abductor a few years back."

Jonas remembered the case. It had haunted law enforcement for well over a decade until the case was finally solved. It involved a string of young girls who had disappeared—including Nikki's own sister. According to the file he had on her, her sister's disappearance had been her motivation for going into law enforcement.

"You gave a detailed description of the car you believe the suspect drove away from the shoot house," Velasquez continued.

"I did. My partner and I followed it about two miles down the road, where we lost it. There are a number of side roads branching off the main road. Our assumption is that they took one of them. The brush is thick enough that it wouldn't be too difficult to hide. We were told to return here."

"What do you know about Ryan Bailey? I understand he was new to your team."

"He was quiet, and a private person, but very intuitive. He brought a good balance to our team. He was engaged to be married. He came from a very well-off family, but he decided not to join his father's business."

"What do you know about his fiancée?"

"Not a whole lot, though I did meet her a couple of times. She works at a restaurant in downtown Nashville."

"What's her name?"

"Shelby Lehar."

Velasquez glanced at his notes again. "We haven't been able

to get ahold of his parents. According to their office, they're out of town. Do you know how to reach his fiancée?"

"I can look up the name of the restaurant where she works." Nikki hesitated. "I'd like to go talk with her and a be a part of this investigation. I need to find whoever did this."

Velasquez stood up and nodded at Jonas to meet him outside the room.

"She's right," Jonas said, once he'd shut the door behind them. "She knew Ryan better than any of us, and she has stellar instincts. We don't have time to bring in someone else—"

"You don't have to convince me." Velasquez's frown deepened. "We need answers quickly. The two of you are going. I want to know who did this."

3

The Peach Rooftop and Grill was located in downtown Nashville on the terrace of a hotel and was popular with both tourists and locals for its spicy peach salsa, peach cobbler, and live music. The views of the city were an added bonus.

Nikki stepped into the elevator ahead of Jonas and pushed the button for the restaurant. "Have you had any BBQ while you've been here?"

"I was hoping for a couple days of R&R once training was over, but after today I'm not sure there's gonna be time."

"I'm a bit partial to my parents' restaurant. It's been in the family for three generations. I started by washing dishes on weekends in high school, then waitressed all through college. There's nothing like sitting in a corner booth with my family and eating my dad's barbeque and coleslaw and my mom's jalapeño corn bread while listening to live music playing in the background."

"Sounds like a stop I need to make before I leave." Jonas shoved his hands into his pockets and leaned back against the elevator wall. "Before we get up there, I wanted to ask you about Madison. She's impressed me with her skills this entire week, but she's taking Ryan's death hard. Personally."

Nikki weighed her answer from the little she knew about Madison. "I'll be honest, I don't know her well. She's been completely focused on the training and doesn't really interact with anyone else much. At least not on a personal level. But I don't think you can blame her for her reaction. She was there when he died. She was trying to save him."

"I know. I just want to make sure she's okay."

Nikki tried to read Jonas's expression. While he had a reputation of being tough and demanding in his training, he clearly had a soft side. And he was right, they'd all been affected by Ryan's death. Over the past six months, she'd come to respect Ryan as a competent member of her team. The fact that he was dead had yet to sink in. She knew from experience that it wouldn't be long before it did.

"Do you want me to talk to her?" Nikki asked, as the elevator came to a stop at the rooftop.

"Would you? Maybe just feel her out. Make sure she's okay."

"Of course. I don't mind at all."

The elevator doors opened, and they stepped into the sunlight and the sound of Kenny Rogers in the background. The restaurant didn't open until eleven, so most of the employees were busy setting up tables and getting ready for the lunch crowd. The spacious terrace had mostly outdoor seating with tables, umbrellas, and fireplaces set up, all with a perfect view of the city.

Nikki glanced again at Jonas, wishing she could read him better. Maybe she'd imagined it, but she'd sensed a connection between him and Madison. Then again, maybe he'd simply been impressed with her skills. Either way, it wasn't any of her business. She shifted her thoughts back to the issue at hand and searched the terrace for Shelby.

"I can't believe I've never been here," Jonas said, taking in the view of the familiar Nashville skyline as they walked to the hostess stand. "This is stunning."

One of the employees walked up to them. "I'm sorry, but we're not open for lunch yet."

"I know." Nikki pulled out her badge. "We need to speak to Shelby Lehar."

"Sure. . .she's over behind the bar."

Nikki nodded her thanks, then headed toward the far side of the covered section of the terrace.

"Nikki. . ." Shelby dropped the rag she'd been using to clean the counter and came around the side of the bar to see her. "I didn't expect to see you here today. I thought you were in training."

"We were," Nikki said, glancing at one of Shelby's coworkers who was putting glasses on the shelf. "This is Deputy US Marshal Jonas Quinn, and we need to talk to you. In private, if possible."

Shelby's brow furrowed at the request. "All right."

She signaled to the bartender that she'd be back before leading them to the other side of the restaurant that had already been set up.

"What's going on?" she asked. "Is Ryan okay?"

Nikki hesitated for a moment. "I'm sorry to have to tell you this, but Ryan. . . He was shot this morning. He didn't make it."

"He's dead?" She dropped into one of the chairs, shaking her head. "I don't understand. He wasn't even on the job this morning. He said he was training at a local shoot house with his team. With you."

"He was there," Jonas said.

"Then how did he get shot? He told me that part of the training included live fire, but he told me it was safe. That you take precautions, so no one gets hurt."

"We do." Nikki glanced at Jonas. "We don't believe it was an accident."

"Wait a minute." Shelby pressed her fingers against her temples and closed her eyes. "You think what. . .he was murdered?"

Nikki frowned, but there was no other way to get around the truth. "Yes, we do."

"Murdered?" Shelby's whole body was shaking. "How is that even possible?"

"Slow breaths, Shelby," Nikki said, kneeling down in front of her. "Can I get you something?"

"I'll get some water," Jonas said.

Nikki nodded at Jonas, then turned back to Shelby. "I know this is hard. We're trying to figure out what happened."

"I just. . .I'm just trying to take this in. It makes no sense. I know his job was dangerous, and I'd accepted that, but Ryan is the sweetest, kindest man who goes out there every day to protect people. Why would anyone kill him?"

"That's what we need to find out. Has he received any threats that you're aware of?"

"No." Shelby grabbed a napkin off the table and blew her nose. "But I'm not sure he'd tell me. He really tried to keep his job and the stress that went along with it out of our relationship. I tried to assure him that I wanted to help support him, but he really didn't talk much about his work."

"Has he been acting any different then?"

"I don't know. . . Maybe. He's been a bit distracted lately, but he told me he was tired working extra hours and that I shouldn't worry about it." She blew her nose again. "I just can't believe he's gone. We were supposed to have dinner tonight and discuss wedding plans, but now. . . What am I supposed to tell his parents? What am I supposed to do?"

Nikki pulled an empty chair toward her and sat down. "I know this isn't easy to process, but can you help us with his parents? We haven't been able to get ahold of them."

"They're out of town. They. . ." Shelby drew in a ragged

breath. "They always go to Colorado for a few weeks this time of year."

"Do we need to call someone for you?"

"I don't know. I can't even think. I don't have family here, just Ryan and a few friends. I haven't lived here that long. I met him at the gym. We just started talking, he asked me out. . ." Shelby glanced down at her engagement ring. "His job worried me. I know it's tough out there for law enforcement, but in a training exercise. . ."

Shelby's voice trailed off as she started crying again.

"Again, we are so sorry for your loss," Nikki said. "Ryan was a valuable member of my team. If you think of anything he said that might help us find who did this—"

"Wait." Shelby looked up and caught Nikki's gaze. "There is one person."

Jonas returned with the water and handed it to Shelby.

"Who's that?" Nikki asked.

Shelby took a long drink of the water, then set it on the table. "Lana Montgomery. His ex-girlfriend. She's never been able to accept that their relationship was over."

"Did she ever threaten either of you?" Nikki asked.

"I don't know if it was her, but someone has been threatening me. Three or four times someone was following me, and I've gotten two voice mails that were electronically altered. And somebody's left notes on my car."

Jonas leaned back against the terrace railing. "When did this start?"

"A couple of weeks ago."

Nikki frowned. "Did you ever tell Ryan or report this to the authorities?"

"The police said I didn't have enough for them to do anything. I didn't want to make a big deal about it, and Ryan. . . He promised he would look into the situation himself."

"Do you know if he confronted her?" Jonas asked.

Shelby shook her head. "He just told me not to worry about it. That he would take care of it. Far as I know, though, nothing ever happened."

"Do you have any photos?"

Shelby pulled out her phone and swiped the screen. "I kept records of everything."

Nikki took the phone from her, quickly scrolled through the photos of the notes that had been left on Shelby's windshield, then handed the phone to Jonas. "But you can't prove Lana was the one who left these, right?"

"No. They weren't signed, and I never got a good look at whoever was following me. I can't even recognize the voice. But. . ." Shelby looked up. "This has to be connected. It's the only thing that makes sense."

"Have you ever met her?" Jonas asked.

"Not in person. I just saw a picture of the two of them in a drawer in his house and I. . .I admit, I looked her up on social media."

"Do you know where she lives?" Nikki asked.

"Somewhere here in the city, though I don't know where. I never asked, and I didn't exactly want to run into her. Not after Ryan told me about her."

"What did he tell you about her?" Jonas asked.

"Not much. Just that they had a falling out and mutually broke up. We started dating about six months later. All I really know is that she's a singer and a regular at some bar in town, though I'm not sure where, and she was always jealous and possessive of Ryan. It was one of the things that made him break up with her. He was tired of her always needing to know where he was and always needing to be with him." Silent tears streamed down Shelby's face. "What am I supposed to do now?"

Nikki stood up. "We're going to do everything we can to find out who did this. We'll also have someone escort you down to the police precinct where you can give a statement."

Shelby's frown deepened. "Now that he's dead, maybe someone will finally believe me."

4

Sunlight streamed through the ceiling of the two-story atrium windows of the Tennessee Bureau of Investigation headquarters as Jonas and Nikki headed toward the elevators. The state-of-the-art building was located in north Nashville and gave law enforcement space to manage the state's crime labs, investigate major crimes, and collect state crime stats. Captain Garrett Addison, an old friend of Jonas, had moved the investigation from the shoot house to the bureau.

"You know Captain Addison?" Nikki asked.

"We go way back, actually. We met shortly after Garret became a criminal investigator with the bureau, and we've worked together on several task forces over the years."

Nikki's phone rang. She pulled her cell out of her pocket and checked the caller ID.

"This is my brother," she said, looking up at Jonas. "I asked him to call me back about Lana. Why don't you go on up and I'll meet you there in a couple minutes. Captain Addison has us set up in the squad room, just right off the elevators."

Jonas nodded, then took the elevator up to where Jack and Madison were already sitting at a couple of desks, engrossed in separate phone conversations. Computer screens hung on the wall, and a coffee bar was tucked into the back corner. He glanced at the box of subs someone had brought in. Breakfast had been hours ago, but today's events had squelched any appetite.

"Jonas?"

"Garrett," Jonas said, turning around and shaking his friend's hand. Garrett's dark hair had grayed some around the temples, but otherwise, he didn't seem to have aged a bit. "Nikki's on her way up. It's good to see you again, Captain."

"Captain." Garrett let out a low chuckle. "I'm still getting used to that. Grab yourself some coffee, and a sandwich if you're hungry. I've already got Jack and Madison working, and I've pulled in a couple of my guys to help as well."

"I'm not hungry, but I could definitely use some coffee," Jonas said, heading to the back of the room with Garrett. Jonas grabbed one of the mugs. "I heard you got married."

"Jordan and I finally tied the knot three years ago, and now we have twin girls."

"Congratulations," Jonas said, filling up his cup, then adding creamer and sugar while Garrett followed suit. "Is Jordan still with the FBI?"

"She works as a consultant, but recently decided to pull back on her hours. At least for now, she's enjoying staying home more. What about you? I thought someone would have caught you by now."

Jonas held up his left hand, empty of a wedding band. "Guess I've been too busy trying to save the world."

"You better be careful," Garrett said. "My biggest regret is waiting so long to marry Jordan and start a family. It's never easy balancing this kind of life with family, but trust me. It can be done. And if you find the right person, it's worth it."

Jonas took a sip of his coffee—too bitter—and glanced at Madison. Her honey-colored eyes were intense as she talked on the phone with someone while tugging on the end of her ponytail.

His mother had tried—more than once—to set him up with several of her friends' single daughters, but so far, he'd been able to avoid the dreaded blind date. Pushing ahead in his career had made him put off dating—and maybe that was a mistake. He'd met Nikki Boyd's husband and two children and had been impressed with how she managed to juggle a career in law enforcement and raise a family.

Maybe it was the fact that he was turning thirty tomorrow. Numbers had never bothered him in the past, but another decade milestone did bring up the question of whether or not he was going to let his career push out a chance for a family.

Madison had impressed him the entire week, and if he was honest with himself, she was one of the best officers he'd ever trained. While she was definitely reserved, she was extremely focused on everything she did. And even though she was only five foot five, she was still strong and fast, which gave her an advantage in hand-to-hand combat. But the reality was he really knew nothing about her. He'd never heard her talk about anything personal. Neither had she spent much time interacting with the rest of the team outside the training sessions. Maybe that's what intrigued him. She was a mystery.

In another place and time he might have considered trying to get to know her better, but unfortunately, that time was not now.

"I wish you were here under different circumstances," Garrett said, pulling Jonas away from his thoughts. "For now, we need to move on this. Tell me what you found out from the girlfriend."

"Her story is compelling," Jonas said. "Someone has been stalking her, and she believes it could be Ryan's ex-girlfriend."

"So, you think we're talking about a jealous ex," Garrett said.

Jonas added some more sugar and cream, then took another sip. It was still bitter, but it would do. "According to Shelby, Lana wants him back. And if she can't have him, then no one should."

"Ryan did come to me a couple weeks ago," Garrett said. "Told me someone was harassing his fiancée, and that she was pretty shaken up about it, but unfortunately he didn't have any evidence that pointed to anyone specific."

"What did you tell him to do?"

"I told him to have her make an official statement and I'd make sure someone looked into it. As far as I know, he never followed up."

"That's interesting."

Garrett set his coffee down on the table and frowned. "We also can't ignore the possibility that we're dealing with someone Ryan arrested."

"Agreed."

Nikki walked into the squad room and made her way over to where they stood. "I just got off the phone with my brother, who, it turns out, has worked with Lana before. She works at the Blue Bird Café and they've sung there together a couple times for their open mic night on Mondays. He said he didn't know her well, but he was pretty sure we could find her at work right now."

"Do you know anything about Ryan's private life?" Garrett asked her.

"Not really." Nikki shook her head. "All I know is that a few months before the wedding he and Lana called things off. It was a mutual break-up as far as I know. At least that was the impression Ryan gave me the one time he mentioned her."

Jonas frowned, not sure he bought the story. "Break-ups are rarely as mutual and cordial as couples want you to think. Usually at least one of them holds a grudge."

"Jack is working through the list of Ryan's arrests," Garrett said, "and in particular any that might have been released recently. I'm not willing to shut that door yet. And Madison's working with the phone company to see if she can track down the voice mails left on Shelby's phone."

"Jonas and I can go talk to Lana," Nikki said.

Garrett nodded. "Check back in with me afterwards."

Lana was on the stage when Jonas and Nikki arrived at the Blue Bird Café, singing a Patsy Cline song to the lunch crowd. The Blue Bird was located in downtown Nashville, and was known for its pulled pork and smoked brisket. Jonas breathed in the tempting aromas from the grill while Lana's smooth voice carried across the room with nothing more than an acoustic guitar to accompany her.

Lana scanned the crowd as the song came to an end and smiled. "Thank you everyone for coming out. I'm going to take a short break, and be back in a few minutes."

She set the guitar down next to her stool, then slipped off the stage.

Jonas and Nikki quickly made their way through the maze of tables toward where they'd seen Lana disappear. A door led to a hallway.

"Lana?" Jonas called out as he followed her into one of the rooms.

Lana turned around in the small dressing room and pointed a handgun at them. "What do you want?"

"I'm deputy US Marshal Jonas Quinn, and this is Agent Nikki Boyd with the Tennessee Missing Persons Special Task Force. I need you to put the gun down."

"I—"

"Now."

Lana dropped the gun onto the dressing table next to her.

"Put your hands behind your back," he said, then motioned for Nikki to handcuff her. "We're here to question you as a person of interest in a murder investigation."

"Murder?" Her dark eyes narrowed. "Whose murder?"

Jonas studied her carefully. "Ryan Bailey."

"Wait a minute. . .Ryan's dead?" Lana's face paled. "He can't be dead. I just saw him." Her chest heaved. "I need some air. Please."

Jonas nodded, then followed her out the side door into a narrow ally where Lana leaned against the wall. Mascara and tears streaked her cheeks.

"I'm sorry," she said, trying to catch her breath. "It's such a shock."

"Do you know this woman?" Nikki asked, holding up her phone and showing her a picture of Shelby Lehar.

"Yes. She's engaged to Ryan."

"She believes you've been stalking her."

Lana's eyes narrowed. "Why would I do that?"

"She says it's because you were trying to break up her and Ryan."

"She's lying."

"Can you prove that?" Jonas asked.

"Why would I try to break them up when Ryan and I were back together?"

"Wait a minute," Nikki said. "Shelby said the two of you broke off your relationship months ago."

"We did, but I. . ." She shook her head. "About two months ago, we ran into each other again. It was purely a coincidence, and I don't know what happened, except we started talking and both realized that we'd made a mistake ending our relationship."

"What about Shelby?" Nikki asked.

"Ryan was planning to call things off with her, but he hadn't yet."

"Why not?" Jonas asked.

"Her family was planning this huge wedding—thanks to Ryan's family—and he wasn't sure how to end things without

making a huge stink. On top of that, Shelby was very possessive, and the closer it got to their wedding, the more controlling
she became. He told me they didn't have as much in common
as he thought, and he told me he believed she was after his
money."

"We could make the same assumption about you," Nikki
said. "You were upset when he broke up with you and maybe
now you're trying to sabotage his relationship with Shelby. "

"I don't care about his money." Lana's shoulders shook. "I
would never have killed him. Why would I? He realized he was
making a mistake if he went ahead and married her. Realized
he'd made a mistake breaking up with me."

Jonas frowned. All they had so far was Shelby's word
against Lana's.

"Do you have any way to prove what you're saying?" Jonas
asked. "Did anyone else know what he was planning to do?"

"Unless he told his best friend, I don't think so. We agreed
to keep our relationship quiet until he broke up with her."

"When was he planning to do that?"

"This weekend, actually, but now. . ."

"Is there any way she might have found out what he was
planning?" Nikki asked.

Lana shrugged. "I suppose it's possible. I wouldn't put it
past her to snoop on his phone, though we were careful and
made sure we were never together in public. But if it was her
following me, and she saw us together. . ."

"You were being followed?" Nikki asked

"In the mornings when I work out. When I drive to work.
It's like she wants me to know that she's following me, but she
never gets close enough for me to ID her. Just enough to scare
me. Like she wants me to know I'm being followed."

"So it's a woman?" Jonas asked.

"The person wears a hoody, but I'm pretty sure it's a woman.
Two days ago, I was running and saw her behind me again. I

turned around and she disappeared. I know it sounds crazy, but it's the truth. I started carrying a gun because I'm so terrified that at some point she might confront me."

"Did you tell the police?"

"No."

"What about Ryan?"

"He was under so much stress that I decided not to tell him. Maybe I was wrong, but I thought I could handle it. Even thought it might have been my imagination. Truth is, we were sneaking around and trying not to get caught. I've felt so much guilt about it—"

"Clearly not guilty enough to tell her the truth," Nikki said.

Jonas tried to read her expression. Was she telling the truth? He glanced at Nikki and frowned, irritated with the drama. They had two women, both claiming they were being followed by the other one. And both had been involved with the same man.

A dead man.

5

Nikki followed Jonas into the entrance of the TBI Headquarters, then pulled off her sunglasses. Madison was sitting on one of the padded chairs in the atrium, typing something into her phone.

Nikki stopped in front of the elevator. "The captain is going to want to hear what Lana said right away, but I think I'll go talk with Madison."

Jonas nodded. "I'll update him and meet you upstairs."

Her phone buzzed as she walked toward where Madison sat. She glanced at the caller ID and frowned. Still nothing from Tyler. She shoved it back into her pocket, ignoring the guilt that surfaced, and instead shifted her focus back to Madison. Someone had given her a TBI T-shirt to replace the bloodstained one she'd been wearing. But it was the troubled look in Madison's eyes that caught Nikki's attention.

"Mind if I join you?" Nikki asked.

"No," Madison said, dropping her phone into her lap. "Of course not."

"It's not exactly the Pacific Northwest, but I've always loved this atrium," Nikki said, sitting down next to her. "Especially when it's quiet like it is right now."

"The greenery is a nice touch, but you're right. It's nothing like the views we have back home." Madison managed a smile. "Someone gave me a clean shirt, but my aunt who lives here in town is bringing me some clothes. I told her I'd meet her down here."

"I know today has been hard on everyone," Nikki said, searching for the right opening, "but you were with Ryan when he died. I just wanted to see how you're doing. Today's been rough."

"It has." Madison's smile faded. "I appreciate your asking, but I'm fine. Just a bit. . .shaken up."

"Can I ask you a personal question?" Nikki asked.

"Okay."

"I was wondering if you'd ever thought about joining a task force, or maybe even the US Marshals?"

"I'll admit, Jonas has impressed me, but I'm not sure I'm cut out for something quite so intense."

"I don't believe that for a second. You'd be a valued asset with your experience. I've been in law enforcement well over a decade now, and I'm impressed with your skills. You're a natural."

"I don't know. I love what I do, don't get me wrong, but I feel as if I'm just finding my feet in this profession." Madison shifted in her chair. "I. . .I recently lost my husband. He was a doctor, handsome, funny. . .sometimes I still can't believe he's gone."

"Oh, wow. . . Madison, I'm so sorry."

"I don't usually tell people, but Luke—my husband—was murdered a few months ago. Which was why today brought back a flood of memoires I thought I was ready to handle. I'm not sure now that I am."

"Ryan's murder was a trigger."

Madison nodded.

"Do you know who killed your husband?" Nikki asked.

"The police still don't have any suspects, and I—" Madison pressed her lips together.

"You're trying to find out who did it," Nikki finished for her.

Madison's brow furrowed. "Most of my friends don't understand my need for closure—my need to know who pulled the trigger. It's why I don't bring it up, *and* why I shouldn't be dumping all of this on you—"

"No. It's okay." Nikki held up her hand. "I know what it's like to lose someone you love."

Madison looked up, waiting, as if she wanted her to continue. Nikki understood the obsession all too well.

"My sister Sarah went missing when she was sixteen," Nikki said. "I was a teacher at the time, but I decided I didn't want anyone else to go through what my family and I went through."

"Is that why you joined law enforcement?" Madison's question shifted the conversation slightly. "The disappearance of your sister."

Nikki nodded. "I've always loved kids. Joining the police force gave me a different way to protect them."

"And then you joined the missing person task force."

"Eventually, yes. At first I started working with law enforcement to make a long-term plan to find my sister. My parents paid for a private investigator to look into the case, but I still went over Sarah's file hundreds of times, memorizing every detail, looking for anything crucial that might have been overlooked. I kept meticulous notes, studied serial abductor and killer cases, and made sure the media kept involved. I was completely focused on finding that one clue that would lead us to Sarah."

But the job continued to be never ending—and personal. For every person they found, there always seemed to be another dozen still missing. The fight against the darkness was hard when there seemed to be no light.

For a moment, she was there again, reliving the details as if it were yesterday. She'd stood on the curb in front of the school in the sunshine waiting for her sister while the sounds of a lawn mower filled the air. She'd checked her watch . . . again. She was late, all because of a pair of shoes she'd impulsively decided to buy at the nearby mall.

She'd assumed that Sarah could wait the extra few minutes it took to try them on and ring them up with the cashier. But when she arrived, Sarah was nowhere to be found. Nikki had questioned everyone she could think of who might know where Sarah was. Then came the desperate 911 call. Hours later, the police interviewed the last person known to have seen Sarah. Another sophomore girl who'd seen her get into a black sedan ten minutes after the last period bell had rung.

She never saw Sarah again.

"Do you ever blame yourself?"

Madison's question pulled Nikki back to the present. After all these years, the grief and pain of Sarah's disappearance could still feel as if it had been yesterday. "I blamed myself and struggled for years with the guilt. I was supposed to pick her up after school that day, but I was late."

"And you wonder what if."

Nikki nodded. "Exactly. And I'll be honest, even though it's been over a decade, sometimes it hits me full force again. If I had been there, I would have been able to save Sarah." She sighed. "But that isn't what happened, and no matter how much I want to change that, I can't. Losing someone you love changes everything. It's easy to tell someone else to stop feeling guilty, but I know what it's like to search for that resolution that never seems to come."

Madison stared at the tiled flooring. "I keep thinking if I

knew why Luke was killed and who killed him, then I could find closure, and yet. . .maybe I never will."

"I've felt so much of what you're describing. The out-of-control feelings. Every day's a struggle, and it's all you can do to hang on. I'm actually surprised you came to the training."

"I think work is my way of coping right now. It keeps me busy, so I don't have to think. This training was planned before Luke died, and I just. . . I decided to come." Madison glanced up, her eyes filled with tears. "But letting go of the guilt. . . I'm still not sure how to do that."

"For me, it was a process that took time," Nikki said. "My faith was an anchor that helped, but for a long time, I went to church because it was expected, while inside, I felt like a hypocrite. I finally started to grasp that God understood the hurt I was going through and why I doubted He cared."

Madison wiped her cheek with the back of her hand. "Today, I kept looking down at Ryan, but seeing Luke instead."

"We all have triggers, especially when we've gone through something traumatic like you have."

"I'd rather people didn't know. I don't want to be treated differently. I don't want Jonas and the others to be soft on me."

Nikki smiled. "I don't think you need to worry about that. You're the best shot on the team."

Madison reached for her bag as a woman walked toward them. "Thank you. I'm not used to being vulnerable, but I think I really needed someone just to listen today."

"Healing takes time. Have grace on yourself, and never forget the good that you're doing."

Jonas was just finishing talking to Jack when Nikki arrived in the squad room.

"Anything new?" she asked, after pulling him aside.

"Traffic cameras caught the vehicle that left the shoot house property. They're using facial recognition to try and ID the driver."

"Good. I spoke with Madison."

"And. . ." he prompted.

"Her story is really hers to tell, but I think she's okay. She's taking Ryan's death personally, though I know we all are on some level. I told her she'd make a great US Marshal if she decided to go in that direction."

"I agree, though for the record. . ." Jonas cleared his throat. "My asking was nothing more than a professional concern."

Nikki grinned. "I never thought otherwise."

"I think I've got something," Jack said, calling them and Garrett over. "We've finally got an ID on our driver."

"Who is he?" Jonas asked.

"Eddie Cobbett. He's your basic thug for hire," Jack said. "According to his record there are three open arrest warrants out on him."

"Do you have an address for him?" Garrett asked.

"Not a current one," Jonas said.

Garrett frowned. "Then we need to find him."

6

J onas glanced up from his computer, irritated that so far, their search for Eddie Cobbett had just led to dead ends. Their suspect had a no-bond felony warrant along with several misdemeanor warrants, and no one had an address on the man. He rubbed the back of his neck, then stood up, needing to figure out a different way to track the man down.

Madison hung up the call she'd been on the last few minutes and blew out a sharp breath, looking just as frustrated as he felt.

He grabbed a mug of coffee from the fresh pot someone had just made and took it to her.

"I've noticed you're a coffee drinker," he said, setting a mug in front of her. "Thought you could use a pick-me-up."

"I could, actually. Thanks."

"One cream and no sugar?"

"You noticed," she said, looking surprised.

"It's my job to notice things."

Any signs he'd seen earlier of her vulnerability had vanished, and in its place was the familiar strength and composure he'd seen all week.

"Any leads yet?" he asked.

"I wish, but no, though I think there might be something to Shelby's story." She took a sip of her coffee, then sat back in her chair. " I'm looking at the voice messages on her phone and the notes left on her car. The woman was definitely being harassed."

"What's the time frame?"

"It matches her story. The texts started a couple of weeks ago."

"Can we trace the sender?"

"So far, no, but I'm working with the phone company on it. And tech is working to see if they can dig up the information on the phone."

"I heard you were from the Pacific Northwest," Jonas said, switching to something more personal.

She glanced up at him. "Yeah.. .the Seattle area."

"I used to live there. In fact, every once in a while I think about moving back closer to my mom, but I don't know. . . Life keeps getting in the way."

"I can't imagine living anywhere else." She took another sip of her coffee. "Especially this time of year. Summer in the south isn't exactly my cup of tea."

"There are things I miss. Skiing in the winter. Visiting Pike Place Market with my mom. And the food. I really miss the food."

"You have family there?" Jonas asked, convincing himself his question was nothing more than professional concern.

"I do." Her phone rang. "I'm sorry, but this might be what we're looking for."

He waited, wondering why it was so hard to hold a conversation that went beyond small talk with a woman.

Maybe that was why he was still single.

Madison scribbled on a piece of paper, then held it up. "I've got his address," she said after hanging up.

An hour later, with a warrant in hand, Jonas banged on the front door of the house with Jack and the team they'd assembled. He could see movement through the curtains. No one was answering, but someone was home.

He ordered the team to surround the house, then motioned at the officer next to him to break down the door. Seconds later, the hinges cracked, and the door swung open.

Eddie headed toward the back of the house, a gun in his hand.

"Police," Jonas shouted. "Drop your weapon and put your hands in the air."

Jonas tore through the house when Eddie didn't stop, then out the back door and around the edge of the swimming pool with Jack following close behind him.

Eddie ran to the back fence and scaled it in flash, with Jonas a few seconds behind him, Jonas jumped over the drainage ditch, hot in pursuit.

Just ahead of him, Jonas saw Eddie throw his gun into the ditch and keep running.

A quarter of a mile down the road, a squad car turned the corner, blocking Eddie's way. Their suspect barreled into the side of the car. He fell backwards onto the ground, then started to get up again.

"Whoa. You're not going anywhere." Jonas aimed his weapon. "Running probably wasn't your smartest move. Dumping your gun in front of a deputy US Marshal wasn't either."

"You have no proof I did that."

"Somehow, I doubt it'll be that difficult to prove."

Jack caught up to them, trying to catch his breath. "Sorry," he said, bracing his hands against his thighs. "Apparently you didn't see the dog."

Jonas looked down at Jack's shredded pant leg. "Are you okay?"

"I think he thought it was a game. Thankfully, he managed to miss my leg."

"Old Brewster wouldn't hurt a fly," Eddie spat.

"Now you tell me," Jack said.

"He threw a weapon in the ditch about fifty feet back," Jonas said. "If you'll grab it, I'll get him to the squad car. I think we might have found our murder weapon.

～

JONAS AND JACK arrived back at the TBI squad room and quickly arranged to get an interrogation set up.

"What is that all over you?" Nikki walked up to Jack with a look of horror on her face. "And your pants?"

"It's nothing," Jack said, brushing past her to his desk.

"Nothing?" Nikki hurried after him. "You're wet, your pants are ripped, and you're covered in burrs."

Jonas folded his arms across his chest. "Your partner failed to tell me he's allergic to dogs, and weeds, and—"

"Everything, really," Nikki finished for him. "I quickly learned working with Jack that he's a magnet. Anything that stings, bites, hisses, and—apparently—barks, somehow manages to find him."

"In my defense," Jonas said, "I told him to get the gun out of the ditch before I knew that, and I did offer to take him to the doctor."

"Wait a minute. . ." Nikki's eyes widened as she turned back to Jack. "You were in a drainage ditch."

"I thought you'd be thrilled," Jack said. "That's where we found the gun that more than likely killed Ryan. On the downside, starting in the next twelve to twenty-four hours, my skin is going to be itchy and burning red from the parsnip sap. I'll just need to avoid the sun for the next few days."

"Do you need some allergy pills?" Madison asked.

"I've been in touch with my allergist and already took some, but thanks."

"I could tell you a dozen stories," Nikki said. "Jack is the best partner I've ever had, but basically he's allergic to the outdoors."

"Which is why"—Jack sneezed—"I married an allergist."

Jonas frowned. "You're kidding, right?"

Jack shook his head. "There are other reasons I married her, but that's the main one. At least that's what she always tells me."

"Don't listen to him." Nikki let out a chuckle. "Jack got the better end of the deal."

"We've got Eddie set up in an interview room," Garrett said, stepping into the room and interrupting their conversation. He stopped in front of Jack. "Are you okay?"

Jack's face reddened. "I just had a bit of a misstep while bringing in our suspect."

"And. . .you're okay."

"I'm hoping to go change, but yeah, I'm fine."

Garrett nodded. "Right. I want you two"—he pointed at Nikki then at Jonas—"to talk to our suspect. "We have one of our examiners testing right now to see if the bullet recovered at the scene of the crime came from our suspect's firearm."

Jonas dropped a file on the table, then took a seat. "It looks as if you were planning a trip. That's interesting, because there are several warrants out on you. But that's not why you're here. We want to talk to you about the murder of Ryan Bailey."

Eddie smirked. "You can't prove anything."

"We actually have a growing pile of evidence against you," Jonas said. "For starters, we have video from a gas station near the shoot house where you dumped the car that was seen fleeing the property. Camo clothes in the bathroom, and of course, the weapon you dumped in the ditch is the same caliber that was used to shoot Ryan."

"There are thousands of the same make and model out there," Eddie said. "That doesn't prove anything."

Jonas sat back in his chair. "It will once we have the testing back."

On cue, Nikki walked into the room and set a file in front of Jonas. "Here's the results."

"Results for what?" Eddie asked. "The firearm test?"

Jonas flipped open the file and quickly scanned its contents. "There's nowhere to run this time, Eddie. We can tie you to the car that was at the shoot house, and now we know your gun is the one that killed Ryan Bailey."

Eddie squirmed in his chair, his jaw tense and his lips pressed together. "You're bluffing."

"Do you really believe that?" Nikki leaned forward. "Who hired you, Eddie?"

"She told me it was a live fire exercise. She told me his death would be blamed on friendly fire and no one would ever know."

"Who?"

"I never saw her and she never used her real name. She hired me online and offered fifty thousand dollars. Ten up front and the rest after I was done."

Jonas stepped out of the room behind Nikki. Garret, Jack, and Madison were waiting for them in the hallway.

"He might not be able to ID who hired him," Jonas said, "but there has to be a money trail."

"I agree," Garrett said, "but we might not need it. You're both going to want to see what Madison found. Shelby told you she didn't have any family and hadn't been here long."

"She did," Nikki agreed.

"Go ahead, Madison," Garrett said.

"When I tried to look into where she'd lived before Nashville, I ran into a snag. Shelby Lehar died twenty-six years ago."

Jonas frowned. "Wait a minute. . .what?"

"She's using a stolen identity," Madison said.

Nikki set her hands on her hips. "Have you been able to track down her real name?"

Madison nodded. "Facial recognition pulled up an old mug shot for a misdemeanor she was charged with. Turns out her real name is Sofia Coleman, but that's not the worst part. Five years ago, she met Jameson Fletcher, a frat boy who came from a wealthy family. A few months after they were married, he was shot in a hunting accident. She was a suspect and questioned by the police, but they couldn't prove she was involved. She ended up with two million dollars."

"Where is she?" Nikki asked.

"We haven't been able to get ahold of Shelby or Lana," Madison said.

Jonas worked to process the information and the implications. "The scenario is eerily familiar, and if we're right, Lana's in trouble."

7

D ark clouds churned above Lana as she followed the GPS on her car's dashboard down the two-lane country road. All she'd seen for the last few miles were scattered farmhouses and fields of corn, soybeans, wheat, barley, and rye, a welcome relief from the stressful city traffic—except her mind wouldn't stop spinning. Ryan was dead, and her entire life had just turned upside down.

Grief from Ryan's death had yet to hit her completely, but the drive had given her time to think. She could understand how Shelby felt. Like it or not, she hadn't been the only one in love with Ryan.

The phone call from Shelby had surprised her as much as Shelby's request for Lana to meet her. Shelby had told her she knew about Lana's relationship with Ryan. How she'd been furious when he'd first told her before going off to his training week, but that their time apart had forced her to look at their relationship in a different light. The bottom line was that she couldn't marry someone who didn't love her, and it was better to know before the wedding than after. And even though their relationship might have ended, Shelby wanted Lana to help her find out who had killed Ryan.

Another flood of emotion gushed through Lana. Ryan had been everything she'd ever wanted, and it wasn't until after their break-up that she'd realized it. Running into him had been awkward, but it had also given them a second chance.

From the beginning she'd tried to dismiss the guilt she felt over the fact that Ryan was going to break Shelby's heart. And she wasn't the only one. Ryan had struggled with finding the right time to break things off. With the couple's wedding plans moving forward, Lana had insisted he talk to Shelby and tell her the truth sooner rather than later, because they'd already dragged things out far too long. At least he'd finally found the courage to tell her. No doubt she wanted to know who'd killed Ryan as much as Lana did.

Shelby was waiting by her car when Lana pulled into the end of a long drive.

"I'm glad you made it before the rains came," Shelby said, opening the car door for her. "It can get pretty muddy."

"I've never been out here," Lana stepped out of her vehicle and dropped her keys and phone into her back pockets. "It's beautiful though, isn't it?"

"I grew up on a farm, so it feels familiar." Shelby caught Lana's gaze. "I know this is awkward. The two woman who were in love with Ryan meeting, but I guess we have even more in common now."

"Finding out who killed him," Lana said. "But it doesn't look like anyone's here. You said we were meeting someone."

"I did, but. . .I lied." The smile on her face disappeared, sending a chill through Lana.

Lana took a step back. "I don't understand."

"I thought you were smarter than this." Shelby pulled a gun from her handbag and pointed it at Lana. "You didn't really think I'm simply going to accept someone stealing my fiancé."

"Wait a minute. . ." Nausea swirled through Lana's gut. "Please don't tell me you killed Ryan."

"I had him killed, and now I'm going to kill you. Drop your phone on the ground—"

"Shelby—"

"Just do it." Shelby waited until Lana had complied, then smashed it with the heel of her boot. "I knew he was seeing someone else, and I had to find out who. He was always late. Always distracted. Never really present. At first I thought it was just wedding jitters. Cold feet like everyone gets, but then he stopped telling me he loved me. Didn't return my calls for hours. Did you think you were going to be able to get rid of me? That I was going to just walk away because you manipulated him into thinking he was still in love with you?"

"Manipulated? I didn't mean for us to get back together, it just happened. And I know it has to hurt, but he really did love me."

A shadow crossed over Shelby's face. "I know you manipulated him to break our engagement. Convinced him to go back to you. If you'd stayed out of the picture we'd be going ahead with our wedding. But instead, you decided to take advantage of him. You confused him."

"I didn't manipulate him. He really didn't love you. I'm sorry, but that's the truth. And getting rid of me. . . You'll never get away with that. It doesn't change the fact that Ryan's dead. And neither of us can have him now."

"Maybe you should have thought about that before you took him from me."

Lana's mind spun. Ryan had told her that he'd made a big mistake in breaking up with her and rebounding with Shelby, but she never imagined that Shelby would take things this far.

"You really did kill him, didn't you?" Lana asked, trying to take in the horrible truth being presented to her.

"I couldn't let you have him. Not when he and I were meant to be together."

"And now that Ryan is dead, what has that accomplished?"

"If you're not going to prison for his death, then I'll have to take care of things myself."

"So that was your plan? Ryan dies and I pay for his death by going to prison?"

"Things didn't go exactly like I planned, but I can fix that. I will fix that. And in the end, it still gets you out of the way."

"Except you'll never get away with it."

"Why not? The police don't know where I am, and even if they do figure out the truth, by then it will be too late. I have enough of his money to disappear for a very, very long time. And if they happen to find you, I'll be long gone, taking time to grieve my fiancé's death. Everyone will understand my getting away from here. And I'll make sure you're the one the police blame for his death."

Shelby waved the gun toward a narrow path away from the driveway. "Go on. Straight ahead. I'll follow you."

"Where?" Lana asked, not moving.

"You'll see soon enough. For now, just walk. And I know how to shoot, so don't try anything stupid."

Cornstalks rustled in the wind to her right. She had no idea what Shelby's plan was, but she did know she never should have come. Never should have gotten out of the car. Never should have trusted Shelby. Grief from Ryan's death had taken her off guard and pulled her to a place she didn't want to be. A place where she wasn't thinking clearly—and that might very well cost her her life.

Lana stumbled when her ankle turned on the dirt path, but she managed to quickly regain her balance. She could run. Maybe that would be the smartest thing to do. Run straight for the tall cornstalks and disappear inside the rows. But then what? She had no doubt Shelby could and would shoot her.

Wasn't Ryan's death proof of that? No, if she didn't want that to happen, she was going to have to find a way to get the upper hand.

Lana glanced up at the two large silver grain bins that were connected by a narrow catwalk ahead of them, trying to figure out what Shelby's plan was.

"Now, you're going to climb up the ladder in front of me," Shelby ordered.

Lana frowned. "Why?"

"It doesn't matter. Just do it."

Lana hesitated at the bottom rung, but the barrel of the gun echoed Shelby's insistent words. She couldn't tell Shelby she was terrified of heights. The only thing left was trying to find a way to appease her.

"Shelby please. Listen to me. I never meant to hurt you. You have to understand that. And Ryan. . . He felt terrible. That was why it took him so long to tell you. He didn't want to hurt you. Neither of us did. We didn't plan it, didn't set out to hurt you. You have to believe me."

"You don't know what it's like to lose someone." Shelby's expression had iced over. "To have no one want you. Ryan changed all of that for me. I felt like for the first time I'd found the man I wanted to spend the rest of my life with. We were going to start a family, and you. . .you took that all away from me."

"You told me you couldn't marry someone who wasn't in love with you, and that you were glad that you had found out before the wedding. There will be someone else out there who loves you completely. I promise—"

"Shut up. He did love me. We both know that."

Lana pressed her lips together. There was no way to reason with the woman. She had her mind set on believing what she wanted to believe. But a broken heart was one thing. Murder was something completely different.

"Up the ladder. Now," Shelby ordered.

Lana climbed up slowly, trying to push back the terror flooding through her. When she reached the top she stood on the catwalk, trying not to give in to the swirling sensation of vertigo.

"What are we doing up here?"

"I grew up here, and I always love coming up here and just looking out over the land. Sunrises and sunsets are especially stunning. I didn't know how much I missed it until right now."

"Shelby?"

Shelby's attention shifted back to Lana. "Do you know what's in these silos?"

"I don't know. Grain? Corn?"

Lana's hands gripped the metal bar of the catwalk and she stared out across the acres of farmland. She didn't want to talk anymore. Didn't want to imagine what Shelby was planning to do to her. There had to be someone nearby who could hear her if she screamed, but all she could see was acres of corn blowing in the breeze. Where was everyone?

"If you're waiting for help to show up," Shelby said, as if reading Lana's mind, "don't bother. They're all working in the east pasture this afternoon." She tugged on the handle of the hatch, then pulled the metal cover open. "Do you know what happens when you fall inside a grain bin without a safety harness?"

Lana glanced inside the silo and felt another rush of vertigo. "No."

"Those enormous grains of dried corn can completely swallow a body."

Lana's gaze jerked back up at Shelby. She had to be kidding. Lana forced herself to take slow breaths. Shelby was just trying to scare her.

"It only takes seconds to sink up to your chest to where you can't move," Shelby continued. "In another few seconds you'll be completely engulfed in the corn and won't be able to breathe. The pressure on your body is horrendous. I've heard it's like being strangled by a thousand boa constrictors because every time you try to move, the corn presses tighter and tighter. You have to fight for every breath, until you don't have enough strength to breathe because of the mountain of corn pressing against you. And there won't be time to get help. It will be too late because it would take hours to pull you out."

Lana gripped the metal bar tightly, terrified her legs were going to give out on her. "You're lying."

"Am I?"

Lana tried to read Shelby's expression, but it was impossible to tell if she was bluffing or telling the truth. Her gaze shifted back to the gun. Maybe it didn't matter. If Shelby had hired someone to kill Ryan, she wouldn't hesitate to kill the person she believed to be responsible for taking him away from her.

"Don't do this, Shelby. Please. I'm sorry for everything that happened but this. . . Please don't do this. This won't fix anything. And it won't make things better for you."

Shelby frowned. "Enough. Begging doesn't become you."

The wind whipped around Lana's face. There had to be a way out. She'd never meant to hurt anyone. Never meant to steal Ryan from Shelby. But that didn't even matter anymore. He was gone, and nothing she did or said was going to bring him back. And clearly nothing she said mattered anymore to Shelby. And by the time someone found her, it would be too late.

8

Nikki drummed her fingers on the console of Jack's car, wishing she'd insisted on driving. Dark clouds were rolling across the miles and miles of farmland surrounding them. She should be used to the urgent response that came with tracking someone down. She'd spent over a decade searching for missing people, and in situations like this, time was never on their side—especially when an abduction was suspected. The first forty-eight hours were always the most crucial, because as every hour passed, their search radius exponentially expanded. Her team had learned to continually revise their plan of action, depending on the situation. What she didn't want today was their search for Lana to turn into another murder.

They'd tried calling both women. Neither had answered. Shelby's phone was off, as Nikki had expected. The woman had managed to wipe out half a million dollars from Ryan's accounts with the goal—Nikki presumed—to disappear. In an organized effort with the phone company, they'd finally located Lana's phone and had been able to track its position, but they still didn't know why she was heading outside of town, or if Shelby had anything to do with it.

"We have a problem." Garrett's voice came through her tactical headset. "We've just lost signal on Lana's phone."

"Where's the last location of the phone?" Jack asked.

"It looks like her vehicle turned left on the gravel road you're about to cross. It leads to a farm. I'm looking it up now."

"Got it," Jack said, pressing on the brakes and making the turn.

"We're pulling in now," Nikki said. "Keep us updated."

She studied the rows and rows of waving corn. Coming here couldn't be random. Shelby had to have a connection to this place. They just had to figure out why here, and what her endgame was.

As soon as Jack parked in front of the farmhouse, Nikki jumped out of the car. To her left were two vehicles, and from the descriptions they'd been given, they belonged to Lana and Shelby. The truck parked next to the house was probably the owner's, but they still didn't know why either Lana or Shelby would be here. She touched the hood of the hatchback. The engine was still warm. On the ground next to it was a smashed cell phone.

"I found Shelby's phone," Nikki said.

"Stay in radio contact and see if anyone's home," Jack shouted to Jonas and Madison as they got out of their vehicle. "Nikki and I will check the barn."

Jonas and Madison headed toward the farmhouse, while Nikki and Jack ran to the barn. Inside, sunlight filtered through the cracks in the walls, an afternoon glow of yellow light in the large, dusty space.

"I don't know how big this property is, but finding them is going to be difficult," Nikki said. "On the positive side, their cars are here, so there's a good chance that wherever they went, they went on foot."

A light rain had started falling as they stepped outside. Jonas and Madison walked toward them with an older man wearing faded jeans and a baseball hat.

"This is Marty Grimes," Jonas said. "He's the owner of the farm."

"Special Agent Nikki Grant." She held up a photo of Shelby on her phone. "Do you

recognize this woman? Her name is Sofia Coleman. She also goes by Shelby Lehar."

Marty shifted his bifocals, then shook his head. "I'm sorry, but no. What's this all about?"

"How long have you lived here?" Nikki asked.

"Twelve, almost thirteen years."

"Did you ever meet the previous owners?" Jack asked.

"No." Grimes shook his head. "My wife and I moved here from Wisconsin, and from what our Realtor told us, the place was hard to sell."

"Why was that?" Nikki asked.

"A man and his son were killed on the property in a grain silo accident, and the wife committed suicide in the house six months after that." Grimes rubbed the stubble on his chin. "Now that I think about, I'm pretty sure their name was Coleman. I think there was a daughter as well, but I don't know what happened to her."

"Can you remember anything else about them?" Jonas asked.

"No, but I know it hit the community hard." Grimes let out a mirthless chuckle. "And despite the neighbors' warnings, I've never run into any ghosts."

"Thank you." Nikki took a step back and spoke to Garrett through her earpiece. "Find everything you can on the Coleman family who used to own this property and update the sheriff on the situation. We need a search organized."

"The silo," Madison said, as Nikki turned back to them. "If

that's the connection. . . If she was here and saw the accident, that's where she has to be."

"Where's the silo?" Nikki asked.

"There are two of them, just north of here," Grimes said. "You can see them from the other side of the barn."

"We're going to need you to stay down here and wait for the sheriff. Make sure he knows where we are."

The wind picked up as they made their way to the pair of silver grain silos towering in the distance. A dog barked, while the skies looked as if they were about to unleash a torrent of rain. But there was no sign of either woman. Nikki pulled her weapon out of its holster and started climbing the ladder of one of the silos ahead of Jack. Jonas and Madison went up the other.

When she reached the top and went around the silo, she saw Shelby—Sophia—on the platform of the other silo pointing a gun at Lana's head.

"Sophia?" Nikki said, starting across the narrow catwalk. "We know that's you're real name. It's Nikki."

Lana was sobbing. The door above the silo was open next to them. "Please, please don't let her hurt me."

"No one needs to get hurt today," Nikki said. "That's why we're here. We've come to help."

"You shouldn't have come," Sophia said. "This has nothing to do with you."

Nikki stopped about six feet from them and motioned to Jonas and Madison to hold up. "Put the gun down, Sophia. We can talk."

"You don't understand. She took Ryan away from me and ruined everything."

"I know you're upset, but I need you to let Lana go." Nikki moved forward a couple more feet. "We can work this out."

"Stop. . . Don't come any closer," Shelby said. "And those

two on the other silo—they better stay right where they are too."

"Please. . ." Lana was sobbing now. "Please don't do this. I never meant to hurt you."

"She's right, Sophia," Nikki said. "What good will come of hurting Lana? It won't bring Ryan back. It won't change anything. I know you loved him. I know you feel lost, but this isn't the way. He's gone, and hurting Lana is only going to make things worse."

"How could this get any worse than it already is?" Sophia waved the gun around. "You don't understand. He was going to marry me. And if I can't have him. . .then she doesn't deserve him either."

Garrett's voice came through Nikki's earpiece. "Sophia saw the accident that killed her father and older brother."

Nikki frowned at the information. Witnessing a traumatic event as a child was often impossible to process. It tore away the child's sense of stability and self, often staying with them into adulthood. And Sophia had never found a way to put those broken pieces back together.

Nikki paused, not sure how hard she should push. "Ryan isn't the first person you've lost, is he, Sophia?"

Sophia took a step back, shaking her head. "Ryan. . .Jameson. . ."

"And you saw what happened to your father and your brother here, didn't you?" Nikki asked. "I heard about the accident, and I'm very, very sorry. You lost a lot that day."

"It changed everything. My mother couldn't help me. I was nine years old and left with strangers."

"It had to have been so hard."

"No one understood how much it hurt. How much it still hurts."

"Sophia. . .look at me," Nikki said, needing to draw her back to reality. She took another couple steps forward until she was standing on the other side of the open silo door. "I know this has been hard for you, but hurting more people... This isn't the answer. You need to let Lana go. Please."

"What does it matter at this point? Ryan's dead. And if I go with you now, I'll spend the rest of my life in prison. She needs to suffer with me."

"Is that really what you want?" Nikki pressed.

"It doesn't matter what I want." Sophia's gaze shifted back to Lana. "This is her fault. Can't you understand? Ryan never really loved her, but she manipulated him into leaving me. And that's what was wrong. That's why I had to stop them. I had to make things right this time."

"Sophia—"

"She ruined everything. If she hadn't come back into the picture Ryan would still be with me." Sophia shoved Lana toward the opening of the silo, then spun around and ran toward the other side of the silo.

Nikki lunged forward, just barely grabbing Lana's hand as Lana toppled over the edge and dangled beneath her.

"Lana, hang on...Jack."

"Jonas...Madison...go after Sophia," Jack shouted as he reached down to grab Lana's other hand.

Nikki felt her grip on Lana began to slip. The bin was half full and it smelled like rotten potatoes. If they dropped her, she'd fall into the grain below, and drown.

9
_____

Jonas raced down the ladder behind Madison then followed Sophia toward the cornfield. Sophia turned back. aimed her weapon, and fired. The bullet slammed into the metal wall of the silo.

"Sophia," Jonas shouted, "it's over. This is only making things worse for you."

Sophia ignored his warning and kept running toward the cornfield spread out to the east of the silo. Shadows were already falling across the acres of crops as the sun made its way toward the horizon. Sophia disappeared into the cornfield and out of sight except for the movement of the cornstalks.

Where does she think she's going?

Jonas ran toward the cornfield. Sophia was out of options and desperate. They'd found her car, so she couldn't drive away, but running wasn't going to get her far.

"We got Lana." Nikki's voice broke through his earpiece. "She's safe."

"Good, but Sophia went into the cornfield. Can you see her from your location?"

"Give me a second. . ."

Jonas stopped at the edge of the field next to Madison, listening for the rustling of the stalks. Sofia could be anywhere.

"Nikki?" he repeated. "Where is she?"

"Ahead of you. . .about fifty feet. Moving east, diagonally, toward the main road."

They pushed through the stalks of corn that were taller than he was. A spiderweb brushed across his face as he navigated the uneven terrain. Rough leaves scraped against him, but he kept moving.

"Contact the sheriff and have him and his deputy head to the other side and cut her off," Jonas said into his earpiece.

"Copy that."

They kept walking through the rows of corn, stopping every ten feet or so to listen for Sophia, but the rain had started falling, muffling her movements. Drops of cold rainwater slid down his face. He blinked. While pursuits in a car were inherently dangerous, tracking down an armed suspect on foot had its own set of dangers. Adrenaline hit, and his body prepared to fight. He drew in a couple deep breaths, forcing the oxygenated blood to his brain and focusing his thinking.

Gunshot fired, ripping through the willowy stalks of corn. He dove for cover, grabbing Madison and taking her down with him.

"Nikki? Where is she?"

"Hold your position. She's turned around and is headed back toward you."

He crouched down and motioned for Madison to stay still next to him. Why was Sophia coming after them? Her smartest move would be to get as far away from them as possible as quickly as she could, but even then it was going to be almost impossible to slip past law enforcement. To come at them made no sense.

But then nothing the woman had done over the past few

days had been rational. Which was why reasoning with her now wasn't possible.

Rain was falling harder now, dripping down his shirt. He could hear Madison breathing next to him as he crouched beside her, watching for movement ahead of them. She was someone he'd want to have on his team on a day-to-day basis. She had good instincts and physically was at the top of her game. He might never be able to connect with her personally, but right now, he had to trust her with his life.

Dogs barked in the distance as the wind rustled through the cornstalks. The sheriff and his team were moving into position, but they weren't close enough yet to stop her.

"She's at your two o'clock," Nikki said. "And it looks like she's still coming back toward you."

"Sophia!" Jonas shouted above the wind and rain. "You need to end this before someone else gets hurt. There's nowhere to run."

There was no response.

"Nikki, where is she?"

"I don't know. I've lost her. The sheriff has the adjacent perimeters covered. You both need to move back now."

"Copy that," Jonas said.

Shadows shifted around them, and the rain continued to fall as he and Madison retreated. They walked back-to-back, weapons drawn, while they searched the rows of corn for movement. A stalk brushed across his arm, shifting his attention to the left. He took in a deep breath to slow his heart rate as he took another step backward.

Where was she?

"Jonas get down!"

Madison shouted the warning a split second before she pulled him to the ground with her. The sharp crack of a gunshot exploded nearby. Madison fired back, managing somehow to hit her mark. Sofia dropped to the ground.

"Man down," Jonas said into his earpiece. "I repeat, man down. Our suspect has been hit."

"We're moving in now," Nikki responded.

Jonas rolled over, turning back to Madison, but she lay still on the ground next to him.

No. . .no. . .no. . .

"Madison?"

She let out a soft groan, but still didn't move.

"Madison," He knelt next to her while Nikki and Jack dealt with Sophia. "Talk to me, Madison."

"My side," she choked out. "It's on fire."

He pulled up her T-shirt, revealing where the bullet had hit her vest.

"Breathe slowly. Slow, deep breaths. The vest stopped the bullet."

Rain ran down her face as she gasped for a breath. "I've heard this feels like getting hit with a hammer. . . I think it feels more like getting hit with a semi."

He undid the side strap of her vest to reveal the bruise that was already forming. "Looks like your quick reflexes probably saved my life."

She looked up at him and smiled. "Just doing my job. I had a good trainer."

He had a crazy urge to pull her into his arms. He moved his hand away from her side, not expecting the confused rush of feelings. He couldn't afford to mix emotions with his job. Especially with someone he would never see again after this week.

"We need to get you out of here," he said. "Do you hurt anywhere else?"

"Trust me. This is enough."

"We've got two ambulances on their way," Nikki said. "Can you help her out of here?"

"Yeah." He put his arm around Madison and helped her up. "How's Sophia?"

"Looks like the bullet was a through and through," Nikki said. "She's fully conscious and should live."

Jonas nodded, then shifted his attention back to Madison, tightening his arm around her waist as they made their way out of the cornfield. Nikki's voice sounded behind them.

". . .you're under arrest for the murder of Ryan Bailey, the kidnapping of Lana Montgomery, and the attempted murder of officer Madison James."

10

N ikki let the hot water run down the back of her neck, wishing she could wash away the stress from the day. Some of the knots in her shoulders had slowly began to loosen, but it was going to take more than hot water to dissolve the rest. Tyler had told her to take as much time as she needed, but she knew that they were going to have to talk. Something was bothering him, and as tired as she was, she couldn't go to sleep until they did.

She turned off the water and quickly dressed before stepping back into the bedroom. Tyler was still awake, absorbed in a book. She watched him for a moment. As former military, he still wore his hair short. Add to that a five o'clock shadow and those familiar brown eyes that could always see straight through her, and yeah . . . He was definitely gorgeous. They'd been through so much together. The death of Katie, Tyler's first wife and her best friend. The search for her missing sister. . .

Falling in love with him had been unexpected, but it had also changed her life. She'd been drawn to his honesty and integrity, and he in turn completed her in a way no one ever had.

Tyler looked up. "Hey,"

She smiled back at him. "Hey."

"How long have you been standing there?"

"Not long. We need to talk."

He set his book down on the bed beside him. "I know."

"Mommy?"

Liam's soft voice sounded from the room next to theirs.

"I'll go get him," Tyler said, starting to get up from the bed.

"It's fine. I'll go."

Liam was lying in his twin bed with his latest Lego project next to him. Having children was more fulfilling than she'd ever expected. Love. Joy. Loss and grief. They were all a part of the journey she and Tyler had chosen to navigate together.

"Hey buddy, you're supposed to be asleep."

"I was. I wanted to show you my airplane."

She sat down on the bed and picked it up. "Have I ever told you how clever you are?"

Liam laughed. "Yes."

"And how much I love you?"

"Yes." He laughed again. "Did you catch a bad guy today?"

"I did, actually."

Hoping to make the world a better place for you, little man.

Liam's eyes drooped.

"I think it's time for someone to go to sleep."

He forced his eyes back open. "I'm not tired."

"Daddy's making pancakes in the morning, but you've got to sleep first."

Liam let out a sigh, kissed her on the cheek, then turned over. "Okay. Good night."

She kissed him on the top of his head, noticing—not for the first time—how much he looked like Tyler's first wife Katie, then left his room, quickly checking on Isabella before heading back to the bedroom.

"Liam's almost asleep," Nikki said, sitting down on the bed next to Tyler, "and Isabella didn't stir when I checked on her."

"Perfect." He leaned over and brushed her lips with a kiss. "How are you?"

"It was a rough day."

"Do you want to talk about it?" he asked. "I saw the news clip about the murder and arrest."

She pulled one of the pillows into her lap and hugged it. "Ryan was a good guy who didn't deserve what happened to him. We were able to arrest the person behind the murder, but it reminded me that life is short and uncertain."

"I'm really sorry."

She nodded. "I also found out today that one of the women on my team lost her husband a few months ago."

"Was he in law enforcement?"

"No. He was a doctor. For some reason it hit me hard. Reminded me of Katie."

Tyler moved closer to her so he could wrap his arm around her shoulder and pull her against him.

"She shared some things with me, and it made me realize that I don't want us to take each other for granted. Everything we have together with Liam and Isabella." She twisted the wedding ring on her finger. "I owe you an apology. This morning—"

"No, I'm the one who's sorry." He kissed the top of her head. "I want you to know that I'm proud of you and what you're doing, but days like this scare me too."

"I know. I can't help but worry about something happening when I'm out there." She pressed her head against his shoulder. "But we can't have our fears push us apart."

"I know." He brushed back a strand of her hair. "Which is why I need to apologize to you. You're the one who always reminds me that sometimes all we can do is trust God. To hold on to him—and each other—when life sucks us into that dark place. I think, I forgot that."

"I needed to hear that again today." She worked to keep the anxiety out of her voice. "You've been distant the past week or so. You know you can tell me anything."

Tyler ran his finger across the back of her hand. "I got a job offer."

"A job offer?" She pulled back. "That wasn't what I was expecting. Why didn't you tell me?"

"Because I wasn't going to. I was going to turn it down."

She shook her head. "I don't understand. Without even telling me? Why?"

"It's in Houston."

"Okay. What kind of job?"

"It's a lot of the same things I'm doing, but I'd be the intelligence manager of a global team."

"Sounds like something you'd excel at." Nikki worked to absorb the news, but it wasn't the job that bothered her. It was the fact that he hadn't come to her about it. "You're worried that if you take it I'd end up resenting you for taking me away from my job and family here."

Tyler nodded, his brow furrowed.

They'd talked about it before. Before Katie had died, she'd been pregnant and was facing being a single mom while Tyler served overseas and was tired of waiting for Tyler to come home after each tour. Her fears had been understandable. As a military wife, she'd known guys who came home missing limbs or dealing with PTSD, and on one level she accepted that reality, because when she married Tyler, she knew she'd signed up for more than just a husband. But after Tyler was shot, she told him she couldn't take it anymore. And in the end, Tyler had left the military for her. While he'd never said a bad word against Katie, Nikki knew that not being able to defend his country anymore had been a tough transition.

Nikki searched for the right response. "I didn't marry you thinking everything would be perfect, but we have to face things together."

"I know, and I'm sorry I didn't tell you right away."

"You're good at what you do, Tyler." She reached for his hand and linked their fingers together. "Maybe it's time for our family to make some changes."

"What about your job?" Tyler asked. "I'm not going to ask you to leave it."

"Maybe it's something to consider. I've worked on the missing persons task force for over a decade now. Maybe it's time I stepped down and started a new season."

"Like?"

"I used to be a teacher. I've been thinking the past few years that I'd like to go back to teaching criminal justice. Train young people to do what I've been doing. At least we can consider it."

He pulled their hands against his chest as he listened. "You're sure about this? You don't have to decide any time soon."

She looked up and caught his gaze. "Maybe I do."

"What do you mean?"

She studied his face, her heart racing. "The doctor left me a message on my phone."

"The test results came back?"

"I'm pregnant, Tyler."

His jaw slacked in surprise. "Wait a minute. . .What? I didn't think you could get pregnant again."

"Trust me, I haven't even had time to process it, but everything came back normal. And the pregnancy test they took was positive."

Having Isabelle had been a miracle. The doctor had said she had a five percent chance of ever getting pregnant, but now God had just given them their second miracle.

Tyler ran his hand over the back of his neck, but the grin on his face told her how he felt. "Wow. . . I wasn't expecting that. A baby?"

She leaned into him again and let him wrap his arms around her. Life was fragile. She knew that all too well. In a matter of seconds, one fatal moment, everything could change forever. She'd lived through it with her sister's disappearance, and again when Katie had drowned. And yet, despite the deep hurt life sometimes brought, there was also so much to be grateful for.

"Maybe you need to take the job," she said, looking up at him.

"Maybe." He leaned in and kissed her slowly, before pulling back and studying her face. "I just want us to be together, and for you to be happy."

"I am happy." She ran her thumb down his jawline, amazed at how grateful they'd found each other. "It doesn't matter to me if we live here or Houston, or the North Pole. As long as we're together and have each other. What else really matters?"

DEAR READER

Dear Reader,

Thank you so much for reading Point Blank! This story brings together some of my favorite characters from two of my series. Nikki, her husband Tyler, and Jack Spencer from my best-selling Nikki Boyd Files series, along with Madison James and Jonas Quinn from my US Marshal series. I had so much fun writing this story because it not only allows readers to catch up with Nikki and Tyler again, but tells how Madison and Jonas first met several years before their first assignment together as US Marshals. If you want to read more of their stories, you won't want to miss either series!

Lisa Harris

Best selling suspense

VENDETTA LISA HARRIS
MISSING LISA HARRIS
PURSUED LISA HARRIS

The fast-paced pursuit of justice in a haunting case that will have you holding your breath until the heart-stopping finish.

THE **ESCAPE** LISA HARRIS
THE **CHASE** LISA HARRIS
THE **CATCH** LISA HARRIS

"This whirlwind fast-paced chase will please fans of Terri Blackstock."
–Publishers Weekly

"You don't get it. I HAVE NOTHING TO LOSE. That plane crash was a second chance at freedom. MY WAY OUT."